ELLERY QUEEN digs deep into the private
lives of the richest family on earth:

Beautiful Karla Bendigo, a woman fit for
a king; Judah, a lush who guzzles cognac;
Abel, a financial genius who spends
a million dollars a day; and the fabulous
munitions maker, King Bendigo
himself, a man so rich, so powerful that
a wit once quipped, "When the King stands
in a draft the whole world sneezes!"

Ellery Queen's job was to keep this
powerful tycoon from being murdered.
With the help of all the King's money and
all the King's men the task looked
simple. But here was a case where the
perfect detective came face to face
with a killer who had contrived
the perfect crime!

• • • • • • • • • • • • • •

THE KING IS DEAD
was originally published by
Little, Brown and Company.

OTHER BOOKS BY ELLERY QUEEN

*THE ADVENTURES OF ELLERY QUEEN

CALENDAR OF CRIME

CAT OF MANY TAILS

THE CHINESE ORANGE MYSTERY

*THE DUTCH SHOE MYSTERY

*THE EGYPTIAN CROSS MYSTERY

†THE FINISHING STROKE

†THE GREEK COFFIN MYSTERY

*INSPECTOR QUEEN'S OWN CASE

*THE MURDERER IS A FOX

*THE NEW ADVENTURES OF ELLERY QUEEN

THE ORIGIN OF EVIL

*Q. B. I. (Queen's Bureau of Investigation)

*THE QUICK AND THE DEAD (originally *There Was an Old Woman*)

*TEN DAYS' WONDER

*Published by Pocket Books, Inc., in a POCKET BOOK edition.
†Published by Pocket Books, Inc., in a CARDINAL edition.

ELLERY QUEEN

THE KING
IS DEAD

POCKET BOOKS, INC. • NEW YORK

THE KING IS DEAD

Little, Brown edition published May, 1952

POCKET BOOK edition published July, 1954
4th printing....................December, 1960

L

POCKET BOOK editions are distributed in the U.S. by Affiliated Publishers, Inc., 630 Fifth Avenue, New York 20, N.Y.

Cast of Characters

THE KING
IS DEAD

1

THE INVASION of the Queen apartment occurred at 8:08 o'clock of an ordinary June morning, with West 87th Street just washed down three stories below by the City sprinkler truck and Arsène Lupin in grand possession of the east ledge, breakfasting on bread crumbs intended for a dozen other pigeons of the neighborhood.

It was an invasion in twentieth-century style—without warning. At the moment it exploded, Inspector Queen was poising a spoon edgewise over his second egg, measuring peacefully for the strike; Mrs. Fabrikant had just elevated her leviathan bottom at the opposite side of the room, preparing to plug in the vacuum cleaner; and Ellery was in the act of stepping into the living room, hands at his neck about to pull down his jacket collar.

"Don't move, please."

There had been no noise at all. The front door had been unlocked, the door wedged back against the wall, and the foyer crossed in silence.

The Inspector's spoon, Mrs. Fabrikant's bottom, Ellery's hands remained where they were.

The two men were standing just inside the archway from the foyer. Folded topcoats covered their right hands. They were dressed alike, in suits and hats of ambiguous tan, except that one wore a dark blue shirt and the other a dark brown shirt. They were big men with nice, rather blank faces.

The pair looked around the Queen living room. Then they stepped apart and Ellery saw that they were not a pair but a trio.

The third man stood outside the apartment, straddling the landing to block the public hall. His motionless back was to-

1

ward the Queen front doorway and he was looking down the staircase.

Blue Shirt suddenly parted company from his twin. He had to pass Inspector Queen at the dropleaf table, but he paid no attention to the staring old gentleman. He went through the swinging door to the kitchen, very fast.

His mate remained in the archway in an attitude of almost respectful attention. His brown shirt added a warm tone to his personality. His right hand appeared, holding a .38 revolver with a pug nose.

Blue Shirt came out of the Queen kitchen and disappeared in Inspector Queen's bedroom.

The Inspector's spoon, Mrs. Fabrikant's bottom, Ellery's hands all came cautiously down at the same moment. But nothing happened except that Blue Shirt came out of the Inspector's bedroom, crossed to the doorway where Ellery stood, stiffarmed Ellery politely out of the way, and went into the study.

The third man kept watching the stairs in the hall.

Mrs. Fabrikant's mouth was working up to a shriek. Ellery said, "Don't, Fabby," just in time.

Blue Shirt came back and said to his partner, "All clear." Brown Shirt nodded and immediately set out across the room, heading for Mrs. Fabrikant. She scrambled to her feet, creamier than the woodwork. Without looking at her, Brown Shirt said in a pleasant voice, "Take the vacuum into one of the bedrooms, Mother, shut the door, and get it going." He stopped at the window.

Arsène Lupin boomed and flew away, and Mrs. Fabrikant fled.

That was when Inspector Queen found his legs and his voice. Jumping to his full five feet four inches, the Inspector bellowed, "Who in the hell are you?"

The vacuum cleaner began to whine like a bandsaw from Ellery's bedroom beyond the study. Blue Shirt shut the study door, muffling the noise. He wedged his back in the doorway.

"If this is a stickup—!"

Blue Shirt grinned, and Brown Shirt—at the window—permitted himself a smile that only briefly shattered his expression. His glance remained on 87th Street below.

"—it's the politest one in history," said Ellery. "You at the window. Would you get nervous if I looked over your shoulder?"

The man shook his head impatiently. A black town car with a New York license plate was just swinging into West 87th Street from Columbus Avenue. Ellery saw its glittering mate parked across the street. Several men were in the parked car.

Brown Shirt's left hand came up, and two of the men in the parked car jumped out and raced across the street to the sidewalk below the Queen windows. As they reached the curb, the car which had turned into 87th Street slid to a stop before the house. One of the men ran up the brownstone steps; the other swiftly opened the rear door of the car and stepped back, looking not into the car but up and down the street.

A smallish man got out of the town car. He was dressed in a nondescript suit and he wore an out-of-shape gray hat. In a leisurely way he mounted the brownstone steps and passed from view.

"Recognize him, Dad?"

Inspector Queen, at Ellery's shoulder, shook his head. He looked bewildered.

"Neither do I."

Brown Shirt was now at the door of the Inspector's bedroom, so that he and Blue Shirt faced each other from opposite sides of the room. Their foreshortened Police Positives dangled at their thighs. Their companion on the landing stepped up to the newel post, and now his right hand was visible, too, grasping a third .38.

Mrs. Fabrikant's machine kept sawing.

Suddenly, out in the hall, the third man backed away.

The smallish man's shapeless hat and undistinguished suit began to rise from the stairwell.

"Good morning," said the smallish man, removing his hat. He had a voice like a steel guitarstring.

Seen close up, he was not so small as he had appeared. He

was several inches taller than Inspector Queen, but he had the Inspector's small bones and the narrow face structure of many undersized men. His head broadened at the temples and his forehead was scholarly. His skin was bland and firm, with an undertinge of indoor gray, his hair mouse-brown with a tendency to scamper. His eyes, which were protected by squarish rimless glasses, had a bulgy and heavy-lidded look, but this was an illusion; his blinking stare was unavoidable. A growing pot strained the button of his single-breasted jacket, which could have done with a pressing. He looked as if he ought to be wearing a square derby and a piped vest.

He might have been fifty, or sixty, or even forty-five.

Ellery's first impression was categorical: *The absent-minded professor.* The rather highpitched Yankee voice of authority went with examinations and blackboards. But professors, absent-minded or otherwise, do not go about the city accompanied by armed guards in powerful cars. Ellery revised. A general, perhaps, one of the intellectual brass, a staff man who moved mountains from the Pentagon. Or an oldfashioned banker from Vermont. But . . .

"My name," twanged the visitor, "is Abel Bendigo."

"Bendigo!" The Inspector stared. "You're not the Bendigo—"

"Hardly," said Abel Bendigo with a smile. "I take it you've never seen his photograph. But you see what I'm up against, Inspector Queen. These security people are members of my brother's Public Relations and Personnel Department, which is under the command of a very hard fellow named Spring. Colonel Spring—I doubt if you've ever heard of him. He tyrannizes us all, even my brother—or, I should say, especially my brother! And so you're Ellery Queen," their visitor went on without so much as a glissando. "Great pleasure, Mr. Queen. I've never got over feeling a bit silly about these precautions, but what can I do? Colonel Spring likes to remind me that it takes only one bullet to turn farce into tragedy. . . . May I sit down?"

Ellery pulled the old leather chair forward, and the Inspector said, "I wish, Mr. Bendigo, you had let us know in advance—"

"The Colonel again," murmured Abel Bendigo, sinking into the chair. "Thank you, Mr. Queen, my hat will do nicely on the floor here. . . . So this is where all the mysteries are solved."

"Yes," said Ellery, "but I believe what's bothering my father is the fact that he's due in his office at Police Headquarters in about twelve minutes, and it's downtown."

"Sit down, Inspector. I want to talk to both of you."

"I can't, Mr. Bendigo—"

"They won't miss you this once. I guarantee it. By the way, I see we've interrupted your breakfast. Yours, too, Mr. Queen—"

"Just coffee this morning." Ellery went to the table. "Will you join us?"

From the side of the room Brown Shirt said, "Mr. Bendigo."

Bendigo waved his slender hand humorously. "You see? Another of Colonel Spring's rules. Finish. Please."

Ellery refilled his father's cup from the percolator and poured a cupful for himself. There was no point in asking this man questions; in fact, there was every point in not. So he stood by the table and sipped his coffee.

The Inspector gulped his breakfast, throwing side glances at his wristwatch in perplexity.

Abel Bendigo waited in silence, blinking. Blue Shirt and Brown Shirt were very still. The man on the landing did not move. Mrs. Fabrikant's vacuum cleaner kept buzzing in a helpless way.

The moment the Queens set their cups down, the visitor said, "What do you gentlemen know about my brother King?"

They looked at each other.

"Got a file on him, son?" asked the Inspector.

"Yes."

Ellery went into his study, Blue Shirt moving aside. When he came back, he was carrying a large clasp envelope. He shook it over the table and a few newspaper and magazine clippings fell out. He sat down and glanced over them.

Abel Bendigo's prominent eyes behind the glasses blinked at Ellery's face.

Finally Ellery looked up. "There's nothing here that amounts to anything, Mr. Bendigo. Sunday supplement stuff, chiefly."

"You know nothing about my brother," murmured the slender man, "beyond what's in those clippings?"

"Your brother is rumored to be one of the five richest men in the world—worth billions. That, I take it, is the usual exaggeration. However, the assumption may be made that he's a man of great wealth."

"Oh, yes?" said Abel Bendigo.

"How great makes an interesting speculation. There is in existence an industrial monster known as The Bodigen Arms Company, munitions manufacturers, with affiliates all over the globe. This company is supposed to be owned lock and stock by your brother King. I say 'supposed to be' because the only 'proof' presented in evidence of his alleged ownership is the rather amusing one that Bodigen is an anagram of Bendigo. If it should happen to be true, I salaam. During World War II a single branch of The Bodigen Arms Company—just one branch out of the dozens in existence—showed profits after taxes of some forty-two millions a year."

"Go on," said Abel Bendigo, blinking.

"Your brother, Mr. Bendigo, is also said to be deeply involved in worldwide oil interests, steel, copper, aluminum—all the important metals—aircraft, shipbuilding, chemicals—"

"Anything, that is," said Inspector Queen, dabbing at his mustache, "relating to materials vital to war. I really must be getting downtown, Mr. Bendigo—"

"Not yet." Bendigo crossed his legs suddenly. "Go on, Mr. Queen."

"Personal data," continued Ellery, "are almost as speculative. Your brother seems extremely shy. Little or nothing is known about his background. A photographer for a Kansas newspaper won a national spot-news photography award two years ago for snapping a picture of King Bendigo and managing to get away with an unbroken plate, although the decoy camera by which he pulled off the trick was smashed to crumbs—by these gentlemen here, for all I know. The photo shows a big man, handsome as the devil—I quote an eye witness—at that time fifty-two years old, which makes him fifty-four today. But he looks little more than forty or so, and he carries himself—I quote again—'with an arrogant self-confidence usually associated with twenty.' 'Dressed to kill,' it says here, and you'll forgive me if I wonder whether the reporter was trifling libelously with the English language when he wrote it."

King Bendigo's brother smiled, but then the corners of his mouth dropped and snuffed the smile out.

"I have in my possession," he said slowly, "two letters. They were addressed to my brother. They're threat-letters.

"Now a man in my brother's position, no matter how careful he is to avoid publicity, can hardly avoid cranks. Colonel Spring's PRPD takes all the necessary precautions against that sort of thing as a matter of routine. These letters, however, are a different run of shad."

Bendigo took two folded sheets of paper from his inside breast pocket. "I want you to examine these, please."

"All right," said Ellery, and he came over.

The Inspector rose, too. "Where are the envelopes?"

"King's secretaries discarded them before their importance was appreciated. My brother's staff opens all his mail for sorting and distribution—all, that is, except letters marked 'confidential' or under special seal. These two letters, I understand, were in the ordinary mail."

Ellery made no move to unfold them. "Was no attempt made to recover the envelopes, Mr. Bendigo? From the wastebasket, or wherever they were tossed?"

"There are no wastebaskets at our offices. Each secretary has beside his desk a chute which leads to a central macerating machine. Discarded paper goes down the chute and is chewed to pulp. The pulp feeds automatically into an incinerator."

"Since smoke," murmured Ellery, "can't be yanked out of a file?"

Abel Bendigo's lips pursed. "We have no use, Mr. Queen, for mere accumulations."

"Let's see those letters, Ellery," said the Inspector.

The two sheets of paper were identical. They were creamy single sheets, personal letter size, of a fine vellum-type stationery, unmarked by monogram or imprint. In the center of each sheet there was a single line of typewriting.

"The six-word message was the first," said Bendigo.

The six-word message was:

You are going to be murdered—

The dash was not casual. It was impressed into the paper, as if the key had been struck at that point with force.

The message on the second sheet was almost identical with that on the first. The only difference was the addition of two words:

You are going to be murdered on Thursday—

As in the first message, the dash had been physically emphasized.

The Queens studied the two messages.

Bendigo waited.

Finally, the Inspector looked up. "Where in these notes does it say that *your brother King* is going to be murdered, Mr. Bendigo? I don't see any name on these. Anywhere."

"The envelopes, Inspector Queen."

"Did you see the envelopes?"

"No, but the staff—"

"Did anyone but the secretaries who opened them—and threw them down the chute to be destroyed—see the envelopes?"

"No. But they are reliable people, thoroughly screened. Of course, Inspector, you'll have to take my word for that. The envelopes were addressed to King Bendigo." Bendigo was not irritated; if anything, he seemed pleased. "What do you think, Mr. Queen?"

"I see what's bothering you. Threatening letters are usually hand-printed on cheap paper—the block-lettering, commonly in pencil, is almost always unidentifiable, and the cheap paper untraceable. These letters are remarkable for their frankness. The writer did not try to cover his tracks. He used expensive, distinctive notepaper which should be easy to trace. Instead of printing capitals in pencil, he typed his message on a Winchester—"

"Winchester Noiseless Portable," snapped the Inspector.

"—virtually inviting identification. It's almost," said Ellery thoughtfully, "as if he *wanted* the letters to be traced. Of course, they could be a practical joke."

"No one," said Abel Bendigo, "jokes about the death of my brother King."

"Then they make no sense," said Ellery, "at least to me. Do they make sense to you, Mr. Bendigo?"

"It's your opinion, then, that these are the work of a crank?"

"No, indeed," murmured Ellery. "They make no sense because they're obviously *not* the work of a crank. The letters are unfinished: the first ends with an emphasized dash, the second adds a fact and ends with another emphasized dash. There is a progression here. So there will be more letters with more information. Since the first letter promises murder and the second promises murder on a Thursday, logically a third letter will specify on which of the fifty-two possible Thursdays the murder is planned to take place. It adds up to cold calculation, not aberration. Why, then, leave an open trail? That's why I say it makes no sense."

The man in the leather chair seemed to weigh Ellery's words, each one carefully.

"How far apart did the letters arrive?" asked the Inspector.

"The second came Monday. The first a week ago."

Ellery shrugged, turning to the mantel and his pipe. "'I don't get it. I mean the purpose of all this, Mr. Bendigo. Your establishment is important and powerful enough to employ a private police force of great efficiency. Determining the authorship of these letters should be a kindergarten exercise to your Colonel Spring. Am I seriously to take it that you're proposing to engage me to do it for him?"

"I haven't made myself clear." Abel Bendigo's blandness remained unmarred. "This matter has nothing to do with Colonel Spring or the security department. I have not permitted it to be put in the Colonel's hands . . . I consider it too special a problem. I'm handling it personally."

"And you haven't got anywhere," grinned the Inspector.

"What worries me—" the prominent eyes chilled—"is that I *have* got somewhere."

"Oh," said Ellery. "Then you know who sent the letters?"

"I believe," said Abel Bendigo, "I do."

The Queens exchanged glances.

"Well," demanded the older man, "and who is it?"

Bendigo did not reply.

Ellery looked at the two guards. They had not relaxed. It was hard to say that they were even listening. "Shall we send these boys out for a beer, Mr. Bendigo?"

"You misunderstand. I'd rather not disclose what I've found because I don't want to prejudice your investigation. I never jump to conclusions, Mr. Queen. And when I reach a conclusion I invariably double-check it. There's always the possibility—though not the probability—that in this matter I'm wrong. I want you gentlemen to tell me whether I am or not."

"And your brother King? What does he think of all this, Mr. Bendigo?"

"He glanced at the letters and laughed. Threats amuse him. They don't amuse me."

"Then he doesn't know the results of your private investigation? Or even that you've been investigating?"

Bendigo shrugged. "I haven't told him. What he knows or doesn't know is another matter." He said abruptly, "I want you both to come with me."

"This morning?"

"This minute."

Inspector Queen stared as if Abel Bendigo were out of his mind.

Ellery smiled. "My father is a salaried employee of the City of New York, Mr. Bendigo. And while I'm a relatively free soul, the necessity of earning a living has managed to foul me up in responsibilities and commitments. You can't walk in here and expect us to get up and walk out with you—with even you, Mr. Bendigo—on five minutes' notice."

"Your father has been taken care of—"

"Hold it." The Inspector deliberately went back to the dropleaf table and sat down. "And how would you go about 'taking care of' me, Mr. Bendigo?"

But Bendigo said patiently, "As for you, Mr. Queen, you're between novels and you are four issues ahead with the editorial work on *Ellery Queen's Mystery Magazine*. And the only investigation on your calender at the present time has been taken out of your hands."

"Has it?" said Ellery. "That's news to me."

"If you'll glance through your morning mail, you'll find a note from a man named Harold P. Consideo terminating your connection with his affairs."

Ellery looked at him. He went to the table after a moment and picked up the letters on his breakfast plate. He shuffled through them and came to one that made him stop and look at Abel Bendigo again. Then he tore off the end of the envelope.

A letter fell out. Ellery glanced through it. The Inspector reached over and took the letter and he read it, too.

"Mr. Bendigo," said Ellery, "what makes you think you can interfere in my life this way?" The man in the chair drummed on the leather. "How well do you know Consideo?"

"I don't know him at all. These things are easily arranged. Let's not waste time on Consideo. Are you ready?"

"Me?" said Ellery. "I think not."

"How long will it take you?"

"Too long, Mr. Bendigo, for your busy schedule."

Bendigo opened his pink mouth. But then he shut it and regarded Ellery earnestly. "Why do you take this attitude?"

"A shoehorn has nothing to say about who buys it or the use it's put to. A man wants to feel that he has. Mr. Bendigo," said Ellery, "I like to be asked."

"And I'm his old man," said his father.

"I apologize. We Bendigos live in something of a vacuum. Of course, you're perfectly right." He leaned forward, pudgy hands clasped like a deacon. "Making sure who wrote these letters is of great importance, and not only to me. The assassination of my brother would be followed by the most serious consequences all over the world." He was choosing his words with care. Now he looked up at them with a smile. "Would you gentlemen accept the assignment?"

Ellery smiled back. "Where are your headquarters?"

"On Bendigo Island."

"Bendigo Island . . . I don't believe I know it. Do you, Dad?"

"I've heard tell," said the Inspector dryly, "but I can't tell you where it is."

"It's not well-known," said their visitor. "And you won't find it on any chart."

"Where is it?"

Abel Bendigo looked regretful. "I really mustn't say, Mr. Queen. It's one of our strictest rules. You'll be taken there and returned to this apartment when the job is done."

"How far away is it?"

"I wish I were free to tell you."

"How long does it take to get there from New York?"

"Planes travel fast these days. Not too long."

Ellery shrugged. "I'm afraid, Mr. Bendigo, I'll have to think it over."

"And *I'm* afraid," said Inspector Queen, getting out of his chair, "I'll have to be moseying on down to Centre Street. Interesting experience meeting you, Mr. Bendigo, and I've never meant anything more in my life."

"Call your office first, Inspector."

"What for?"

"You'll find that, as of this morning, you're on leave of absence. On full pay."

"Now I know this is a pipe dream!"

The Inspector, russet about the ears and neck, stamped past Brown Shirt into his bedroom. Abel Bendigo quietly waited. Ellery heard his father's voice, on his direct wire to Police Headquarters, raised in outrage, as if a leave of absence on full pay were cruel and unusual punishment. When the Inspector came out, however, he was looking thoughtful.

"Nobody seems to know how it happened or why!"

Bendigo smiled again. "Mr. Queen, you'll change your mind?"

"I can't very well change it when I haven't yet made it up."

Bendigo rose, glancing at his wristwatch. Something final glittered from his eyeglasses. "I was asked not to use this unless it became necessary, Mr. Queen. You've left me no choice." He handed a long envelope to Ellery. Then he turned to one of the windows, clasping his hands at his back.

The Inspector glared at the envelope. It was addressed by hand to *Mr. Ellery Queen, New York City.* The reverse was heavily sealed with wax.

Ellery broke the seal. The envelope contained a single sheet of very stiff notepaper. The embossing at the top of the sheet made him glance quickly at their visitor.

The letter was entirely handwritten:

MY DEAR MR. QUEEN:

This request has no official status and is made in strictest confidence. Regardless of your decision, I must ask you to destroy this letter immediately upon reading its contents.

Will you put your professional services at the disposal of bearer?

In doing so you would be performing an act of high citizenship, in a matter in which your government has a vital interest but in which it cannot participate by the normal means, for reasons which I may not disclose.

It would be helpful, in the event you undertake the assignment, if your father would make a special point of joining you.

Yours sincerely,

Ellery studied the famous signature for a long moment. "Mr. Bendigo, are you aware of the contents of this letter?"

"I have a fair idea of what it says," was the dry reply.

"But why me?" muttered the Inspector.

"What, Inspector?" Abel Bendigo turned.

"Excuse us, Mr. Bendigo, for just a few minutes," said Ellery.

Bendigo said nothing.

BLUE SHIRT stood aside and the Queens went into Ellery's study. Ellery shut the door in the blank face and carefully turned the key.

Mrs. Fabrikant's vacuum cleaner was still keening behind the bedroom door.

"I don't get it," murmured Ellery. "Granted that King Bendigo is large pumpkins, that his activities touch on national interests, and that the Bendigo name drags enough weight to get a letter like this out of Washington—why either of us?"

"If this isn't a forgery, son."

"Somehow I don't see forgery in that fellow's horoscope."

"Call Washington," said his father. "Just for the hell of it."

Ellery put the call through with some excitement and no conviction. Yet six minutes later, against all reason, he heard the voice of the letter writer in his ear. There was no mistaking those dry, easy tones.

"No, it's all right, Mr. Queen, I was hoping you'd check. When B. asked for a letter, I wrote it with care." The speaker chuckled. "In spite of the seal."

"May I talk freely, sir?"

"This is a private line."

"Was it B.'s idea to hire me?"

"Yes."

"You're aware, of course, of the nature of the case?"

"Yes, indeed. Someone is threatening His Majesty's life." The dry tones were drier than usual. "B. thinks he knows who it is, wants confirmation. Since he does, I reminded him that a brace of good heads is preferable to one, and I suggested your father go along, too. I have something—I think I used the word 'special'—in mind for Inspector Queen. Are you going to accept?"

"Yes, sir."

"Good! The United States government is extremely—if unofficially—interested in keeping up to date on the state of His Majesty's health. Is your father there?"

"Yes, sir."

"Let me talk to him."

Inspector Queen said, "Yes, sir?" and then he listened for a long time. After which he said, "Yes, *sir*," and hung up.

"I thought that last paragraph concealed a weenie," muttered Ellery. "What does he want you to do, Dad?"

"Give him a confidential report on Bendigo Island. What's on it, who's on it—plant, personnel, plans, purposes, detail maps if possible—the whole picture, Ellery."

"Do you mean to say our own government doesn't know—!"

"Apparently not. Or what they know is sketchy or not up to date. So I've got to grow a tail in my old age," said the Inspector incredulously, "and make like the Trojan horse."

"What fun."

They grinned at each other suddenly, shook hands, and then Ellery went into his bedroom to calm Mrs. Fabrikant, give her some money and instructions about the apartment, and pack a bag. Before leaving he burned the Washington letter and envelope in the brass ashtray on his night table and used the nozzle of Mrs. Fabricant's vacuum cleaner to suck up the ashes.

THE TWO CARS skirted La Guardia Airport and drew up before a hangar with a gilded roof on which was lettered in black the single giant word, BENDIGO. The hangar was filled with aircraft of varying sizes and types, but all uniformly golden and inscribed with the unqualified name. An immense passenger plane loomed before the hangar, its motors warming up. Attendants in black and gold coveralls swarmed over the plane.

Blue Shirt carried the bags. A Bendigo plane was taking the air from one of the field runways, and Ellery asked him,

"Where's that one going? Or is such a question on Colonel Spring's *verboten* list?"

"Buenos Aires, Johannesburg, Teheran—I wouldn't know, sir. Hurry, please."

Brown Shirt was friendlier. "We'll be on the plane with you. . . . Help you up the step, sir?"

The Inspector growled, "Not if you want to stay healthy!"

They found Abel Bendigo waiting for them in the big ship. Its interior made them blink. It was fitted out like a private railroad car, with deep leather chairs, lamps, books, a central bar, and several compartments. The attendants—Ellery counted five, and he suspected others—wore black and gold uniforms. There were no women attendants and no other passengers.

"We're taking off at once, gentlemen," said Abel Bendigo abruptly. "The stewards will see to your wants. I'll have to ask you to excuse me. My work . . ." His voice trailed off as he turned away. Two dark-suited, middle-aged men carrying portfolios were waiting for him at the door of one of the compartments. He brushed by them and they followed him quickly. A moment later the compartment door was shut.

Rather pointedly, Ellery thought.

The ship began to move.

"Would you take seats, please?" said Brown Shirt's pleasantly chill voice.

He strapped them into two of the armchairs.

"You forgot the electrodes," muttered the Inspector.

Ellery said nothing. He was watching Blue Shirt. Blue Shirt was moving from window to window, pulling down metalvaned black blinds and securing them to the sills.

"ALL this hush-hush," said Ellery. They had felt the lift of the ship and heard the motors settle down to a comfortable thunder, and Ellery had even made a note of the take-off time, but these were mechanical observations in a hopeless cause. "How secret can you keep an island?"

"There probably aren't five men in the United States who know where it is."

"How do you know?"

"I heard an earful from one of the brass who'd been head of liaison at Bendigo Midwestern headquarters, in Illinois, till about two years after the war. He was feeling brotherly after six Martinis—I'd got his son out of a bad jam in New York."

"I don't get the point of it all," said Ellery, staring at the blinded windows.

"Seems this King Bendigo's always been a secretive gent," said the Inspector reflectively. "Some men never grow up. Play the same games, on a bigger scale. He probably had a dark cellar as a kid, a secret hideout, and buried treasure you got to with a map drawn in blood.

"Take this island of his. There's no earthly reason the General could see why Bendigo would need an island home office. Or why, if he had to have an island, he'd make a mystery of its whereabouts. During the war he operated from the mainland, like anybody else."

"Then Bendigo Island is a postwar development?"

"Yes and no. The way I heard it, the island was owned by one of our allies. England or France, maybe, but I'm guessing. It was one of those islands that never got onto a map, like so many in the Pacific, only this one is supposed to be in the Atlantic."

"I don't believe it. I mean that it's not on the map."

"I'm not asking you to believe it," said his father. "I'm telling you what I heard. The likeliest explanation is that it's on the map, all right, but as an uninhabited island. Maybe surrounded by dangerous reefs and off the regular sea and air lanes.

"Well, during the war," continued the Inspector, "the government that owned the island decided to prepare it for an emergency hideout. It may have been during the Battle of Britain, if it was England. If it was France, it was probably after the fall of Paris but before De Gaulle fell afoul of F.D.R.

"Anyway, the British, or the French Resistance, or what-have-you, began secret construction on the island. It was then known as Location XXX, and only a few of the top brass in

Washington knew anything about it. It was done with the consent of the United States government, of course—for all I know, with us supplying most of the materials.

"According to the General's story, they built for keeps—a tremendous administration building, a lot of it underground, shelters, barracks, arsenals, factories, a couple of airfields—the works; they even dredged out an artificial harbor. The idea was that if the government of the country that owned the island had to leave home base in a hurry, this was where they'd evacuate to. The whole shoreline was camouflaged and the waters around the island mined. The development of radar made it possible to anticipate the approach of aircraft, too."

Ellery said darkly, "I've never heard a syllable of this."

"You weren't supposed to. It was one of the best-kept secrets of the war. As it turned out, the island was never used. The installations were finished just about when the European phase of the war ended. And after Hiroshima, atomic developments made the whole project seem kind of silly."

"And Bendigo bought it?"

"Leased it on a ninety-nine-year lease. Complete, just the way they'd built it, right down to the radar. The lease was cleared with Washington, but even if Washington didn't like the idea they couldn't do much about it. Bendigo had been too important during the war. And he's still at it."

The Inspector stopped. One of the uniformed stewards was approaching.

"Would you gentlemen care for your luncheon now?"

Brown Shirt was strolling their way.

"Later, I think," Ellery said. "Unless we land soon?"

"I can't say about that, sir," said the steward.

"Don't you know when we set down? I'm not asking you where. I'm just asking when."

"I can't say about anything, sir, but lunch." The steward retreated, and Brown Shirt turned away.

"Relax," grinned Inspector Queen. "These people are said to go through a screening that makes an F.B.I. atomic project clearance look like a vag booking in the Squedunk Corners pokey." Then he looked grim. "This island of Bendigo's is no joke. Bendigo's supposed to have a private army there. For that matter, his own navy and air force, too."

"Navy?" said Ellery incredulously. "Air force? You mean shooting stuff?"

The Inspector shrugged. "I can only tell you what the General told me. Maybe he was pulling my leg. But he mentioned at least two ex-warships, a light cruiser and a heavy cruiser, and a system of submarine nets and underwater detectors, as well as a couple of submarines. The shoreline's still camouflaged and the radar works twenty-four hours a day. You might say it's a whole new little country. Autonomous. Whom would Bendigo have to account to? I guess that's why Washington is so interested."

"His Christian name begins to impress me. Shooting stuff . . . What's he expect, an invasion?"

"Don't be childish. Nobody invades a man as powerful as King Bendigo. Not because you couldn't wipe him off the map he isn't on, but because he's in too many places at the same time. He's spread all over the globe. Bendigo Island's just the —the concentration of his personality, his court, you might say. It's just that, by the way, from what the General said. Bendigo's added a real palace to the island. . . . No, I imagine the shooting stuff—his 'army,' his 'navy,' his 'air force'—it's all kind of automatic. It goes with power. It's for show, like a throne. No self-respecting royalty without it."

"But it's . . . outmoded, all that," complained Ellery. "He can't be a boy playing with lead soldiers. What are a couple of warships and a few planes in the world of A- and H-bombs? Beanshooters. I don't get it."

The Inspector shrugged again and looked around. The steward anticipated him. There was a bottle at his elbow immediately, and a glass.

Ellery squirmed in the chair. He got up. But then he sat down again.

The Inspector sipped, leaned back, closed his eyes. The motors flowed on like a waterfall. He felt sleepy suddenly.

But his arm was prodded and he opened one eye.

"His family," Ellery mumbled.

"Hm?"

"His family. Does it consist of his brother Abel and himself exclusively? Is King married? Children? Parents? What do you know about him personally, Dad?"

The Inspector struggled awake. "There are three brothers, not two. No sisters, and if their parents are living the General doesn't know about them. Only one of the brothers is married, and that's King himself. No children. Take a snooze, son."

But Ellery said, "Who's the third brother? Where does he fit?"

"Hmm?" The Inspector opened the eye again. "Judah?"

"Who?"

"Judah Bendigo. He's the middle one. King's the eldest of the three. Abel's the baby. Abel is sort of the Prime Minister —he and King are very close. But Judah . . . the General didn't know *what* he did in the outfit. Didn't see Judah do anything but lap up brandy. His impression was Judah's a lush."

"Who is King's wife?"

"The Queen. Who else?" murmured his father with a drowsy grin. "Queen Karla . . . well, almost. The General said Karla's of real royal blood. From Europe. A princess, or grand duchess, or something."

"Now tell me she's a raving beauty, and I'll take on Blue Shirt with one hand behind my back!"

"A knockout, the General said. He had to visit the island several times."

Ellery muttered, "And the Court Jester? Of course, there's a Court Jester."

"Max is his name," nodded the Inspector. "An ex-wrestler, big as a house. Follows King around, works him out, body-guards him, keeps him laughing. Everything but the cap and bells. Shut up, will you? I'm an old man."

And the Inspector shut the other eye, decisively.

ABEL BENDIGO joined them at lunch. He seemed less pre-occupied. The two middle-aged secretaries did not appear.

The stewards had set the table for only two, and Ellery remarked that in an organization as perfectly oiled as this it seemed a mighty slip—or was one of them to be starved?

"I never eat lunch," said the Prime Minister with a smile. "Interferes with my afternoon work. A glass of buttermilk sometimes, or yoghurt. But don't let that stop you gentlemen. The chef was detached from my brother's Residence staff especially for the occasion."

The lunch was superb, and the Inspector tackled it with gusto. Ellery ate absently.

"Are your brothers as Spartan as you are, Mr. Bendigo?" asked the Inspector. "My, this is delicious."

"Very nearly. King has simple tastes in food, as I have, and Judah—" Abel Bendigo stopped smiling—"Judah hardly eats at all."

"Judah?" said Ellery, looking up.

"Another brother, Mr. Queen. Will you have some brandy? I'm told this is exceptional, though I don't drink myself."

"Judah," said Ellery. "And Abel. The 'King' doesn't seem to follow, Mr. Bendigo. Or was he a king in Israel from the womb?"

"I think," said Bendigo, "he was." And he looked up. The Queens looked up, too. Blue Shirt and Brown Shirt loomed there.

"What now?" asked the Inspector humorously. "The execution?" Nevertheless he quickly swallowed the last of his brandy.

Bendigo said slowly, "We've come about halfway, gentlemen. From here until we land these two men will remain with you. I'm sure you'll understand, if not appreciate, the necessity to stick to rules. I regret it, but I must ask you to make no attempt to get your bearings. These men are under the strictest orders to prevent it." He got up suddenly. "You'll see me on the island." Before either could open his mouth the Prime Minister had retired to his compartment again.

The twins did not move.

"Halfway," muttered the Inspector. "That means about eight hours out. At, say, three hundred m.p.h., the island's around twenty-four hundred miles from New York. Or is it?"

"Or is it?" said Ellery, looking up at Brown Shirt.

Brown Shirt said nothing.

"Because, of course, we can be flying around in circles. . . .
Funny way Bendigo put that parting crack of his, Dad. Why
you'll see me on the island instead of the more natural *I'll
see you on the island?*"

Hours later, in the middle of a nap, Ellery was answered.

He awoke at a touch to find himself in total darkness, and
when he heard his father's outraged exclamation he knew that
they had both been blindfolded.

3

WHEN the dark cloths were removed, the son and the father
found themselves standing with Brown Shirt and Blue Shirt
beside the big ship, on a great airfield.

The midafternoon sun rode an intense sky, and they blinked
in the backwash of glare.

Abel Bendigo was close by talking to an undersized man.
Behind the undersized man stood a squad of tall soldiers, at
attention. The undersized man had prim shoulders and large
hips and he was dressed in a beautiful black and gold military
uniform. The black cap he wore sported a linked-globe-and-
crown insignia above the visor and the legend PRPD. This
officer, who was smoking a brown cigaret, turned from time
to time to stare at the Queens with the friendliness of a fish.
Once he shook his head as if it were all too much for him to
bear. However, he bore it—whatever it was—with resignation. The Prime Minister talked on.

They faced a camouflaged administration building. Men in
black and gold suits moved above in the glassed circle of the
control tower. Ground crews swarmed about a dozen large

hangarlike structures, also camouflaged. Planes flitted about,
field ambulances raced, commissary trucks trundled; all were
painted black and gold. A very large cargo ship was just
taking the air.

A high wall of vegetation surrounded the field, screening
off the rest of the island. The vegetation seemed semitropical
and much of it had the underwater look of Caribbean flora.
And Ellery had never seen a sky like this in the North Tem-
perate Zone. They were in southern waters.

He had the queerest feeling that they were also in a foreign
land. Everyone about him looked American and the airfield
buildings betrayed a functional vigor inseparable from advanced American design—Frank Lloyd Wrightism at its angri-
est. It was the air that was alien, a steel atmosphere of discipline, of trained oneness, that was foreign to the American
scene.

And then there was the flag, flapping from a mast above
the control tower. It was like no flag Ellery had ever seen, a
pair of linked globes in map colors surmounted by a crown
of gold, and all on a black field. The flag made him uncom-
fortable and he looked away. His glance touched his father's;
it had just come from the flagpole, too.

They said nothing to each other because the Shirts were so
attentively at their elbows, and because there was really nothing to communicate but questions and doubts which neither
could satisfy.

The Prime Minister finished at last, and the hippy little
man in the splendid uniform waved the squad of soldiers
away. They wheeled and marched to the administration building and disappeared. Bendigo walked over with his companion. The Shirts, Ellery noted, stiffened and saluted. But it was
not Abel Bendigo they saluted; it was the hippy little man.

"Sorry to have kept you waiting," Bendigo said, but he did
not explain why. "This is the head of our Public Relations
and Personnel Department, Colonel Spring. You'll probably
be seeing something of each other."

The Queens said a word or two.

"Anything I can do, gentlemen," said Colonel Spring, offering a limp white hand. His eyes remained fishy. His whole face was marine—greenish white and without plasticity, like the face of a drowned man.

"Isn't the question rather, Colonel," Ellery asked, "anything *we* can do?"

The underwater eyes regarded him.

"I mean, your PRPD seems to lean heavily to the military side. What are our restrictions?"

"Restrictions?" murmured Colonel Spring.

"Well, you see, Colonel," remarked Inspector Queen, "there's never any telling where a thing like this can lead. How free are we to come and go?"

"Anywhere." The white hand fluttered. "Within reason."

"There are certain installations," said Abel Bendigo, "which are out of bounds, gentlemen. If you're stopped anywhere, you'll understand why."

"And you'll be stopped," said the Colonel with a smile. "You're going directly to the Home Office, Mr. Abel?"

"Yes. Excuse us, Colonel."

The little officer rather deliberately ground the butt of his *cigarillo* under his boot heel. Then he smiled again, touched his visor with his delicate fingers, and turned curtly away.

The Shirts instantly followed.

"Valuable man," said the Prime Minister. "Gentlemen?"

The Queens turned. A black limousine had come up on silent treads and a footman in livery was stiffly holding the door open. To the front door was attached a gold medallion, showing two linked globes surmounted by a heavy crown.

Like a coat of arms.

THE airport was on high ground, and when the car drove through the screen of vegetation the Queens had a panoramic view of half the island.

They realized at once why this island had been selected as the site of a government-in-hiding. It was shaped like a bowl with a mound in the center. The shoreline, which was the edge of the bowl, was composed of steep and heavily wooded cliffs, so that from the sea no evidence of human occupancy or construction in the interior would be visible. The mound in the middle of the bowl, where the airfields lay, was at approximately the same elevation as the wooded cliffs at the shoreline. Between the central airfields and the cliffs on the rim, the ground sloped sharply to a valley. It was in this valley, invisible from the sea, that all the building had been done.

The sight was startling. It was a large island, the valley was great, and as far as the eye could see the valley was packed with buildings. Most of them seemed industrial plants, vast smokeless factories covering many acres; but there were office buildings, too, and to the lower slopes of the hillsides clung colonies of small homes and barracklike structures which, Abel Bendigo explained, housed the workers. The small homes were occupied by minor executives. There was also, he said, a development of more spacious private dwellings on another part of the island; these were for the use of the top executives and the scientific staffs and their families.

"Families?" exclaimed the Inspector. "You mean you've got housewives and kids here, too?"

"Of course," replied the Prime Minister, smiling. "We provide a normal, natural environment for our employees. We have schools, hospitals, recreation halls, athletic fields—everything you'd find in a model community in the States, although on a rather crowded scale. Space is our most serious problem."

Ellery thought preposterously: *Lebensraum.*

"But food, clothing, comic books," said Inspector Queen feebly. "Don't tell me you produce all that!"

"No, though if we had the room we certainly would. Everything is brought in by our cargo fleets, chiefly airborne."

"You find planes more practicable than ships?" asked Ellery.

"Well, we have a problem with our harbor facilities. We prefer to keep our shoreline as natural-looking as possible—"

"There's the harbor now, Ellery!" said the Inspector.

"I'm sorry," said Bendigo, suddenly austere. He leaned forward to say something to the chauffeur in a low tone. The car, which was speeding along inside the rim of woods, immediately turned off into a side road and plunged down to the valley again. But Ellery had snatched a glimpse, through a break in the vegetation, of a horseshoe-shaped bay very nearly landlocked, across the narrow neck of which rode a warship.

The chauffeur had gone slightly pale. He and the footman sat rigidly.

"We didn't really see anything, Mr. Bendigo," said Ellery. "Just a heavy cruiser. One of your naval vessels?"

"My brother's yacht *Bendigo*," murmured the Prime Minister.

Inspector Queen was staring down into the valley with glittering eyes. "Yacht my sacroiliac," he snapped. "These food and other supplies, Mr. Bendigo. Do you give the stuff away, or how do you handle it? What do you pay your people off in?"

"Our banks issue scrip, Inspector, accepted by Company stores as well as by individuals all over the island."

"And when a man wants to quit, or is fired, does he take his Bendigo scrip with him?" asked Ellery.

"We have very few resignations, Mr. Queen," said the Prime Minister. "Of course, if an employee should be discharged, his account would be settled in the currency of the country of his origin."

"I don't suppose your people find unions necessary?"

"Why, we have unions, Mr. Queen. All sorts of unions."

"No strikes, however."

"Strikes?" Bendigo was surprised. "Why should our employees strike? They're highly paid, well housed, all their creature comforts provided, their children scientifically cared for—"

"Say." Inspector Queen turned from the window as if the thought had just struck him. "Where do all your working people come from, Mr. Bendigo?"

"We have employment offices everywhere."

"And recruiting offices?" murmured Ellery.

"I beg your pardon?"

"Your soldiers, Mr. Bendigo. They are soldiers, aren't they?"

"Oh, no. The uniforms are for convenience only. Our security people are not—" Abel Bendigo leaned forward, pointing. "There's the Home Office."

He was smiling again, and Ellery knew they would get no more information.

THE Home Office looked like a rimless carriage wheel thrown carelessly into a bush. Trees and shrubbery crowded it, and its roofs were thickly planted. From the air it was probably invisible.

Eight long wings radiated like spokes from a common center. The spokes, Abel Bendigo explained, housed the general offices, the hub the executive offices. The hub, four stories high, stood one story higher than the spokes, so that the domed top story of the central building predominated.

Not far away, Ellery noticed some mottled towers and pylons and the glitter of glass rising from the heart of a wood. The few elements of the structure that could be seen extended over a wide area, and he asked what it was.

"The Residence," replied the Prime Minister. "But I'm afraid we'll have to hurry, gentlemen. We're far later than I'd intended."

They followed him, alert to everything.

They entered the Home Office at the juncture of two of the spokes, through a surprisingly small door, and found themselves in a circular lobby of black marble. Corridors radiated from the perimeter in every direction. An armed guard stood at the entrance to each corridor. They could see office doors, endless lines of them, each exactly like the next.

In the center of the lobby rose a circular column of extraordinary thickness. A door was set into it at floor level, and Ellery guessed that it was an elevator shaft. Before the door was a metal booth, behind which stood three men in uniform. The collars of their tunics bore the gold initials PRPD.

Abel Bendigo walked directly to the desk of the booth. To the Queens' astonishment, he offered his right hand to the central of the three security men. This functionary quickly took an impression of the Prime Minister's thumb while the man to the right whisked an odd-looking card, like a section of

X-ray film set in a cardboard frame, from one of a multiplicity
of file drawers before him. This film was placed in a small
machine on the desk, and the Prime Minister's thumbprint
was inserted in the bottom of the machine. The central man
looked through an eyepiece carefully. The machine apparently
superimposed on the fresh thumbprint the transparent control
print on file, in such a way that any discrepancy was revealed
at a glance. This was confirmed a few moments later when the
Queens' thumbprints were taken and their names recorded.

"Films of your prints will be ready in a short time," said
Bendigo, "and they will go into the control file. No one, not
even my brother King, can get into any part of this building
without a thumbprint checkup."

"But these men certainly know you and your brother!" protested Inspector Queen.

"Exceptions don't make the rule, Inspector. They break it.
Will you step in, gentlemen?"

It was a self-service elevator. It shot upward, and a moment
later they preceded their guide into a strange-looking reception room.

It was shaped like a wedge of pie with a bite taken out of
its pointed end, the bite being formed by the section of elevator
wall giving into the room. They discovered later that the whole
pie represented by the floorplan of the dome was composed of
three pieces, of which the reception room was the narrowest
and smallest. King Bendigo's private office took up half the
circle. The third room, for King's staff of private secretaries,
and the reception room made up the other half-circle. The
elevator had three doors, one to each of the rooms.

The outside wall of the reception room was composed entirely of fluted glass bricks. There were no windows, but the
air was cool and sweet.

The room was stark. There were a few functional armchairs of black leather, a low copper table six feet in diameter,
a small black desk and chair, and that was all. Not a lamp—
the two side walls themselves glowed—not a vase of flowers,
not a picture. And no rug on the floor, which was made of
some springy material in a black and gold design. There was

not even the solace of a loud voice, for no receptionist received them in this queer reception room, and it was so thoroughly soundproofed that a voice could not be heard fifteen feet away.

Abel Bendigo said: "My brother is tied up just now." How he knew this Ellery could not imagine, unless the Prime Minister had memorized his sovereign's schedule for days in advance. "It will take—" Bendigo glanced at his wristwatch—"another twenty-three minutes. Make yourselves comfortable, gentlemen. Cigarets and cigars on the table there, and if you'd care for liquid refreshment, there's a cabinet in that wall. And now please excuse me. I was to have sat in at this conference from the beginning. I'll be back for you when King is free."

There were two doors with conventional knobs in the reception room, one in each of the straight walls. Abel Bendigo slipped through the lefthand door and shut it before either man could catch a glimpse of what lay beyond.

They looked at each other.

"Alone," said Ellery, "at last."

"I wonder."

"You wonder what, Dad?"

"Where it's planted."

"Where what's planted?"

"The ear. Of the listening business. If this is where His Nibs keeps visitors waiting, you don't think he'd pass up the chance to find out what's really on their minds? Ellery, how's this setup strike you so far?"

"Incredible."

The Inspector sank uneasily into one of the black armchairs.

Ellery strolled over to the elevator door. Like the one in the lobby, it had sunk into the floor on their arrival and had risen shut again. The door section fitted so cunningly into the curved shaft wall that it took him a long moment to locate the crack which outlined it.

"You'd need a nuclear can-opener to get this open." Ellery went over to the door in the righthand wall. "I wonder where this goes."

"Probably an outer office."

Ellery tried the door; it was locked. "For his forty-nine secretaries. Do they wear uniforms, too, I wonder?"

"I'm more interested in King King. What are the odds he wears ermine?"

"Nobody trusts anybody around here," Ellery complained. He was over at the door in the lefthand wall now.

"Better not," advised his father. "It might open."

"No such luck." Ellery was right; the door to King Bendigo's office, through which they had seen Abel hurry, was fast. "Sealed in, that's what we are. Like a couple of damned anchovies."

The Inspector did not smile. "We're a long way from Eighty-seventh Street, son."

"Stiff upper." But the quip did not amuse even its author.

Ellery surveyed the small black desk. It was of heavy metal, screwed to the floor. Its empty swivel chair, of the same metal, faced the smooth cylindrical section of the elevator.

"I wonder why the receptionist isn't here."

"Maybe he had to go to the men's room."

"I doubt if the Bendigo code recognizes hand-washing as a legitimate excuse for dereliction of duty. Besides," Ellery tried a few drawers, "the desk is locked. No, here's a drawer that isn't." It was the bottom drawer, a deep one.

His father saw him stare, then drop into the chair. "What is it?"

"Dictaphonic gadget of some sort." Ellery was doubled over. "Of a type new to me. I wonder if . . ." There was a *click!* and a faint whirring sound. Ellery whistled softly. "Do you suppose this can be hooked up to the big boy's office?"

The Inspector jumped out of the armchair. "Careful, son!"

"He'd want records of private talks. Too bad we won't have the chance to lift the record of the one that's going on in there right now—"

"*—overexcited. Sit down, Mr. Minister.*"

The easy male voice boomed in their ears. The Queens whirled. But, except for themselves, the reception room was empty.

"The machine," whispered the Inspector. "Ellery, what did you touch?"

"Does double duty." The voice had not resumed, but the whirring sound continued. "Records the sound, but the pressure of something here amplifies the sound simultaneously— Here it is! You have to keep your finger on this stud."

The man with the easy voice was laughing. It was the laugh of a big man. It filled the room like a wind.

"*—no climate for temper, Mr. Minister. Abel, help Señor Minister to a chair.*"

"*Yes, King.*" Abel's voice.

"Bendigo the First," whispered the Inspector.

"*Are you all right?*" The easy voice was amused.

"*Thank you.*" This was a bubbly voice with a strong South American accent, struggling to control its fear and anger. "*It is difficult to remain calm, my dear sir, when one has been abducted by brigands from one's home in the middle of the night and spirited out of one's country by an unlawful foreign aircraft!*"

"*It was necessary to have a private conversation within walls whose ears we could trust, Mr. Minister. We regret the inconvenience to you.*"

"*Regret! Do not trifle with me. This is kidnaping, and you may be very sure I shall make an international incident of it, with the strongest possible representations to your government!*"

"*My government? Just where do you think you are?*" The voice was still amused, but a power-switch had been flicked on.

"*I will not be intimidated!*" The foreign voice was shouting now. "*I know very well what you are after, Señor King Bendigo. We have access at last to the secret files of the defunct régime. The new government, which I have the great honor to serve as Minister of War, will not be so complaisant, I promise you! We shall confiscate the Guerrerra works under the powers vested in El Presidente by the National Resources Decree of the fourteenth May, and we will have no dealings with The Bodigen Arms Company or any other of your creature subsidiaries, Señor!*"

Thunder smote the machine in the receptionist's desk.

"Smacked something, His Majesty did," whispered Inspector Queen.

"Let's hope it wasn't Señor Minister of War."

"You miserable anteater—!" It was a bellow.

"Anteater?" screamed the foreign voice. *"You insult, you insult! I demand to be flown back to Ciudad Zuma immediately!"*

"Sit down! How much of this drivel do you think I'm going to stan—" The growl stopped. Then the powerful voice said impatiently, *"Yes, Abel. What is it?"*

There was a long silence.

"The sweet *sotto voce* of reason," murmured Ellery. "Or Abel's passed him a note."

They heard King Bendigo laugh again. This time the voice said smoothly, *"Forgive me for losing my temper, Señor. Believe me, I respect the position of your government even though it is hostile to our interests. But there are no viewpoints —no matter how opposing, Mr. Minister—which can't be reconciled."*

"Impossible!" The angry voice registered several decibels fewer.

"To establish a private cordiality, Mr. Minister? Known, let us say, only to us and to you?"

"There is nothing more to be said!" But now it was merely fuming.

"Well, Abel, it looks as though we're in for a licking."

Abel murmured something; the words did not come through.

"Unless, Mr. Minister, you don't quite see how . . . Let me ask you: Did your predecessor in the War Ministry manage to salvage his yacht in the revolution, Señor?"

"She saved the traitor's life," said the foreign voice stiffly. *"He made his escape in her."*

"Oh, yes. You must have admired her, Señor—your enthusiasm for pleasure craft is well-known. And she's one hundred and twenty feet of sheer poetry, as my brother Judah would say. Did say."

"She was beautiful." The War Minister spoke in the wistful,

bitter way of the lover who has lost. *"Had the swine not got to her in time . . . But I presume on your schedule, Señor King—"*

"Her sister is yours."

There was a silence.

"She's identical in every respect, Mr. Minister, except that her designer tells me she's even faster. And speed in a ship is a quality not to be despised, Señor, as your predecessor discovered. Who knows? The politics of your country tend to be somewhat unstable—"

"Señor, you bribe me!" the Minister of War replied indignantly. But it was not as if he were really surprised. His tone had a flinch in it. *"I thank you for your gift, Señor King Bendigo, but I repudiate it with scorn. Now I wish to leave."*

"Good boy," breathed the Inspector. "He made it."

"After a bit of a tussle," grinned Ellery. "Ah, there's Abel calling time again. Conference in the box. Do they pitch to the Señor or pass him?"

"Here it comes!"

"Gift?" came the dark, rich voice. *"Who said anything about a gift, Mr. Minister? I had something quite legal in mind."*

"Legal . . . ?"

"I'm offering her for sale."

The harassed man laughed. *"At a discount of five per cent, perhaps, because we are such cordial friends, Señor? This is absurdity. I am not a wealthy man—"*

"I'm sure you can afford this, Mr. Minister."

"I am sure I cannot!"

"Don't you have twenty-five dollars?"

There was a very long silence indeed.

"Struck him out," said the Inspector.

"I believe, Señor Bendigo," said the foreign voice, and for the first time it was without heat or distress, *"that would make a bargain I could not afford to ignore. I shall purchase your yacht for twenty-five dollars."*

"Our agent will call on you in Ciudad Zuma next Friday, Mr. Minister, with the bill of sale and the other documents

necessary for your signature. Needless to say, the other docu-
ments are equally important to the transfer of title."

"*Needless to say.*" The foreign voice stopped for an instant,
then it went on amiably: "*Love of the sea is in the blood of
my family. I have a son in the Naval Ministry, Señor Bendigo,
who is also an ardent yachtsman. There will be no difficulty
about the other documents, none whatever, if you will sell me
also the eighty-foot* Atalanta IV, *which has only recently, I believe, come off your ways. Possession of such a prize would
make my son Cristoforo a happy young man. At the same
purchase price, of course.*"

"*You have a nose for bargains, Mr. Minister,*" said King
Bendigo gently.

"*I also keep them, my friend.*"

"*Take care of it, Abel.*"

After a moment, they heard a door open and close.

"*And I mean a nose,*" came King Bendigo's growl. "*How
good an investment is that sucker, Abel?*"

"*He's the intellectual strong man of the Zuma régime.*"

"*He'd better stay that way! Who's next?*"

"*The E–16 matter.*"

"*The mouth-twitcher? I thought that was settled, Abel.*"

"*It isn't.*"

"*The trouble with the world today is that it has too many
little crooks running it under the delusion that they're big
crooks! All they do is shoot the cost of history higher—they
don't change the result a damn. Send him in.*"

There was a lull, and Ellery mumbled, "In big stuff they
send 'em in direct. I wonder if there's another elevator to
H.R.H.'s office. Bet there is."

"Shut up!" said his father, straining.

King Bendigo was saying heartily, "*Entrez, Monsieur.*"

A buttered voice said something in rapid French, but then,
with a foreign accent that was not French and was spread with
irony, added in English: "*Let us dispense with the amenities.
What do you want?*"

"*The signed contracts, Monsieur.*"

"*I do not have them.*"

"You promised to have them."

"That was before you raised your prices, Monsieur Bendigo. I hold the folio of Defense in my country, not of clairvoyance."

"Is this your personal decision?" They heard a drumming sound.

"No. Of the entire Cabinet."

"Are you slipping, Monsieur le Ministre?"

"I have been unable to persuade my colleagues."

"You evidently used the wrong arguments."

"You did not provide me with the right ~~~. Your prices are so high that they would wreck the budget. New ~~~ are out of the question—"

The rich voice was frigid. *"This is an annoyance. What of your word?"*

The buttery voice slipped. *"I must repudiate it. I have no choice. It is too risky. A contract with Bodigen Arms at such a price might unseat us. The Actionist Party—"*

"Let's be realistic, Mr. Minister," said King Bendigo's voice suddenly. *"We know the influence you exert in the power group of your country. We admit the risks. What is your price to take them?"*

"I wish to terminate this conversation. Please have me flown back."

"Damn it all—!"

Abel's voice said something.

"What, Abel?"

The brothers played another counterpoint in murmurs. Then the big voice laughed.

"Of course. But before you go, Mr. Minister, may I examine that stickpin you're wearing?"

"This?" The European voice was surprised. *"But certainly, Monsieur Bendigo. How could it interest you?"*

"I'm a collector of stickpins. Yours struck my eye at once ... Beautiful!"

"It is merely a reproduction in gold and enamel of our national emblem. I am happy that it strikes your fancy."

"*Mr. Minister, you know what collectors are—perfect idiots. I must have this pin for my collection.*"

"*I shall send you one this week. They are obtainable at numerous shops in the capital.*"

"*No, no, I want this one—yours, Monsieur.*"

"*I gladly present it to you.*"

"*I make it a rule never to accept gifts. Permit me to buy it from you.*"

"*Really, Monsieur, it is no more than a trifle—*"

"*Would you accept two hundred and fifty thousand dollars for it?*"

"*Two hun—*" The voice choked.

"*Deposited in a New York bank under any name you designate?*"

The Queens gaped at each other.

After a very long time, in a voice so low as almost to be inaudible, the Defense Minister said, "*Yes . . . I will sell it.*"

"*Take care of it, Abel. Thank you for coming, Mr. Minister. I'm sure, on re-examining the situation, you'll find some means of persuading your distinguished compatriots that no sacrifice is too great for a nation to make in this crisis in world history.*"

"*Monsieur has given new strength to my persuasive powers,*" said the foreign voice in a tone compounded of bitterness, irony, and self-loathing; and the Queens heard it no more.

WHEN the door opened and Abel Bendigo reappeared, Inspector Queen was in the armchair with his head thrown back and Ellery was smoking a cigaret at the glass outer wall, staring as if he could see through it, which he could not.

The Inspector rose immediately.

"Sorry to have kept you waiting, gentlemen. My brother can see you now." Abel stood aside.

The Inspector went in first, Ellery followed, and Abel shut the door.

The hemispherical architecture of King Bendigo's office had been cleverly utilized to impress. The door from the reception room was near the end of the straight wall, so that the visitor on entering the office faced, first of all, the curved glass wall at its narrowest. He naturally made a half-turn toward space, and the long diameter of the room struck him like a blow. And near the other end, behind a desk, sat King Bendigo. The approach to him looked eternal.

There was little furniture in the office. A few heavy pieces designed to fit the curve of the outer wall, several uncompromising chairs and occasional tables, and that was all. As in the reception room, there were no paintings, no sculptures, no ornamentation of any kind. Nothing distracted the eye from that big desk, or the big chair that stood behind it, or the big man who sat in the chair.

The desk was of ebony, and there was nothing on its glittering surface.

The chair was of some golden material.

It was only later that Ellery was able to notice what was set into the straight wall near the desk. It was a room-high safe door. The door, a foot thick, was partly open. On its inner surface, behind glass, was the mechanism of a time-lock.

And just inside the safe leaned a troglodyte. His powerful jaws chewed away at something—chewing gum, or candy. He was so broad that he seemed squat; yet he was taller than Ellery. His face was gorillalike and he stared as a gorilla might stare. His stare never left the visitors' faces. He was dressed in a gaudy black and gold uniform and he wore a beret of black leather with a gilt pompom. He looked ridiculous and deadly.

But that came later. During the endless approach to the eminence of that ebony desk, they could see nothing but the man enthroned behind it.

King Bendigo did not rise. Even seated, he was formidable. He was one of the handsomest men Ellery had ever seen, with pure dark features of an imperious cast, bold black eyes, and thick black hair with a Byronic lock. His ringless hands, resting on the desk, were finely proportioned; they looked capable of breaking a man's back or threading a needle. He wore a business suit of exquisite cut and workmanship which draped itself impeccably at every movement of his torso.

There were deep lines in his face, but he looked no more than forty.

Ellery had the most curious sense of unreality. *Every Inch a King*, starring . . .

There were no introductions.

They were not offered chairs.

They were left standing before the desk, being inspected by those remarkable black eyes, while Abel went around the desk to murmur into his brother's ear.

Abel's attitude was interesting. It was all deference, but without an obsequious slant. Abel, with his lack of stature or grandeur, with his eyeglasses shining earnestly, with his body slightly inclined as he reported to his brother, was a picture of dedication.

Ellery tingled with the annoyance of something not quite grasped.

"Detectives?" They instinctively tightened before the black flash in those eyes. "So that's where you've been! Abel, I've told you those letters are the work of a crank—"

"They're not the work of a crank, King." There was a quiet stubbornness in Abel's voice that aroused Ellery's respect. "On that point Mr. Queen agreed immediately."

"Mister who?" The eyes made another survey.

"Queen. This gentleman is Inspector Richard Queen of the New York police department, and this is his son Ellery."

"Ellery Queen." The eyes became interested. "You have quite a reputation."

Ellery said, "Thank you, Mr. Bendigo."

"And you're his father, eh?" The eyes turned on Inspector Queen and at once turned back to Ellery.

And that takes care of me, thought the Inspector.

"So you think there's something in this, too, Queen."

"I do, Mr. Bendigo, and I'd like to discuss—"

"Not with me, Queen, not with me. *I* think it's a lot of damned foolishness. Play detective all you want to, but don't annoy me with it." King Bendigo turned in his chair. "Who's next, Abel?"

Abel began murmuring in the royal ear, and the royal eyes were immediately abstracted.

Ellery said: "Are you through with us, Mr. Bendigo?"

The handsome man looked up. "Yes?" he said sharply.

"Well, I'm not through with you."

The King leaned back, frowning. Abel straightened up and his prominent eyes began to shuttle between them. The Inspector rested against a chair, folding his arms expectantly.

"Well?" said King Bendigo.

"Nothing has been said about a fee."

The stare was degrading. "I didn't hire you. My brother did. Talk it over with him."

Abel said, "We'll discuss your fee this evening, Mr. Queen—"

"I'd rather discuss it now."

The King looked up at his Prime Minister. His Prime Minister shrugged ever so slightly. The stare went back to Ellery.

"Really?" drawled the man in the gold chair, and Ellery could have hurdled the desk and throttled him. "And what is this fee of yours, Queen?"

"My services come pretty high, Mr. Bendigo."

"What is the fee?"

It was at this point that Ellery, to conceal the blood in his eye, glanced away, and that was when he first saw the uniformed gorilla standing inside the doorway of the safe, animal eyes fixed on him, jaws grinding away. The King's jester . . . He felt himself tighten all over, and in the next moment all the pressure of hostility and outraged pride that had been building up came to a head.

"I won't talk total fee, since I don't know just what the investigation entails. I want a retainer, Mr. Bendigo, balance left open."

"How much of a retainer?"

Ellery said, "One hundred thousand dollars."

Behind him there was a choked paternal sound.

Abel Bendigo was looking at Ellery thoughtfully.

But King Bendigo neither choked nor took stock. He merely waved and said to his brother, "Take care of it," and then he waved at Ellery and Inspector Queen and said impatiently, "That's all, gentlemen."

Ellery said: "I'm not finished, Mr. Bendigo. I want my retainer in ten certified checks of ten thousand dollars each. You are to have the payees' lines left blank, so that I can fill in the names of ten different charities."

He knew instantly he had taken the wrong tack. Where money was concerned, this man was invulnerable. Money was a power-tool. Anyone who failed to use it as a power-tool was beneath contempt.

King Bendigo said indifferently, "Give it to him, Abel, any way he wants it. Anything, just so they stay out of my hair." In the identical tone, without stopping, he said, "Max'l."

The beast in the beret shot out of the safe, grimacing horribly.

Ellery dodged. The Inspector jumped out of the way like a rabbit.

King Bendigo threw his head back and roared. The wrestler was grinning.

"All right, all right, gentlemen," said the big man, still laughing. "Go to work."

IN the elevator, Inspector Queen broke the rather sick silence.

"I picked this up from the floor on the way out, son. It was at that far wall, all the way across the office from his desk. He must have cracked it between his fingers for exercise and then tossed it away for the help to throw in the trash."

"What is it, Dad?" Ellery's voice shook a little.

His father opened an unsteady hand. On it lay the fragments of the stickpin they had heard King Bendigo buy from his second visitor for two hundred and fifty thousand dollars.

4

THE SHIRTS were waiting for them in the lobby. Ellery found himself passing the security desk with a stiff back. But the three uniformed men paid no attention to them.

Brown Shirt said, "This way," and Blue Shirt held the outer door open.

Outside, the son and the father breathed again. The sun was low in the west and the western sky was strawberry, copper, and mother-of-pearl. A small, powerful black car gold-initialed PRPD was at the entrance. Blue Shirt took the wheel and Brown Shirt got into the rear seat between them.

Neither Queen felt talkative. Each gazed through his window at the countryside. They might have been traveling along the Mohawk Trail in a quiet fold of the Berkshires, with a city of mills and small homes at their feet, except for the pelagic vegetation and the memory of what they had just heard and seen.

"Who," inquired Ellery, "is at whose orders?"

"We're taking you to the Residence, Mr. Queen," replied Brown Shirt. "Mr. Abel has arranged everything."

"How free are we to move about?"

"You've been given a temporary A–2 rating, sir."

"What's that mean?" asked Inspector Queen, astonished.

"You may go anywhere you want, sir, except those installations marked *Restricted.*"

"From what we've seen, that sounds risky. We're not known on the island."

"You're known," Blue Shirt assured him from the front seat.

The Inspector did not look assured.

The car entered a densely wooded area. There were flashes

41

of flying color everywhere, but these were the only evidences of wildlife.

"Beauty for its own sake?" asked Ellery skeptically.

"Karla likes them," said Brown Shirt.

"Mrs. Bendigo?" The Inspector was scrutinizing the woods closely without seeming to do so.

"King's queen," said Ellery.

He had seen it, too, but he and his father continued to look at opposite terrains. There were camouflaged gun emplacements in these woods. Big guns, of the coast artillery type. Probably the whole wooded area bristled with them. And how much of this jungle itself, Ellery wondered, was real?

THEY came upon King Bendigo's home suddenly.

They could see only a little of it because of the trees and shrubs which choked it. The landscaping was positively untidy. Some of the trees were taller than the buildings, and there were heavy branches that actually brushed windows. Even the towers had been so treated that, while they were visible against the sky from the ground, to an airborne eye they must blend into the greenery.

Secrecy again. The original planners had probably been responsible for the camouflage, but then why, when he leased the island, hadn't Bendigo had these trees and the encroaching underbrush cleared away? Was he afraid someone would try to take his precious midocean anchorage away from him?

The Residence stood only four stories high, like the Home Office, but it covered a wider area. The section immediately before them would have been a courtyard had it not been overgrown with shrubbery planted at random. Even the paved driveway ran between two erratic files of trees whose upper branches twined overhead to form a ceiling. Embracing all of this were two projections of the building, running outward from a sort of parent body. From the angle formed by the arms, Ellery suspected others. Brown Shirt, who remained spokesman of the duo, confirmed this and explained the oddity of the architecture. The building was constructed on a plan similar to that of the Home Office, except that where the Home Office had eight arms, the Residence had five.

They were received in a great hall by flunkies in livery. Black and gold. With knee breeches and stocks. The Inspector goggled.

Here, at least, the functional temporized with fussier modes. The furniture was massively modern, but there were medieval French and Swedish tapestries on the walls and a sprinkling of old masters among new, the new chiefly abstractions. Everything in the hall was immense, the hall itself being three stories high; and it was only here and there that one saw a traditional object—such as the classic canvases—as if someone in the household insisted on at least a smattering of an older environment.

A footman conducted them through one of the five portals into a wing, and just inside this corridor Blue Shirt indicated a small elevator. They were whisked up one floor, and they got out to be marched along a soundless hall to a door. The door was open. In the doorway, dwarfed by its dimensions, stood a small bald man in a black suit and a wing collar. He bowed.

"This is your valet," said Brown Shirt. "Whatever you need to supplement what you've brought with you, gentlemen, just inform this man and he'll provide it at once."

"Jeeves?" said Ellery tentatively.

"No, sir," said the valet Britannically. "Jones."

"Your point, Jones. Does protocol demand evening clothes at dinner?"

"No, sir," said the valet. "Except on given occasions, dining is informal. Dark suit and four-in-hand."

"They'll take my tan gabardine and like it," said the Inspector.

"Yes, yes, Dad," said Ellery, soothingly. "Here, Jones, where are you off to?"

"To draw your tubs, sir," said Jones; and he sedately vanished.

The Queens turned to find the Shirts receding shoulder to shoulder.

"Here, wait!" cried the Inspector. "When do we get to see—?"

But they were already far down the corridor.

THEIR sitting room was almost a grand salon, and the two bedrooms were magnificent affairs with lofty ceilings, canopied beds, and historic-looking furnishings. Here, at least, the *décor* was traditional—*ancien régime*, as cluttered with gingerbread as any suite in the Tuileries under the Grand Monarch. Fortunately, as Ellery hastened to discover, tradition did not extend to the sanitary arrangements; but he was amused to find the telephones discreetly hidden in buhl cabinets whose surfaces were intricately inlaid with gold, tortoise shell, and some white metal in the scrollwork, cartouches, and curlicues so dear to the times of Louis Quatorze.

Inspector Queen was not amused at all. He went about from room to room antagonistically examining the grandeur into which they had been thrust; and he reserved his most hostile glare for the valet, who was patiently awaiting an opportunity to undress him. To avoid a homicide, Ellery conveyed Jones to the door.

They bathed, shaved, and dressed in fresh clothes from their suitcases, and then they waited. There was nothing else to do, for they could find no newspapers and the magnificent leather-bound books turned out to be discouraging eighteenth-century works in French and Latin. And from the windows nothing could be seen but foliage. The Inspector occupied himself for some time searching the suite for a secret transmitter, which he was positive was planted somewhere in the sitting room; but after a while he grew tired of even this diversion and began fuming.

"Damn it, what kind of runaround is this? What are we supposed to do, rot here? I'm going downstairs, Ellery!"

"Let's wait, Dad. All this has a purpose."

"To starve us out!"

But Ellery was frowning over a cigaret. "I wonder why we've been brought to the island."

The Inspector stared.

"Abel hires us to investigate a couple of threatening letters received, he says, through the mail. The mail undoubtedly is flown here daily from the mainland by Bendigo's planes. If those letters came through the mail, then, they emanated from the mainland. Why, then, does Abel ask us to investigate *on the island?*"

"Because he thinks the letters came from the island!"

"Exactly. Someone's slipping them into the pouches or into the already sorted Residence or Home Office mail." Ellery ground out his cigaret in a Royal Sèvres dish which was probably worth more than he had in the bank. "Which somebody? A clerk? Secretary? Footman? Guard? Factory hand? Lab worker? For anyone like that, the Prime Minister doesn't have to make a special trip to New York, with a side visit to Washington, to engage the services of a couple of outsiders. That kind of job could be polished off by Colonel Spring's department in about two hours flat."

"So it gets down to . . . what?" Ellery looked up. "To somebody big, Dad."

But the Inspector was shaking his head. "The bigger the game, the less likelihood that Bendigo would call in an outsider."

"That's right."

"That's right? But you just said—"

"That's right, and that's wrong, too. So none of it sets on the stomach. In fact," and Ellery fumbled for another cigaret, "I'm positively bilious."

That was when the telephone tinkled and Ellery leaped to answer it, almost knocking his father down. Abel Bendigo's calm twang said he was terribly sorry but his brother King was being a bit difficult this evening and in Abel's considered judgment it would be a lot smarter not to press matters at the moment. If the Queens didn't mind dining alone . . . ?

"Of course not, Mr. Bendigo, but we're anxious to get going on the investigation."

"Tomorrow will be better," said the Yankee voice in the tones of a physician soothing a fretful patient.

"Are we to wait in these rooms for your call?"

"Oh, no, Mr. Queen. Do anything you like, go anywhere you please. I'll find you when I want you." Perhaps to get by the ironical implications of this statement, the Prime Minister said hurriedly, "Good night," and hung up.

Dinner was served in their suite from warming ovens and other portable paraphernalia by a butler and three servingmen under the cadaver's eye of a perfect official who introduced himself as the Chief Steward of the Residence and thereafter uttered not a single word.

It was like dining in a tomb, and the Queens did not enliven the occasion. They ate in silence, exactly what they could not afterward recall except that it was rich, saucy, and French, in keeping with the *décor*.

Then, in the same nervous silence, and because there was nothing else to do, they went to bed.

*　　*　　*

THERE was no note from Abel Bendigo on their plates the next morning, and the telephone failed to ring. So after breakfast Ellery proposed a tour of the Residence.

The Inspector, however, had developed a pugnacious jaw. "I'm going to see how far they'll let me go. Where do you suppose the royal garage is?"

"Garage?"

"I'm borrowing a car."

He went out, his jaw preceding him, and Ellery did not see him until late afternoon.

Ellery prowled about the five-armed building alone. It took him all morning to make its acquaintance. Certainly he made the acquaintance of nothing more animate, for he saw none of the Bendigo family during his tour and the servants in livery and minor officials of the household whom he ran across ignored him with suspicious unanimity.

He was stopped only once, and that was on the top floor of the central building. Here there were armed guards in uniform, and their captain was politely inflexible.

"These are the private apartments of the family, sir. No one is allowed to enter except by special permission."

"Well, of course I shouldn't want to blunder into anyone's bathroom, but I was given to understand by Mr. Abel Bendigo that I could go anywhere."

"I have received no orders to admit you to this floor, Mr. Queen."

So Ellery meekly went back to the lowlier regions.

He looked in on the state dining room, the grand ballroom, salons, reception rooms, trophy rooms, galleries, kitchens, wine cellars, servants' quarters, storerooms, even closets. There was an oak-and-leather library of twenty thousand volumes, uniformly bound in black Levant morocco and stamped with the twin-globes-and-crown, which more and more took on the color of a coat-of-arms. The standardization of the books themselves, many of them rare editions raped of their original bindings, made Ellery cringe. None that he sampled showed the least sign of use.

Shortly before noon Ellery found himself in a music salon, dominated by a platform at one end large enough to accommodate a symphony orchestra. In the center of this stage glittered a concert grand piano sheathed in gold. Wondering if this splendid instrument was in tune, Ellery climbed to the platform, opened the piano, and struck middle C. An unmusical clank answered him. He struck a chord in the middle register. This time the horrid jangle that resulted impressed him as far too extreme to be accounted for by mere neglect, and he raised the top of the piano.

Six sealed bottles, identical in every respect, lay in a neat row on the strings.

He took one out with curiosity. It was bell-shaped, with a slender neck, and of very dark green glass, so dark as to be opaque. The antiqued label identified the contents as *Segonzac V.S.O.P. Cognac*. The heavy seal was unbroken, as were the seals of its five brothers, at which Ellery sighed. He had never had the good fortune to savor Segonzac Very Special Old Pale Cognac, for the excellent reason that Segonzac Very Special Old Pale Cognac was priced—where it could be found at all —at almost fifty dollars the bottle. He replaced the heavy glass bell on its harmonious bed and lowered the top of the grand piano with reverence.

A man who cached six bottles of cognac in a grand piano was an alcoholic. The middle Bendigo brother, Judah, had been reported by the Inspector's military *tête-à-tête* as an alcoholic. It seemed a reasonable conclusion that this was Judah Bendigo's cache. The incident also told something of the musicality of the Bendigo household, but since this was of a piece with the evidence of the library, Ellery was not surprised.

Apparently Judah Bendigo scorned his brother's vineyards. Unless the Segonzac label was another possession of the all-powerful King . . . It was a point Ellery never did clear up.

The discovery in the music salon led Ellery to poke and pry. An alcoholic who hides bottles in one place will hide them in another. He was not disappointed.

He found bottles of Segonzac V.S.O.P. hidden everywhere he looked. Seven turned up in the gymnasium, four around the hundred-foot indoor swimming pool. Ellery found them in the billiard room and the bowling alley. He found them in the cardroom. And on one of the terraces, where he lunched in solitude, Ellery felt the flagstone under his left foot give and, on investigating, stared down at another of the bell-shaped bottles nestling in a scooped-out hole beneath the flag.

In the afternoon he toured the vicinity of the Residence. Wherever he went he turned up the dark green evidence of Judah Bendigo's ingenuity. The outdoor swimming pool, cleverly constructed to resemble a natural pond, was good for eight bottles, and Ellery could not be sure he had found them all. He did not bother with the stables—there were too many grooms about—but he took an Arab mare out on the bridle path and he made it a point to probe tree hollows and investigate overhead tree crotches, with rewarding results. Another artificial stream, this one stocked with game fish, was a disappointment; but Ellery suspected that if he had worn hip-boots he could have waded in any direction through the broken water and found a bottle wedged between the nearest rocks.

"And I didn't begin to find them all," he told his father that evening, in their sitting room. "Judah must carry a map around with him, X marking the spots. There's a man who likes his brandy."

"You might have lifted a couple of bottles," grumbled the Inspector. "I've had a miserable day."

"Well?"

"Oh, I putt-putted around the island. Isn't that what a tourist is supposed to do?" And while he said this, in a tone of lifelessness, the Inspector rather remarkably took a roll of papers from an inner pocket and waved them at his son.

"I will admit," said his son, eying the papers, "this enforced vacation is beginning to bore me, too." He leaned forward and took the papers. "When do you suppose our investigation begins?"

"Never, from the look of things."

"What's the island like, Dad?" Ellery unrolled several of the papers noiselessly. Each showed a hasty sketch of an industrial plant. Others were rough detail maps.

"It's no different from any highly industrialized area in the States. Factories, homes, schools, roads, trucks, planes, people . . ." The Inspector pointed at the papers vigorously.

Ellery nodded. "What kind of factories?"

"Munitions mostly, I guess. Hell, I don't know. A lot of places had *Restricted* signs on 'em with armed guards and electrified fences and the rest of the claptrap. Couldn't get near 'em."

There was one series of sketches of rather queer-looking plants, a scale-frame indicating enormous size.

"Meet anybody interesting?" Ellery pointed to the peculiar sketches and looked inquiring.

"Just Colonel Spring's lads. The working people seem an unfriendly lot. Or they're shy of strangers. Wouldn't give me the time of day." The Inspector's reply to the silent part of their conversation was a shrug and a shake of the head. Ellery studied the sketches with a frown.

"Well, son, I guess I'll take me a bath in that marble lake they gave me to splash around in." The Inspector rose and took his notes back.

"I could use one myself."

His father tucked the papers away in his clothes, and Ellery knew that unless a body search were made, the sketches would not leave their hiding place this side of Washington, D.C.

THAT night they passed through the gold curtain.

The feat was accomplished by means of a piece of paper. At six o'clock a footman with overdeveloped calves delivered a velvety purplish envelope, regally square, and backed out with the kind of bow the Inspector had never seen outside a British period movie. The bow indicated that it was hardly necessary to open the envelope. But they did, and they found inside a sheet of richly engraved and monogrammed stationery of the same color and texture covered with gold ink writing in a firm feminine hand. Inspector Richard Queen and Mr. Ellery Queen were requested to appear in the private apartments of the Bendigo family at 7 P.M. for cocktails and dinner. Dress was informal. The signature was *Karla Bendigo*. There was a postscript: She had heard so much of the Queens from her brother-in-law Abel that she was looking forward with delight to meeting them, and she concluded by apologizing—with what seemed to Ellery significant vagueness—for having been "unable to do so until now."

They had hardly finished reading the invitation before their valet appeared with a dark blue double-breasted man's suit, dully gleaming black shoes, a pair of new black silk socks, and a conservative blue silk necktie. Ellery relieved the man of them and nudged him out before the snarl formed in the Inspector's nose.

"Try them on, Dad. Chances are they won't fit, and you'll have an excuse for not wearing them."

They fitted perfectly, even the shoes.

"All right, wise guy," growled the Inspector. "But the school I was brought up in, if your guests want to show up in their underwear the host strips, too. Who the devil do these people think they are?"

So at five minutes of seven, Ellery in his best oxford gray and the Inspector uneasily elegant in Jones's finery, the Queens left their suite and went upstairs.

Different guards were on duty in the foyer on the top floor. They were under the command of a younger officer, who scrutinized Karla Bendigo's invitation microscopically. Then he stepped back, saluting, and the Queens were passed through the portals, feeling a little as if they ought to remove their shoes and crawl in on their stomachs.

"That head will roll," murmured Ellery.

"Huh?" said his father nervously.

"If we snitch on him. He didn't fingerprint us."

They were in a towering reception room full of black iron, hamadryads in marble, giant crystal chandeliers, and overwhelming furniture in the Italian baroque style. Across the room two great doors stood open, flanked by footmen in *rigor mortis.* An especially splendid flunky wearing white gloves received them with a bow and preceded them to the double door.

"Inspector Queen and Mr. Ellery Queen."

"Just a little snack with the Bendigos," mumbled the Inspector; then they both stopped short.

Coming to them swiftly across a terrazzo floor was a woman as improbably beautiful as the heroine of a film. But Technicolor could never adequately have reproduced the snowiness of her skin and teeth, the sunset red of her hair, or the tropical green of her eyes. Even allowing for the art, there was a fundamental color magic that startled, and it enlivened a person that was disquieting in form. A great deal of the person was on display, for she was wearing a strapless dinner gown of very frank décolletage. The gown, of pastel green velvet, sheathed her to the knees; from the knees it flared, like a vase. Despite her coloring, she was not of Northern blood, Ellery decided, because she made him think of Venezia, San Marco, the Adriatic, and the women of the doges. Studying her as she approached, he saw earth in her figure, breeding in her face, and no nonsense in her step. A Titian woman. Fit for a king.

"Good evening," she exclaimed, taking their hands. Her voice had the same coloring; it was a vivid contralto, with the merest trace of Southern Europe. She was not so young,

Ellery saw, as he had first thought. Early thirties? "I am so happy to receive you both. Can you forgive me for having neglected you?"

"After seeing you, madam," said Inspector Queen with earnestness, "I can forgive you anything."

"And to be repaid with gallantry!" She smiled, the slightest smile. "And you, Mr. Queen?"

"Speechless," said Ellery. Now he saw something else—a sort of grotto deep beneath the sunny seas of her eyes, a place of cold sad shade.

"I have always adored the flattery of American men. It is so uncomplicated." Laughing, she took them across the room.

King Bendigo stood at an Italian marble fireplace taller than himself, listening in silence to the conversation of his brother Abel and three other men. The lord of Bendigo Island looked fresh and keen, although Ellery knew he must have had a long day at his desk. The jester, Max'l, was at a table nearby helping himself to canapés with both murderous hands. Occasionally, while his great jaws ground away, he looked around at his master like a dog.

In an easy chair opposite King sprawled a slight dark man in rumpled clothing. On his sallow face, with its intelligent features, he wore a slight dark mustache; it gave him a gloomy, almost sinister, look. It was an odd face, with a broad high forehead, a nose sharply and crookedly hooked, and a chin that came to a premature point. A bell-shaped dark green bottle stood at his elbow and he was rolling a brandy snifter between his palms as his head lolled on the back of the chair. From the slits of his deeply sunken eyes he was studying Ellery, however, with remarkable alertness.

King greeted them graciously enough, but in a moment he had turned aside with Abel, and it was Karla Bendigo who introduced the other men. The slight dark man in the easy chair was Judah Bendigo, the middle brother; he did not rise or offer his hand. He merely squinted up at them, rolling the snifter between his palms. Either he was already drunk, or rudeness was a hereditary Bendigo trait. Ellery was glad when they had to turn to the group at the fireplace.

One of the three was small, stout, and bald, with the unemotional stare of a man to whom nothing has value but the immediate moment. Their hostess introduced him as Dr. Storm, Surgeon-General of Bendigo Island and her husband's personal physician, who lived on the premises. It did not surprise Ellery to learn that the second man, a tall lean swarthy individual with a catty smile, was also a permanent resident; his name was Immanuel Peabody, and he was King Bendigo's chief legal adviser. The third man of the group looked like a football player convalescing from a serious illness. He was young, blond, broad-shouldered, and pale, and his face was rutted with fatigue.

"Dr. Akst," Karla Bendigo said. "We seldom see this young man; it is a rare pleasure. He buries himself in his laboratory at the other side of the island, fiddling with his dangerous little atoms."

"With his what?" said Inspector Queen.

"Mrs. Bendigo insists on making Dr. Akst out some sort of twentieth-century alchemist," said the lawyer, Peabody, smiling. "A physicist can't very well avoid the little atom, but it's hardly dangerous, Dr. Akst, is it?"

"Say it is dangerous, Doctor," said Karla playfully. But she flashed a glance at the lawyer. It seemed to Ellery the glance was resentful.

"Only in the sense that an experimenter," protested Peabody, "is always monkeying with the unknown."

"Can we talk about something else?" asked Dr. Akst. He spoke with a strong Scandinavian accent, and he sounded younger than he looked.

"Mrs. Bendigo's eyes," suggested Ellery. "Now there's a subject that's really dangerous."

Everyone laughed, and then Ellery and the Inspector had cocktails in their hands and Immanuel Peabody began to tell the story of an old criminal trial in England, in which testimony about the color of a woman's eyes delivered the defendant to Jack Ketch. But all the while Ellery was wondering if his father knew that the tired young man with the

humorless Scandinavian voice was one of the world's most
famous nuclear physicists. And he thought, too, that in trying
to gloss over the nature of Dr. Akst's work on Bendigo Island
Immanuel Peabody had only succeeded in calling attention
to it. For the rest of the evening Akst made a point of effacing
himself and, playing the game, Ellery ignored him.

Karla Bendigo did not refer to him again.

DINNER was sumptuous and interminable. They dined in the
adjoining room, a place of suffocating grandeur, and they
were served by an army corps of servants. The courses and
wines came in a steady parade, many of the delicacies blue-
flamed in chafing dishes, so that the whole incredible feast was
like a torchlight procession in a medieval festival.

Immanuel Peabody kept pace, with fat and deadly little
Dr. Storm not far behind, Peabody telling with the utmost
cheerfulness gruesome stories of criminal lore, with Dr.
Storm's surgically bawdy. To these last, Max'l was the most
appreciative listener; he winked, leered, and guffawed between gulletfuls, missing nothing. Max'l wore his napkin
frankly under his chin and he ate with both elbows guarding
his plate; he removed one of them only to batter Ellery's ribs
at a particularly gusty witticism of Dr. Storm's.

To the Queens' disappointment, neither had been placed
beside King or Karla Bendigo. The Inspector was trapped
between the loquacious lawyer and the wicked little Surgeon-
General, while Ellery sat diagonally across the table between
the taciturn physicist, Akst, and Max'l—the father being
talked to death, the son given Coventry on one side and a
beating on the other. The arrangement was deliberate; nothing here, Ellery knew, happened by chance.

Since most of the lawyer's and the physician's conversation
was directed toward the Queens, they found little opportunity
to talk to the Bendigos. Karla murmured to Abel at her end
of the field-long table, occasionally sending a word or a
crooked little smile their way, as if in apology. At the other
end sat King, listening. Once, turning suddenly, Ellery found

their host's black eyes fixed on him with amusement. He tried after that to cultivate at least an appearance of patience.

It was a queer banquet, full of tense and mysterious undercurrents, and not the least of them swirled about Judah Bendigo. The slender little man slumped to the left of his brother King, ignoring Max'l's feeding antics—Max'l sat between Judah and Ellery—ignoring Storm's sallies and Peabody's forensic yarns, ignoring his food . . . giving all his attention to the bottle of Segonzac cognac beside his plate. No servant touched that bottle, Ellery observed; Judah refilled his own glass. He drank steadily but slowly throughout the evening, for the most part looking across the table at a point in space above Immanuel Peabody's head. His only recognition of the menu was to drink two cups of black coffee toward the end, and even then he laced them with brandy. The first cup emptied his bottle, and a servant quickly uncorked a fresh bottle and set it beside him.

The dinner took three hours; and when at exactly 10:45 P.M. King Bendigo made an almost unnoticeable gesture and Peabody brought his story to an end within ten seconds, Ellery could have collapsed in gratitude. Across the table his father sat perspiring and pale, as if he had exhausted himself in a desperate struggle.

The rich voice said to the Queens, "Gentlemen, I must ask you to excuse Abel and me. We have work to do tonight. I regret the necessity, as I'd looked forward to hearing some stories of your adventures." Then why the devil, thought Ellery, did you order Peabody and Storm to monopolize the conversation? "However, Mrs. Bendigo will entertain you."

He did not wait for Karla's murmured, "I will be so happy to, darling," but pushed his chair back and rose. Abel, Dr. Storm, Peabody, and Dr. Akst immediately rose, too. Abel followed his tall brother through one door, and the doctor, the lawyer, and the physicist trooped out through another. The Queens watched them leave, fascinated. It was exactly as if the long dinner had been a scene in a play, with everyone an actor and the curtain coming down to disperse them in their private identities, each registering relief in his own fashion.

As Ellery drew Karla Bendigo's chair back, his eyes met his father's over her satiny red hair.

In three hours, with all the principals present, not one word had been said about the reason for the Queens' presence on Bendigo Island.

"Shall we go, gentlemen?"

King's wife took their arms.

* * *

At the door, Ellery looked back.

Side by side at the littered table sat Max'l and Judah Bendigo. The ex-wrestler was still stuffing himself, and the silent Bendigo brother was pouring another glassful of cognac with an air of concentration and a hand that remained steady.

5

KARLA'S APARTMENT was on another planet, a gentle world of birds and flowers, with casements overlooking the gardens and a small fireplace burning aromatic logs. Watercolors splashed the walls, glass winked in the firelight, and everything was bright and warm and friendly.

A maid, not a flunky in livery, served coffee and brandy. Karla took neither; she sipped an iced liqueur.

"Coffee keeps me awake. Brandy—" she shrugged—"I find I have lost my taste for it."

"Your brother-in-law's influence?" suggested the Inspector delicately.

"We can do nothing with Judah."

"Why," asked Ellery, "does Judah drink?"

"Why does anyone drink? . . . Rest your feet on the footstool, Inspector Queen. Dinner was exhausting, I know. Immanuel Peabody is a fascinating raconteur, but he has never

learned that the pinnacle of brilliance in storytelling is knowing when to stop. Dr. Storm is a pig. One of the world's great
internists, but a pig nevertheless. Am I being dreadful? It is
such a relief to allow myself to be a woman on occasion, and
gossip."

The sadness in her eyes interested Ellery. He wondered how
much Karla Bendigo knew of the threats against her husband's life, if she knew anything at all.

The Inspector was apparently wondering, too, because he
said, "Your husband bowled me over, Mrs. Bendigo. One of
the most dynamic men I've ever met."

"That is so characteristic, Inspector!" She was pleased. "I
mean, your feeling that. It is the invariable reaction of everyone who meets Kane."

"Who meets whom?" Ellery asked.

"Kane."

"Kane?"

"Oh, I forget." She laughed. "Kane is my husband's name.
K-a-n-e."

"Then the name King—"

"Is not properly his name at all. We are playthings of the
press, *n'est-ce pas?* The newspapers referred to Kane so long
and so often as 'the Munitions King' that he began to use the
word 'king' as a name. In the beginning it was a family joke,
but somehow it has hung on."

"Does his brother Judah address him as King?" asked Ellery. "I don't believe I heard Judah utter a word all evening."

She shrugged. "Judah took it up with as much enthusiasm
as he ever shows for anything. Judah's affinity for cognac often
leads him into childish irony. He uses 'King' as if it were a—a
title. Even Abel has fallen into the habit. I am the only one
who still addresses my husband by his given name."

Ellery began to perceive a ground for the sadness in her eyes.

SHE told the story of how she and her husband had met.

It was in an ultrafashionable restaurant in Paris under characteristic Bendigo circumstances. They were at adjacent tables,
each in a large dinner party. She had noticed the big, dark,

Byronic-locked man with the flashing black eyes when his party entered; it included two members of the French cabinet, a high British diplomat, a famous American general, and Abel Bendigo—there were no women—but it was on the Munitions King that all eyes fastened.

The buzz that filled the restaurant caused Karla to inquire who he was.

She had heard of him, of course, but she had always discounted the stories about him as the inflated gossip of the bankrupt society from which she came. Now, seeing him in the flesh, she was equally sure the stories must be true. In the world in which she lived, men were either cynical petrifications in high places or useless, usually impecunious, exquisites. Among these people he stood out like a Roman candle. He was all radiant energy, heating and exciting the pale particles among which he moved.

Being a woman, Karla had immediately turned her glance elsewhere.

"I remember feeling thankful that my better profile happened to be turned toward his table," Karla said, smiling. "And wondering if it were possible to make a conquest of such a man. He was said to have very little to do with women. That, of course, is a challenge to any woman, and I was bored to death by my friends and my life.

"I suppose some of this showed in what was visible to him. Which was a great deal, I fear," she added, "for this was immediately after the war and I was wearing a particularly shameless creation of Feike-Emma's. Still, I was surprised when the Baroness Herblay, who was called behind her back 'Madame Roentgen' because nothing escaped her eye, whispered to me behind her lorgnette that *Monsieur le Roi* had been staring at me for some time with the most insulting intensity—'insulting' was the word she used, hopefully."

The Baroness explained at Karla's raised brow that "Monsieur le Roi" was what the leftist French press had taken to calling Mr. King-of-the-Munitions Bendigo.

"I looked around," Karla murmured, "and met Kane's eye. Mine was very cold, intended to freeze him into an awareness that I was not some modiste's mannequin to be looked over with insolence. Instead, I met such a heat in his . . .

"I looked away quickly, feeling myself blush. I was not a convent girl. The war had made us all a thousand years old. Still, at the moment, I was feeling exactly like one. He was so . . . uniquely attractive. . . . And then I howled like a chambermaid, which was the effect Baroness Herblay sought, I am sure, for she was a wicked old woman and she had stabbed my ankle with the stiletto she wore in place of a heel. So I looked up through tears of pain to find him, very darkly imperious and amused, stooping over my chair.

" 'Pardon me, if I startled you,' he said in schoolboy French. 'But I had to tell you that you are the most beautiful woman I have ever seen.'

"Of course, in American English it sounds—how do you say?—corny," continued Karla with a twinkle, "but there is something about the French language which gives this sort of sentiment a tone of ever-fresh glamour. And expressed—no matter how awkwardly—in Kane's deep, rich American voice, it sounded as if it had never been said before.

"My cousin, Prince Claudel, was at the head of our table. Before I could find my tongue, Claudel rose and said frigidly, 'And I must tell you, Monsieur, that you are a presuming boor. You will please retire immediately.' "

"There was a brawl," chuckled Inspector Queen.

"A duel," guessed Ellery.

"Nothing of the sort," retorted Karla, resting her shining head on the back of her chair, "although either would have delighted the Baroness. Baron Herblay, who had grown old in the intrigues of Europe, whispered in Claudel's ear, and I saw my cousin go amusingly pale. It was Bendigo money which had supported Claudel in exile while he plotted the destruction of the revolutionary régime in our country and his return there, which would mean eventually his elevation to the overturned throne. Claudel had never laid eyes on Kane Bendigo; it was a minor matter to the Bendigos, handled through agents and bankers in Paris.

"Meanwhile, Kane stood over me paying no attention what-

ever. It was a coldblooded display, and the restaurant had
fallen silent—that horrible public silence which undresses you
and leaves you no place to hide.

"Claudel said nervously, 'Monsieur, I spoke hastily, perhaps.
But you must realize, Monsieur—you have not been presented—'

"And, without looking up at him, Kane said, 'Present me.'

"Whereupon, even paler, Prince Claudel did so."

"Since this is a romance," grinned Ellery, "I suppose you
slapped his face and swept out of the restaurant."

"No," said Karla dreamily, "for this was a realistic romance.
I knew the source of our family's support and I had undergone
too much privation during the war to jeopardize it over a
breach of etiquette. Besides, he was so handsome. And his
breach had, after all, been committed over me. . . . But then
he made it very difficult for me to remain flattered."

"What did he do?" asked the Inspector.

"He ordered all non-redhaired women out of the restaurant."

"He *what?*"

"He passed a law, Inspector Queen. Only redhaired women,
he decreed in a penetrating voice, should be allowed. And he
summoned the *maître* and ordered the poor man to escort all
brunette, blonde, and grayhaired ladies from the premises. The
maître wrung his hands and hurried off, while Kane stood by
my chair with perfect calmness. The restaurant, of course, was
in an uproar.

"I was furious with him. I was about to rise and leave when
the Baroness dug her claws into my arm and hissed at me,
whispering something about the Prince. I glanced at my cousin
and I could see that he was about to do something suicidally
heroic. Poor Claudel! He's had such a hard time of it. So I had
to pretend to be amused, and I smiled up at the tall author
of the scene and acted as if I were enjoying myself. As, secret-
ly, I was."

Karla laughed again, from deep in her throat. "The *maître*
returned with the manager. The manager wrung his hands, too.
Monsieur was obviously jesting . . . it was of a truth impossible . . . these distinguished personages. . . . But Monsieur

very calmly said that he was not jesting in the least. There was room in the planetary system, he said, for only one sun, which at its most beautiful, he reminded the manager, was of the color red. All non-redhaired women must leave at once.

"The manager threw up his hands and sent for the owner of the restaurant. The owner came and he was adamant. It could not be done, the owner said with respect but firmness. Such an act would be not merely immoral and unprecedented, it would be commercial suicide. He would instantly lose the patronage of the most elevated diners in Paris. He would be sued, wrecked, ruined. . . .

"At this point Kane looked over at Abel, and Abel, who had been quietly listening, rose from their table and came to his brother. They conferred for a moment, then Abel took the owner aside and there was another inaudible conference. While this was going on, Kane said to me soothingly, 'A thousand apologies for this annoyance. It will be over in a moment.' I had to smile up at him again to keep Claudel in hand. . . .

"Then the owner rejoined us, and he was paler than my cousin. If Monsieur Bendigo and his guests would be so gracious as to retire to a private suite, for a few moments only. . . . Monsieur Bendigo smiled and said that would be agreeable to him—if I joined his party."

"And you did?"

"I had to, Mr. Queen, or Prince Claudel would have assaulted him where he stood. I went to Claudel and whispered that I was being most terribly diverted—leaving Claudel speechless—and then I permitted Kane to escort me from the room. The last thing I remember," laughed Karla, "was Baroness Herblay's open mouth.

"Fifteen minutes later the owner of the restaurant presented himself to Kane in the private suite, informed him that all ladies who were not so fortunate as to possess red hair had been 'removed from the premises,' and bowed himself out again. At this Kane nodded gravely, and he said to me, 'I am reasonably sure you were the only redhaired woman present, but if we find that I've made a mistake, I will take appropriate action on some other ground. Will you do me the honor of dining with me and my friends?' And we went back into the restaurant, and not a woman was there—just a few men who had remained out of curiosity. Needless to say, Claudel, the Herblays, and the others had all left."

"But what on earth made the owner change his tune?" asked Ellery. "I assume he was well paid for it, but it seems to me no amount of money, after a stunt like that, would keep his business solvent."

"It was no longer his, Mr. Queen," said Karla. "You see, on the spot, on Kane's instructions, Abel had purchased the restaurant!"

FOUR days later—four of the most exciting days in her life, Karla said—they were married. They spent a prolonged honeymoon on the Continent, to the despair of Abel. But Karla was overwhelmingly in love, and it was not until two months later that her husband brought her in state to Bendigo Island.

"Where you've been ever since?" asked the Inspector. "Must get pretty lonely for a woman like you, Mrs. Bendigo."

"Oh, no," protested Karla. "I could never be lonely with Kane."

"But doesn't he work very hard?" murmured Ellery. "Late hours, and all that? From what I've gathered, you don't see much of your husband."

Karla sighed. "I have never felt that a woman should stand between her husband and his work. It is probably my European training. . . . We do have our interludes, however. I often accompany Kane on business trips, which take him all over the world. We spent most of last month, for example, in Buenos Aires, and Kane says we will be going to London and Paris soon." She refilled their brandy glasses, her hand shaking slightly. "You must not feel sorry for me," she said in a light tone. "It is true, I sometimes miss the company of women of my own class, but one must sacrifice something for being married to a phenomenon. . . . Did you know that my husband was a famous athlete in his day?"

It was all rather pathetic, and when Karla insisted on showing them her husband's trophy room they followed her like tourists into what looked like a museum. The room was sternly Greek in spirit, an affair of pure-line marble and slender columns, and it was full of athletic trophies won, Karla Bendigo said, by her extraordinary husband in his youth.

"This is a phase of the great man that never gets into the magazine articles," remarked Ellery, glancing about at the plaques and scrolls and cabinets containing memorial footballs, baseballs, skis, statuettes, cups, lacrosse sticks, foils, boxing gloves, and a hundred other testimonials to athletic prowess. "Did Mr. Bendigo actually win all these?"

"We rather discourage magazine writers, Mr. Queen," said Karla. "Yes, these were all won by Kane at school. I don't think there's a sport he didn't excel in."

Ellery paused to study one silver cup for water polo, on whose surface the name Kane appeared brighter than the other engraving.

"That one," observed the Inspector over Ellery's shoulder, "looks as if the name Kane's been re-engraved."

Karla looked, too, and nodded. "Yes, it has. I asked Kane about that myself when I first saw it."

"Abel. Judah." Ellery turned suddenly. "I wondered why Biblical influence didn't extend to the other brother. It did, didn't it, Mrs. Bendigo? Kane—K-a-n-e—isn't his name, either. It was . . ."

"C-a-i-n. That is right, Mr. Queen."

"Can't say I blame him."

"Yes, for obvious reasons he always loathed it. When he entered private school—some military school, I think—even as a boy he insisted on changing it. He told me he had won this water polo trophy in his Genesis phase, as I always call it, so he had it re-engraved later to read K-a-n-e."

"From his appearance, Mrs. Bendigo," said the Inspector, "your husband must keep up a lot of these sports. When does he get the time?"

"He doesn't. I have never seen him do anything but wrestle and box a little with Max."

"What?" The Inspector looked around the trophy room.

"He takes no exercise to speak of," laughed Karla. "I told

you Kane is unique! He keeps his figure and muscles in trim by massage twice a day. For all his stupidity, Max is a skillful masseur and Kane, of course, is Max's religion. Careful food habits—you saw how sparingly he ate tonight—and a constitution of steel do the rest. Kane has so many facets to his personality! In many things he is a little boy, in others a peacock. Did you know that for years now he has been judged one of the world's ten best-dressed men? I will show you!"

King's wife dragged them to another room. It was a large room; it might have been an exclusive men's shop. Closet after closet, rack after rack, of suits, overcoats, sportswear, dinner jackets, shoes—he had everything, in wholesale lots.

"He can't possibly find the time to wear all of these," exclaimed the Inspector. "Ellery, take a gander at that lineup of riding boots! Does he ride much, Mrs. Bendigo?"

"He hasn't been on a horse for years. . . . Isn't it fabulous? Kane comes in here often, just to admire."

They were inspecting this kingly wardrobe with appropriate murmurs when a deep voice said behind them, "Karla, why would our guests be interested in my haberdashery?"

He was in the doorway. His handsome face was fatigued. His voice held a cross, raspy note.

"You would not deprive your wife of the pleasure of boasting about her husband?" Karla went to him quickly, slipped her arm about his waist. "Kane. You are very tired tonight."

She was frightened. There was no trace of it in her expression or attitude, and her voice was merely anxious, but Ellery was sure. It was almost as if she had been caught in the act of treason, discovery of which meant merciless punishment.

"I've had a long day, and some of it was trying. Would you gentlemen join me in a nightcap?" But his tone was icy.

"Thank you, no. I'm afraid we've kept Mrs. Bendigo far too long as it is." Ellery took his father's arm. "Good night."

Karla murmured something. She was smiling, but her face was suddenly bloodless.

Bendigo stood aside to let them pass. The Inspector's arm jerked. A security guard stood at attention just outside the door. They were about to step into the corridor when Bendigo said, "One moment."

They stopped, alert to some new danger. It was puzzling and annoying. Every word this man uttered seemed full of traps.

King Bendigo, however, sounded merely absent. "Something I was to show you. Abel told me not to forget. What the devil was it, now?"

Blocking the corridor at the turn loomed the ape, Max'l. He was holding up a wall as he smoked a long cigar. He eyed them with a grin.

"Yes?" Ellery tried to relax.

"Oh." King's hand went to his breast pocket. "Another of those letters came tonight. By the late plane. It was in the general mail."

He dropped the envelope into Ellery's hand. The envelope had been slit open. Ellery did not remove its contents; he was looking at Bendigo's face.

He could see nothing there but weary indifference.

"You've read this, Mr. Bendigo?" asked Inspector Queen sharply.

"Abel insisted. Same brand of garbage. Good night."

"Kane, what is it?" Karla was clinging to him.

"Nothing to concern you, darling—" The door shut in their faces.

Max'l followed them at a distance of six feet all the way to the door of their suite. Then, to their alarm, he closed the gap a bound.

"Here!" The Inspector backed up.

Max'l's sapper of a forefinger struck Ellery in the chest, staggering him.

"You ain't so tough. Are you?"

"What?" stammered Ellery.

"Na-a-a." Max'l turned on his heel and rolled contemptuously away.

"Now what in hell," muttered the Inspector, "was *that* for?"

Ellery bolted the door, rubbing his chest.

THE third note was almost identical with its predecessors. The same elegant stationery, the same type—of a Winchester Noiseless Portable—and virtually the same message:

You are going to be murdered on Thursday, June 21—

"June twenty-first," said the Inspector thoughtfully. "Adds the date. Less than a week from now. And again he ends up with a dash, showing there's more to come. What the devil else can he say?"

"At least one other thing of importance." Ellery was scanning, not the enclosure, but the envelope. "The exact hour, maybe the exact hour and minute, on Thursday, June twenty-first. Have you noticed this envelope, Dad?"

"How can I have noticed it when you've hoarded it like a miser?"

"Proves what we suspected all along. King says it was found with the mail brought in by tonight's mail plane. That ought to mean that it went through somebody's post office. Only, it didn't. Look."

"No stamp, no postmark," mumbled his father. "It was slipped into the pouch on arrival."

"An inside job, and no guesswork this time."

"But this is so dumb, Ellery. Doesn't he care? A school kid would know from this envelope that the origin of these notes is on the island. I don't get it at all."

"It's pretty," said Ellery, with a faraway look. "Because they don't need us, Dad. Not the least bit. And right now I don't care a toot if they do hear all this in their spy room."

"What are you going to do, son?"

"Go to bed. And first thing in the morning—assert myself!"

6

THE NEXT MORNING Ellery asserted himself. He deliberately set out to make as much trouble as he could.

Leaving his father at the Residence, Ellery ordered a car.
One showed up in the courtyard with Blue Shirt behind the
wheel and his alter ego at the door.

"I don't want company this morning, thank you," Ellery
snapped. "I'll take the wheel myself."

"Sorry, Mr. Queen," said Brown Shirt. "Get in."

"I was told I could go anywhere."

"Yes, sir," said Brown Shirt. "We'll take you wherever you
want to go."

"My father took a car out without a wet-nurse!"

"Our orders this morning are to stick with you, sir."

"Who gives these orders."

"Colonel Spring."

"Where does Colonel Spring get them?"

"I wouldn't know, sir. From the Home Office, I suppose."

"The Home Office is where I want to go."

"We'll take you there, sir."

"Jump in, Mr. Queen," said Blue Shirt amiably.

Ellery got into the car, and Brown Shirt got in beside him.

At the Home Office Ellery strode into the black marble
lobby with a disagreeable face. The Shirts sat down on a
marble bench.

"Good morning, Mr. Queen," said the central of the three
security men behind the desk. "Whom did you wish to see?"

"King Bendigo."

The man consulted a chart. He looked up, puzzled. "Do
you have an appointment, sir?"

"Certainly not. Open that elevator door."

The three security men stared at him. Then they conferred in whispers. Then the central man said, "I'm afraid you don't understand, Mr. Queen. You *can't* go up without an appointment."

"Then make one for me. I don't care how you do it, but I'm talking to your lord and master, and I'm doing it right now."

The three men stared at one another.

From behind him, Blue Shirt said, "You don't want to make trouble, Mr. Queen. These men have their orders—"

"Get Bendigo on the phone!"

It was a crisis Ellery thoroughly enjoyed. Brown Shirt must have touched Blue Shirt's arm, because both fell back; and he must have nodded to the central security man, because that baffled official immediately looked scared and sat down to fumble with the controls of his communications system. He spoke in a voice so low that Ellery could not hear what he said.

"The King's receptionist says it's impossible. The King is in very important conference, sir. You'll have to wait, sir."

"Not down here. I'll wait upstairs."

"Sir—"

"*Upstairs.*"

The man mumbled into the machine again. There was a delay, then he turned nervously back to Ellery.

"All right, sir." One of the trio pressed something and the door in the circular column sank into the floor.

"It's not all right," said Ellery firmly.

"What, Mr. Queen?" The central man was bewildered.

"You've forgotten to check my thumbprints. How do you know I'm not Walter Winchell in disguise? Do you want me to report you to Colonel Spring?"

The last thing Ellery saw as the elevator door shut off his view was the worried, rather silly, look on Brown Shirt's face. It gave him a great deal of satisfaction.

The elevator discharged him in the wedge-of-pie reception room. This time the black desk was occupied. The man behind the desk wore a plain black suit, not a uniform, and he was the

most muscular receptionist Ellery had ever seen. But his voice
was soft and cultured.

"There's some mistake, sir—"

"No mistake," said Ellery loftily. "I'm getting tired of all
this high-and-mightiness. King Kong in his office?"

"Have a seat, please. The King is in an extremely—"

"—important conference. I know. Doesn't he ever hold any
unimportant conferences?" Ellery went to the lefthand door
and, before the receptionist could leap from behind the desk,
pounded coarsely on the panel. It boomed.

He kept pounding. It kept booming.

"Sir!" The receptionist was clawing at his arm. "This is not
allowed! It's—it's—"

"Treason? Can't be. I'm not one of your nationals. Open up
in there!"

The receptionist got him in a stranglehold. The other hand
he clamped over Ellery's mouth and nose.

Things began to turn blue.

Ellery was outraged. Taking his own bad office manners into
due consideration, this sort of treatment smacked more of
bouncer in a Berlin East Zone rathskeller than the dutiful cleri-
cal worker of a civilized democracy. So Ellery slumped, feign-
ing submission, and when the muscular receptionist's hold relaxed, Ellery executed a lightning judo counterattack which
sent his captor flying backward to thump ignominiously on his
bottom.

Just as the door to King Bendigo's private office opened
and Max'l peered out.

Ellery wasted no strength parleying with the gorilla. Having
the advantage of surprise, there was only one way to deal with
such as Max'l, and Ellery did so. He stiffarmed the King's
jester in the nose and walked in past the outraged carcass.
What must follow in a matter of seconds he preferred not to
linger over in his thoughts.

The hemispherical room seemed full of distinguished-looking
men. They were seated or on their feet about the King's desk,
and they were all staring toward the door.

Behind him Ellery could hear the receptionist shouting and

a drumming of boots. Max'l was up on one knee, nose bleed-ing, beret askew over his left eye, and his right measuring Ellery without the least rancor.

Ellery trudged the long mile to Bendigo's desk, sidestepped one of the distinguished-looking men, planted both fists on the ebony perfection, and stared at the man in the golden chair malevolently.

The man on the throne stared back.

"Wait, Maximus." The voice was furry. "Just what do you believe you're doing, Queen?"

Ellery felt Max'l's hot breath on the back of his neck. It promised neither comfort nor cheer.

"I'm looking for the answer to a question, Mr. Bendigo. I'm sick of evasions and double talk, and I won't stand for further delays."

"I'll see you later."

"You'll see me now."

Abel Bendigo was in the group, looking on inscrutably. Out of the corner of his eye Ellery also noticed Immanuel Peabody and Dr. Akst, the lawyer's mouth open, the physicist regarding him with an interest not evident the night before. The dis-tinguished strangers looked merely confused.

"Do you have any idea," demanded the master of Bendigo Island, "what you have interrupted?"

"You're wasting time."

The black eyes dulled over. Bendigo sank back.

"Excuse me, gentlemen, just a moment. No, stay where you are. You guards, it's all right. Shut that door." Ellery heard a scuffling far behind him, the click of the distant door. "Now, Queen, suppose you ask me your question."

"Where on your island," said Ellery promptly, "will I find a Winchester Noiseless Portable typewriter?"

Had he asked for the formula of the H-bomb, Ellery could not have met a more absolute silence. Then one of the dis-tinguished visitors permitted himself an undistinguished titter. The giggle shot King Bendigo out of his golden chair.

"In the course of your stupid, inconsequential investiga-tion," thundered the King, "you disrupt what is probably the

most important conference being held at this moment anywhere on the face of the earth. Mr. Queen, do you know who
these gentlemen are? On my left sits Sir Cardigan Cleets, of
the British government. On my right sits the Chevalier Camille
Cassebeer, of the Republic of France. Before me sits the Honorable James Walbridge Monahew, of the United States Atomic
Control Commission. And you dare to break in on the de-
liberation of these gentlemen—not to mention mine!—in order
to locate a *typewriter?* If this is a joke, I don't appreciate its
humor!"

"I assure you, Mr. Bendigo, I'm not feeling the least bit
devilish—"

"Then what's the meaning of this? Explain!"

"Gladly," said Ellery. "You've fouled your island up with
so many locked doors, armed guards, orders, restrictions, and
other impediments to an investigation, Mr. Bendigo, that it
would take me five years to do the job properly, and even then
I wouldn't be sure I'd covered them all. And I don't have five
years, Mr. Bendigo. I want action, and on Bendigo Island it's
obvious that to get it you have to go to the top. I repeat:
Where on your island will I find a Winchester Noiseless Portable typewriter?"

The black eyes dulled even more. And the fine hands on
the desk top trembled a little. But when the big man spoke, it
was in a low voice.

"Abel . . ."

Then his control broke. The fine hand became a club, smash-
ing the air. *"Get rid of this lunatic!"*

Abel hurried around the desk to whisper into his brother's
crimson ear. . . .

As Abel whispered, the crimson began to fade and the big
fist came undone. Finally King nodded shortly, and his black
eyes looked Ellery over once more.

Abel straightened up. "We don't have such information at
our fingertips, Mr. Queen." There was something secretive and
yet amused in his unhurried twang. "I can tell you that all the
typewriting machines in the Home Office are electrics, standard
in size and weight; we use no portables in this building at all.

There may be some, of course, elsewhere on the island, in the personal possession of employees—"

"If you can't give me any more concrete information than that," said Ellery, "I want permission to search the private apartments of the Residence. Specifically, the Bendigo living quarters." He added brutally, looking Abel in the eye, "Nothing like starting in the feedbox, Abel, is there?"

Abel blinked. He blinked very rapidly indeed, and he kept blinking.

That's where I'll find it, thought Ellery.

King Bendigo snapped, "All right, Queen, you have our permission. Now get out, before I let Max'l boot you out."

ELLERY picked his father up in their suite.

"I made myself as obnoxious as possible," he concluded his recital of his adventures in the Home Office, "and I made one discovery, Dad—no, two."

"I know the first," grunted his father. "That you were born with the luck of the leprechaun."

"We'll find the murderous portable somewhere in the Bendigo living quarters," said Ellery. "That's one. The other is that King is an even more dangerous man than I thought. He has not only the power of a tyrant, but a tyrant's whims as well. And he'll become more whimsical when he recognizes power in others. It's a trait I don't trust. Let's see if Abel's carried out his lord's command."

Abel had. They were not stopped by the guards. The officer in charge looked pained, but he saluted and stepped aside without a word.

Each member of the family had a private suite, and the Queens searched them in turn. There was no sign of a machine in Karla Bendigo's suite, and no sign of Karla. They found a typewriter in the King's study, and one in Abel's, but these were standard machines of a different make. They were approaching Judah's quarters when Ellery noticed for the first time, across the corridor from Judah's door, a large and massive-looking door of a design different from any he had seen

THE KING IS DEAD

in the Residence. He tried it. It was locked. He rapped on it.
He whistled.

"Steel," he said to his father. "I wonder what's in here."

"Let's find out," said the Inspector, and he went for the
officer in charge.

"This is the Confidential Room, sir," said the officer. "For
the use of the King only, and of whoever's helping him.
Usually it's Mr. Abel."

"Where the deeper skulduggery is planned, hm?" said Ellery. "Open it, please, Captain."

"Sorry, sir. No one may enter this room except by special
permission."

"Well, you've got your orders. I've been granted special
permission."

"Nothing was said about the Confidential Room, sir," said
the officer.

"Then get something said."

"One moment, sir."

The officer strode away.

The Queens waited.

"Confidential Room," grunted the Inspector. "Fat chance
we have to get in there. I suppose that's where he and Abel
work nights when they don't want to go back to the Home
Office."

The officer came back. "Permission refused, sir."

"What!" exploded Ellery. "After all that—"

"Mr. Abel assures Mr. Queen that there is no Winchester
Noiseless Portable typewriter in the Confidential Room."

They watched the officer march away.

"It looks, Dad," said Ellery, "as if Mr. Judah Bendigo
is elected."

He was. They found a Winchester Noiseless Portable in
Judah's study.

JUDAH BENDIGO was still in bed, snoring the spasmodic snores
of the very drunk. The Inspector set his back against the bedroom door while Ellery looked around.

There was nothing like Judah's suite anywhere in the Residence. Karla's had been feminine, but it lacked depth and breadth. These were the cluttered, comfortable quarters of a man of intelligence, culture, and artistic passions. The books were catholic in range, visibly read, and many were rare and beautiful volumes. The paintings and etchings were originals and could not have been gathered by any but a man of acute perception and taste. Many were by artists unknown to Ellery, which pleased him, for it was evident that Judah set no store by mere reputation, seeing greatness still unrecognized elsewhere. At the same time, there were two little Utrillos which Ellery would have given a great deal to own.

One entire wall was given over to music recordings. Perhaps twenty-five hundred albums, a fabulous record collection which must have taken many years to put together. Ellery saw numerous recordings which had long been out of print and were rare collectors' items. Palestrina, Pergolesi, Buxtehude, Bach, Mozart, Haydn, Handel, Scarlatti. Beethoven, Schumann, Brahms, Bruckner, and Mahler were heavily represented; there were whole volumes of Gregorian chants; and one long shelf was devoted to ethnic music. But Bartók was there, too, and Hindemith, and Shostakovitch, and Toch. It was a collection which embraced the great music of the Western world since the ninth century.

On a table, in a velvet-lined case which was open, glowed a Stradivarius violin. Ellery touched the strings; the instrument was in perfect tune.

And he opened the Bechstein piano. No bell-shaped bottles here! Here, Judah Bendigo found such subterfuge unnecessary. In the corner of the room behind the piano, piled high, stood six cases of Segonzac cognac.

Ellery glanced at the bedroom door with an unhappy frown.

He shook his head and went to the Florentine leather-topped desk on which the Winchester portable stood.

He did not touch it.

Suddenly he sat down and began to rummage through drawers.

The Inspector watched in his own silence.

"Here's the stationery."

There was a large box of it—creamy single sheets, personal letter size, of a fine vellum-type paper without monogram or imprint.

"You're sure, Ellery?"

"It's of Italian manufacture. The watermarks are identical. I'm sure."

He took one of the sheets from the box and returned the box to its drawer. The sheet he inserted in the carriage of the machine.

"He'll wake up," said the Inspector.

"I hope he does. But he won't. He's stupefied and this is a Noiseless. . . . I don't get it. If this is the same machine—"

Ellery brought out the third threatening note, propped it against a bottle of Segonzac on the desk, and copied its message on the blank sheet.

The machine made a pattering sound. It was soothing.

Ellery removed the copy and set it beside the original. And he sighed, unsoothed. The evidence was conclusive: The latest message threatening King Bendigo's life and setting the date for Thursday, June the twenty-first, had been typed on this machine. Slight discrepancies in alignment, ink flaws in the impression of certain characters, were identical.

"It is, Dad."

They looked at each other across Judah's quiet room.

After a while the Inspector said, "No concealment. None at all. Anybody—Abel, King—could walk in here at any hour of the day or night and in ten seconds find the stationery, the typewriter, make the same test, reach the same conclusion. Or Colonel Spring, or any security guard on the premises. Max'l could do it!"

"Abel did do it."

Brother proposing to take the life of brother, and taking no precautions of any kind against discovery. And another brother discovering this and—most baffling of all—seeking confirmation where no confirmation was even remotely called for. . . .

"Maybe," said the Inspector softly, "maybe Judah's being framed, Ellery, and Abel knows it or suspects it."

"And would that present a problem?" said Ellery, gnawing his knuckles. "On the top floor of the central building of this fortified castle, in the private apartment of one of the royal family? Does that sort of thing require 'experts' flown from New York? When they've got a complete law-enforcement organization here, with undoubtedly the most advanced facilities? All the exploration of that theory would require, Dad, is the simplest sort of trap. A mere fingerprint checkup, for that matter." He shook his head. "It doesn't make sense."

"Neither does this!"

Ellery shrugged. He fished in his pocket and produced a pocketknife.

"What are you going to do, Ellery?"

"Go through the motions. What else can I do?" Ellery opened the knife to its sharpest blade and carefully nicked both sides of the lower case *o* in Judah Bendigo's typewriter.

"What's the point of that? We know they're being typed on this machine."

"Maybe they were all typed at the same time, long ago. If the *o*'s on the next note are undamaged, they were, and we'll probably be at a dead end. But if they show these nicks, and if we can get a round-the-clock check on who enters this room . . ."

ELLERY said to the captain of the guard, "Get Colonel Spring on the phone for me."

The officer stiffened. "Yes, sir!"

The other guards stiffened, too.

"Colonel? This is Ellery Queen. I'm calling from—"

"I know where you're calling from, Mr. Queen," said Colonel Spring's high voice. "Enjoying your visit?"

"I'd rather answer that question in person, Colonel. If you know where I am, suppose you come here at once."

"Something wrong?" The Colonel sounded alert.

"I'll wait for you."

The drowned face of Colonel Spring appeared in six minutes. He was not smiling or limp now.

"What is it?" he asked abruptly.

"How much are these guards," asked Ellery, "to be trusted?"

The guards, including their officer, were rigidly at attention. Their eyes bulged.

"These men?" Colonel Spring's aqueous glance washed over them. "Completely."

"That goes for all shifts on duty up here?"

"Yes. Why?"

But Ellery said, "They're utterly devoted to the King?"

The little man in the splendid black and gold uniform put one hand on a hip and cocked his fishlike head. "To King Bendigo, you mean? They'd lay down their lives for him. Why?"

"I'll settle for incorruptibility," murmured Ellery. "Why, Colonel? Because, as of this minute, I want a twenty-four-hour-a-day report on the identity of every person who enters the private apartment of Judah Bendigo."

"Mr. Judah? May I ask *why?*"

"You may, but I'm not going to answer, Colonel Spring."

The little man produced a brown cigaret and snapped it to his lips. The captain sprang forward with a lighter.

"Thank you, Captain," said the Colonel. "And is this authorized, Mr. Queen?" He puffed in short, stabbing puffs.

"Check with Abel Bendigo. If he withholds authorization, tell him Inspector Queen and I will expect to be flown back to New York within the hour. But he won't. . . . This report, Colonel, is to be confidential. No one—except Abel Bendigo, and I'd really prefer not to except even him—no one is to know the check is being made. For simplification, maids and other servants are to be barred from Judah Bendigo's rooms on some plausible pretext until further notice. If any leak whatever occurs, or the job isn't done thoroughly, Colonel—"

The green in Colonel Spring's complexion deepened. But he merely said, "I've never had any complaints, Mr. Queen."

In the elevator Inspector Queen said dryly, "I wonder how much *he* can be trusted."

Ellery was wondering, too.

7

THE FOURTH LETTER turned up on the afternoon of the following day.

The day began with a humorous ultimatum from the King's Surgeon-General. Dr. Storm's quarters in the Residence were combined with a hospital wing, reserved for the use of the Bendigo family. Here, against a background of the most advanced equipment, with the assistance of a staff of medical and dental assistants and laboratory technicians, Dr. Storm supervised the daily ritual of examining into the health of the master of the Bendigo empire. The medical examination took place each morning before King Bendigo's breakfast.

On this particular morning the stout little doctor, brandishing a clip of reports, waddled past the guards into the family dining room, as King and his queen were rising from the table, to announce abruptly that there would be no work for his eminent patient that day.

"Something is wrong?" Karla asked quickly.

"Rot," growled King. "I feel fine. A bit pooped, maybe—"

"A bit pooped, maybe," mocked Dr. Storm. "A bit pooped, certainly! I don't like you this morning. I don't like you at all. And it's a heavy, humid day. Bad for you, at your age. You'll do nothing today but relax."

"Go away, Stormy," frowned King Bendigo. "Abel's had to run over to Washington and I have a thousand things on my calendar. It's out of the question."

"I'll go away," said the Surgeon-General, showing his sharp little teeth, "and I won't come back. Do you think I enjoy this exile? Oh, for an excuse, an excuse."

"Why do you stay?" King was smiling.

"Because I detest *genus homo*. Because I've conquered all

78

their little universes and staggered all their little minds and shocked all their little ethical sensibilities, and because you've given me a great hospital to play with—and a wealth of raw material. And because, my lord, I'm in love with you. You're not to go near the Office today, do you hear? Not a step, or find another fool."

"But my appointments, Stormy—"

"What will happen? A dynasty will fall? You'll make ten million dollars less? To hell with your appointments."

"Darling," begged Karla. Her hand was on her husband's arm and her eyes were very bright.

"You, too, Karla?" The great man sighed and turned to inspect himself in a mirror. He stuck out his tongue. "Aaaaa. Does look starchy—"

"It isn't your tongue at all. It's your muscle tone and vascular system. Do you stay, or do I go?"

"All right, all right, Doctor," said the King tolerantly. "What are your orders?"

"I've given them to you. Do anything you like except work. Fly a kite. Get plastered. Make love to your wife. What do I care?"

So that afternoon, oppressed by the heat, nerves jangling, prowling restlessly, the Queens came upon an extraordinary scene. Passing by the Residence's gymnasium, they heard masculine shouts and looked in to find royalty at play. Near the indoor pool there was a regulation prize ring, and in the ring the master of the island was wrestling with Max'l. The two men wore high laced shoes and tights; both were naked from the waist up. Max'l was completely furred; the King's torso was as smooth as a boy's. Beside the other man's bulk, he looked slim.

As the Queens entered, Bendigo broke a vicious arm-lock by a backward somersault, and the next moment he had spun Max'l about and applied a full nelson. Max'l raised his great arms, hands clenched, and exerted all his strength in a downward pressure. But King's eyes flashed and he held on. And then Max'l sagged and he began to wave his fingers frantically.

"Give up, Maximus?"

"Yah, yah!"

Laughing, King increased the pressure. Max'l's eyes popped in his contorted face. Then, with a sort of contempt, King unlocked his hands and turned away. The great furred body crashed to the mat and lay still. After a moment Max'l rolled over and crawled to a corner of the ring, where he sat dejectedly, like an exhausted animal licking his wounds. He kept rubbing the back of his neck.

King spied them and waved gaily as he vaulted out of the ring.

"Do you wrestle, Queen?"

"After what I just witnessed—no, thank you!"

King laughed. "Karla. Our wandering guests."

Karla looked up. She was in a French bathing suit, lying with goggles on under a sun lamp at the edge of the swimming pool. She sat ⌐ ⌐ ⌐.

"There you both are. I sent all over the Residence looking for you to ask you to join us. Where have you been hiding?"

"Here and there, Mrs. Bendigo. It's a jittery day."

King Bendigo was looking down at them, smiling. Ellery wondered what would happen to a man this potentate caught making love to his wife.

Max'l was on his feet now, looking foolish.

And in the pool was Judah Bendigo. There was no sign of Abel.

Judah's white, emaciated body, wearing green bathing trunks, was floating in the pool like a broken lily pad. On the edge of the pool lay a bottle of Segonzac and a glass. As Ellery looked at him, Judah opened his eyes. They were bloodshot and bleared, but they did not blink. To Ellery's stupefaction, one lid moved down and up in an unmistakable wink. And then both eyes closed and Judah paddled a little, moving lazily toward the bottle and the glass.

Karla was saying, "Why don't you two cool off in the pool? There are dressing rooms down here, and we have a central guest-supply room from which we can provide anything."

"I wouldn't bare my scrawniness before a beautiful woman, even at my age," said the Inspector, "if my hide was baking off. Don't mind if I do," he said to an attendant, who had come up with a portable bar. "But my son here, he's kind of proud of his physique—"

"Not any more," said Ellery, glancing at King.

The big man laughed. "You're slighter than I am, but Darius—my receptionist at the Office—tells me you're a powerful boy. Do you box, Queen?"

"Well . . . yes."

"Don't let Kane tempt you into a boxing match, Mr. Queen," said Karla. "There is a photograph in the trophy room —did you notice it the other evening?—showing my husband standing over the prostrate form of a champion?"

"Champion?" said the Inspector. "What champion?"

"The heavyweight champion of the world," chuckled King Bendigo. "It was a long time ago—I was in my early twenties. He was barnstorming up around my way, putting on exhibitions and pushing over the yokels, and some of my local admirers persuaded me to climb into the ring with him. I got in a lucky right cross in the first twenty seconds, he went down, and one of my newspaper friends snapped a flash photo of it. He ran like hell, as I recall it, and so did I! That photo is one of my proudest possessions.—Maximo! How you feeling?"

"We wrestle again," grunted Max. "I'll break your arm this time. Come on!"

"No. I feel like showing off. Let's put the gloves on, Max'l. I'm going to knock your block off."

"Oh, this has been the loveliest day," sighed Karla. "Go on, Max'l. Knock his off. I'd love to see your block flying off, darling. . . ."

"You heard the Madame," grinned King Bendigo. "Toss me my gloves."

Two pairs of eight-ounce boxing gloves hung over one of the ring posts. One pair was the regulation color, the other had an iridescent purple cast. It was these gloves that Max'l tossed with a growl down to his master. Ellery noticed a great many pairs of boxing gloves hanging on one of the gymnasium walls; none of them was purple. His stomach crawled.

It was as King was drawing on the left glove that it happened. His big hand stuck midway into the glove, and with a scowl he withdrew his hand. Then he probed with his forefinger.

It came out hooked about a wad of paper.

Cream-colored paper.

Bendigo unfolded it. He exclaimed with annoyance and whirled as if to accuse someone of something. As he whirled, the sole of his gym shoe slipped on the apron of the pool and, with a comical shout, he tumbled backwards into the water, landing with a splash that soaked Ellery and the Inspector to the skin.

Karla, who had not seen him withdraw the note from the boxing glove, cried out in terror; but then, at the sight of her lord and master threshing and floundering about in the pool, she burst into laughter.

"Oh, Kane, I can't help it! That was so funny! Judah, don't just float there like a dead stick. Help him!"

The great man sank, came to the surface, howled, got a ⸻uthful of water, and sank again. Judah sat up in the pool, ⸻artled. Then he swam over to his brother with quick strokes and seized the royal chin.

"A miracle! A miracle!" Judah cried. "Ozymandias revealed! Who's got a hook to barb this foot of clay? And watch out for typhoons!"

As Ellery and the Inspector dragged the spluttering man out of the pool, Ellery was thinking that it was the first time he had heard Judah Bendigo's voice.

"Kane, I'm so sorry. Darling, are you all right? But I've never seen you lose your dignity before. Humpty-dumpty!" Karla laughed and laughed, holding his head tenderly.

He shook her off, jumped to his feet, and strode out of the gymnasium. His face was black.

Max'l, who had stood stupidly in the ring through it all, vaulted to the floor and ran after his master.

Karla stopped laughing.

"He is angry," she said slowly. "He laughs a great deal, but never at himself. . . . What was that piece of paper? Another of those threatening notes?"

Then she did know.

"I'm afraid so, Mrs. Bendigo." Ellery had picked up the paper as it fell from Bendigo's hand and had slipped it into his pocket. He produced it now, and Karla and his father read it with him.

Judah was sitting on the edge of the pool, calmly pouring himself a drink.

It was the same kind of paper, and the typing had been done on a Winchester Noiseless Portable.

This time the message said:

You are going to be murdered on Thursday, June 21, at exactly 12:00 o'clock—

"I can't believe it," Karla said. "I have known about the others—I wormed it out of Kane—but it is all so silly. So uselessly melodramatic." She drew her robe about her. "Excuse me," she said faintly. "I will dress."

She ran toward the dressing rooms.

And that was when they turned around to find that Judah Bendigo was gone.

With the bottle and the glass.

NEITHER of the Queens bothered to change his wet clothing. They hurried upstairs and dashed for the private elevator.

"The nicks in the *o*," muttered the Inspector. "Six small *o*'s, and every one has the double nick. Now the question is—"

"Your report, Captain," Ellery said to the officer of the guard. "Let me have it, please!"

The officer thrust a time-sheet into Ellery's hand.

They retreated as pell-mell as they had come.

IN their own rooms, with the door locked, they bent over the report.

There was one name on it.

No one had entered or left Judah Bendigo's quarters since Ellery had nicked the *o*'s in Judah Bendigo's typewriter but Judah Bendigo.

Not only had Judah Bendigo's typewriter been used in the

composition of the fourth threatening note, but it could only
have been Judah Bendigo who used it.

*   *   *

"ALL RIGHT," said the Inspector, pacing. "So now we *know* it.
It's Judah Bendigo on the level, and the time is definitely set
for Thursday, June twenty-first, twelve o'clock, and that's
that."

"That's not that. Twelve o'clock what?"

"What?"

"Noon or midnight. There's going to be a fifth note."

"I don't care about that, Ellery. Right now the important
thing is that we know it's Judah. Only now that we know it,
what do we do about it?"

"Report to Abel."

"Who's in Washington."

Ellery shrugged. "Then we wait till he gets back."

"Suppose," said his father, "suppose Abel doesn't get back
till Friday, June twenty-second?"

Ellery tapped his lip with the edge of the note.

"Or suppose he gets back in time. We report. He says,
'Thank you, gentlemen, that's what I thought, here's your hat
—take off!' So we fly into the sunset, or whatever the devil
direction New York is from here—and I ask you, *Why?* What
were we needed for in the first place?"

"And what," mumbled Ellery, "what do they do with Brother Judah? Skin him alive? Hang him by the neck till he can't
even swallow Segonzac? Slap his skinny little wrist?"

"Climb out of those wet clothes, son. No sense getting
pneumonia on top of a first-class skull ache."

They undressed in silence.

8

WHAT FOLLOWED was intolerable. For what followed was nothing at all. All the next day Abel did not return to the island. Karla could not see them—she was reported ill, nothing of importance, but Dr. Storm was keeping her in bed. King Bendigo returned to the Home Office and, as if to make up for the day he had lost, remained there until far into the night, working with Peabody. The Queens saw Judah two or three times; he waved amiably but managed to keep out of their way. They had long since discussed the advisability of tackling Judah on their own initiative, without waiting for Abel, but they decided against this.

There was literally nothing to do.

So they wandered over the island.

"Maybe," remarked the Inspector, "I can add to my little bundle of notes and sketches."

Even the Shirts had disappeared. At least, no block was put in their path and no one, so far as they could make out, trailed them.

On the second day after the incident of the boxing glove, they were exploring a part of the island neither had seen before. There were no factories or workers' homes here. It was a barren place, an area of sand dunes and leathery scrub, with the blue glass of the sea rolling in to smash into splinters against the cliff walls. This was one of the spit ends of the island, exposed to the sea on three sides, and it had probably been left in its natural state because of the difficulty of effective camouflage.

"But not entirely," said Ellery. "If you'll look up there— where the thick stuff starts growing—you'll see something that looks like the biggest leaning birch tree you ever saw. Only it's a sixteen-inch gun."

"Who'd want this Godforsaken place, anyway?" snarled his father. "What's that?"

"What's what?"

The Inspector was a little ahead, to one side of a dune, and when Ellery joined him with a stride the stride stopped short.

The cliff wall crumbled at their feet to make a steep but negotiable path down to the beach. Between the shoreline and the base of the cliff there was a concrete building. It was not a large building, and its few iron-barred windows were so small that it looked like a fort in miniature. Palm trees had been planted about the structure, which was streaked and slashed with green and dun-colored paint. From the sea it was probably indistinguishable from its background.

Around the entire area rose a twelve-foot metal fence topped with barbed wire.

Ellery pointed to some camouflaged cables. "Electrified."

There was a little blistery bulb of a lookout on top of the building, with a narrow embrasure through which machine-gun muzzles protruded. Uniformed men, heavily armed, patrolled the enclosure.

"Soldiers of the Kingdom of Bendigo," said Ellery through his teeth. "They must get lonely way out here. Maybe they'll loosen up to a kind word."

Ellery scrambled down the path, the Inspector at his heels. Bits of shale flew from under their feet. The sun was hot.

As they reached the base of the cliff they came upon a small Residence car. There was a key in its ignition lock, but the car was empty. They looked around. There was no beach road. They had had to leave their car up on the cliff some distance away, where the road ended.

"Now how the dickens did this car get down here?"

"A tunnel." Ellery pointed. "Plugged up—see the camouflaged door? It must lead up through the rock and join the main road somewhere back there. Cliff doors, God help us! I tell you, Dad, these people never grew beyond the age of eight."

"They're little hellers, though," said his father dryly.

"Halt!"

The gate was locked. Just inside were two soldiers armed with submachine guns. The guns were trained on the Queens' bellies through the gate. Between the soldiers loomed an officer with a sun-black face and eyes of the color and warmth of oyster shell.

A little to one side, smoking a brown cigaret, stood Colonel Spring.

"Good morning," said Ellery to Colonel Spring.

The Colonel smoked.

"What do you want?" The officer had a harsh, mechanical voice.

"Nothing especially. Just rubbernecking—Major, is it? I'm still not familiar with your insignia system." Maybe Spring didn't like to interfere in the routine duties of his subordinates. He was standing there as if he had never seen them before. "May we come in, Colonel, and look around?"

Colonel Spring smoked.

"Your passes!" rapped the officer.

"What is this place, anyway?" muttered the Inspector.

All right, Colonel, if that's your game . . . "Yes, what are you boys playing at way out here, Major?"

"Your passes!" There was no humor in that robot voice.

The Queens stopped smiling.

"We don't have any passes," said Ellery carefully. "Colonel Spring can tell you who we are."

"I know who you are. Your pass."

"We have King and Abel Bendigo's personal permission to go anywhere on the island. Hasn't the word come down?"

"Produce it!"

"Produce what?" Ellery was growing angry. "I've told you. Your King said we could go anywhere we pleased."

"In this place you must produce a written pass signed by Colonel Spring. This is forbidden ground. If you have no pass, leave at once. Do you have a pass?"

"Well, I'll be damned," said the Inspector.

Ellery deliberately looked the Colonel over. The hippy,

elegant little man in the uniform might have been watching
the antics of a cageful of trained fleas. "All right, Colonel, here
we are and there you are. Inspector Queen and I want a pass.
Make one out."

The little Colonel smiled. "Certainly, Mr. Queen. But then
you'll have to have it countersigned by King Bendigo or Abel
Bendigo. Those are the rules. Apply to my office in the usual
way. Good morning." He poised the smoldering brown butt
of his cigaret delicately, dropped it, and ground it with the
heel of his boot into the shaly sand.

"Come on, son," said Inspector Queen.

Four things happened almost simultaneously.

The only visible door of the concrete building opened and
the chubby figure of Dr. Storm appeared, carrying a medical
bag; behind him towered an enormous guard.

Ellery snatched a pair of binoculars from his pocket, clapped
them to his eyes, and trained them on one of the barred
windows of the building.

Colonel Spring stiffened and said something to the officer
in a sharp voice.

The officer jumped forward, shouting to the lookout in the
blister. Apparently the current charging the fence was operated from the tower. The officer seized the gate and unlocked
it.

"Arrest these men," said Colonel Spring.

The binoculars were torn from Ellery's grasp by the officer
and the next moment the Queens were in the grip of the two
armed soldiers.

They were dragged into the enclosure.

"For . . . the love of . . ." The Inspector choked. One of the
soldiers had an easy hold on the Inspector's necktie. The old
gentleman slowly grew purple.

A cool small voice kept saying to Ellery, *This is ridiculous,
it's something you're reading in a book,* as his fist kept cracking against flesh and faces stared into his and blue sky and
blue sea and white sand and green palms whirled and pain
jolted him from every direction and finally exploded in his

middle and he found himself prone on the sand with his nose grinding into some shale and a crushing weight on his back.

And then he was lifted clear and smashed to his feet and things came back a little. His father stood nearby, deathly pale, brushing himself off with blind puny strokes. The door of the concrete building was closed again. Dr. Storm, looking like a portly old penguin in his black suit and white shirt, was talking cheerfully to Colonel Spring.

They were ringed with armed soldiers.

Nobody looked menacing.

Nobody even scowled.

Part of the job. All in the day's work. . . . Ellery found himself doubled up, clutching his groin.

Colonel Spring was smoking another brown cigaret, head lowered, listening with a frown to Dr. Storm.

"My rules aren't made to be broken, Doctor."

Dr. Storm kept talking cheerfully.

The men holding him up kept holding. Ellery felt grateful. His father was still brushing himself futilely. A Bendigo plane streaked by deep in the sky.

"All right." Colonel Spring shrugged.

He said something to the officer, turned on his heel, and walked over to the building. The door opened instantly. He stepped inside. The door crashed.

"You may leave now, gentlemen."

Ellery looked up. It was Dr. Storm, smiling.

"May . . . !" He heard a strangled voice, sounding nothing like his own.

"I know, I know," said the Surgeon-General of Bendigo Island. "Your male ego is offended—"

"Offended!" gurgled Ellery. He kept digging his fists into his groin. "I want an explanation. I want an apology. I want this man alone in a room with me. I want *something!*"

"You won't get it," said Dr. Storm. "You're lucky I happened to be here. And if you'll take my advice, Mr. Queen, you'll never come here again." And the fat little doctor waved, went through the gate, climbed into the empty car, backed around, and drove into the hole in the cliff.

A moment later there was no hole, just cliff.

"Outside," said the officer's thumb. His oyster eyes had not changed expression.

Ellery felt swollen fists at the ends of his arms.

"Come on, son," said his father urgently. "Do you think you can make it back to our car?"

ELLERY did not start the car. The pain was going away from his groin, but his nose burned where the shale had cut it and his body ached in a dozen places.

The Inspector sat limply, hands in his lap, staring at the peaceful sea.

They sat there, without a word, for a long time.

Then his father said, "Who was it you spotted in that building?"

"Dr. Akst." His tongue tasted bitter.

"Akst? The big blond young physicist?"

"Yes."

"Can that be Akst's hush-hush lab? Where he fiddles around with his atoms? That would explain the electrified fence, the guards—"

"It's too small a building for physical research. Anyway, Akst had his hands up to the bars. They were manacled."

"Manacled!"

"He's a prisoner." Ellery stared at his overstuffed hands. "I wondered why we hadn't seen him around. He's been tapped for out."

"Oh, come on," said the Inspector vehemently. "That's a bit thick even for this hellhole. After all—"

"After all what? That enclosure is Bendigo Island's version of Dachau. Who's to tell His Mightiness the King what he can or can't do? He's squatting on this island in the ocean, absolute monarch of it and everyone on it."

"But Akst—a man like Akst—"

"Disappears. Or false reports are cleverly broadcast. That wouldn't be a problem, Dad."

"But *why?*"

"*Lèse-majesté*. Treason to the Crown. Or he's found that

what he's been working on sticks in even his scientific craw. Who knows why? Probably Akst's loyalty came under suspicion. He was investigated, or he's in the process of being investigated. Or he's refused to go on, and this is a little persuasive treatment. Meanwhile, he's in chains in the King's private concentration camp. . . . Are there courts on Bendigo Island, I wonder?"

* * *

THE Inspector patched up Ellery's wounds, gave him a hot bath, and made him lie down. Ellery did not sleep. It was impossible to sleep.

Inspector Queen paced and paced. They had a nameless need to remain together. Had his father gone into the next room, Ellery would have followed.

At last he jumped out of bed and dressed in fresh clothes.

"How about lunch, son?"

"No."

"Where you going?"

But Ellery was already limping up the corridor. The Inspector hurried after him.

When they got to the Home Office, Ellery marched up to the desk with the air of a man who is prepared to slash and broadax a path to his objective.

"Open that elevator door. I want to see this King of yours!"

The central of the three security men said, "Yes, sir."

Thirty seconds later, the muscular receptionist was holding the door of the big office open.

"Interrupting me seems your only strong point, Queen," said the powerful voice at the other end of the room. "Well, come in."

The receptionist closed the door behind them softly.

King Bendigo was seated behind his desk. In a chair by his side sat Immanuel Peabody, immersed in some papers. A man they had never seen—a large stout man with flabby cheeks—stood facing them. The large stout man was standing between two armed soldiers.

Bendigo seemed calm and relaxed, one hand on the desk. As Ellery and his father approached, the handsome man lazily moved a finger and the soldiers stepped to one side, yanking the stout man with them.

"Mr. Bendigo—" began Ellery.

"Is this what you came for?" said the King, smiling.

His other hand appeared. In it was Ellery's pair of binoculars.

Ellery stared at him across the ebony desk. The black eyes were sparkling. Bendigo clearly had been expecting him. He wanted some entertainment, and what would entertain him best, Ellery saw suddenly, was the outraged fury of a helpless man.

The only defense was a feeble one. Having no choice, Ellery used it. He reached across the desk, took his binoculars from the arrogant fingers, and turned on his heel with a matching arrogance.

"Just a moment, Queen."

He felt calm. He would never lose his temper with this man again.

"When you were given carte blanche we thought you, as a man of intelligence, would understand that it was only relative. This is the original tight little isle; we like to keep our secrets. You're a guest here. We don't expect our guests to go snooping in our closets."

"Especially," said Ellery, "those with the skeletons in them?"

"Put it that way if you like. By the way, do you have a camera—any photographic equipment?"

"No."

"Do you, Inspector Queen?"

"No."

"Well, just in case. Cameras are not permitted on Bendigo Island. They are confiscated and smashed, and the film burned, whenever and wherever found. There are also certain . . . forfeits involved. That's all, gentlemen."

He turned toward Peabody.

"Mr. Bendigo."

Bendigo looked back sharply. "Yes?"

"As long as we're going down the Mosaic tables," said

Ellery, "I think I ought to tell you that my father and I have guns with us. Are guns on your contraband list, too?"

Bendigo laughed. "No, Queen. We're very fond of guns here. You may have all the guns you can carry." His lips thinned until they almost disappeared. "But no cameras," he said.

Again their glances crossed.

And this time Ellery was able to smile.

"We understand, Your Highness," he said gravely.

"*Wait!*" King Bendigo sat taller on his throne. At the note in his voice Immanuel Peabody, for the first time, looked up from his papers. "I don't believe you do understand, Queen," Bendigo said slowly. "No, I don't believe you do. . . . Sit down and watch what you interrupted. Over there!"

His thumb stabbed toward two chairs at the curved wall.

Ellery felt a twitch of alarm. The drawl had been unpleasantly without inflection. It reminded him of the voice of the robot officer behind the electrified fence. He was vaguely sorry now that he had come. To conceal his apprehension, he went abruptly to one of the chairs. The Inspector was already at the other, looking gray.

They sat down, tense without knowing quite why.

"You may go ahead now," said Bendigo curtly to Peabody.

Peabody rose. His master leaned back and closed his eyes for a moment. It was theatrical, but it failed to give the reassurance of playacting. For in another moment Bendigo had opened his eyes and turned them on the large stout man between the two soldiers. And what glittered in the black arctic depths of those eyes made the Queens look at the large stout man really for the first time.

His knees sagged, as if his body were too heavy for his legs. His flabby cheeks were pale and wet, although air conditioning made the office very pleasant. He kept screwing up his eyes, as if he were having trouble focusing; occasionally, he would blink. His whole appearance was that of an exhausted man who feels he must pay the closest attention to the proceedings. Ellery had seen men look like that who were defendants in murder cases.

And it occurred to him suddenly that the rhetorical question he had asked in the car after their experience at the concentration camp was being answered here and now.

Yes, there were courts on Bendigo Island. This was one of them, the highest.

The large stout man with the rubbery knees was about to be tried.

And when Immanuel Peabody began to speak, there was no doubt left. He spoke in the crisp, confident tone of the experienced prosecutor. King Bendigo listened with the aloof gravity of the supreme judge.

Peabody was outlining the charge. It had something to do with the stout man's failure to carry out certain instructions. Ellery could not follow it closely, for his thoughts were a bottleneck of jammed impressions—the handsome immobility of Bendigo, the slightly nervous fuss the lawyer's fingers made as he talked, the desperate concentration of the stout man, the glow of the glass brick walls, the powerful mastication of Max'l's jaws as he rapidly fed himself hulled nuts in the doorway of the open safe, apparently his favorite lounging place. Had Max'l been there all the time? . . .

Peabody became more specific. He enumerated dates, names, facts. None of them meant anything to Ellery, who was growing more and more confused. All he could gather was that something or some things the accused had done or had not done had resulted in the severance of an important secret contact somewhere in Asia, which in turn had brought about the loss of an armaments contract. At least it seemed to concern an armaments contract, although Ellery was not sure even of that; it might have involved oil, or raw materials, or ships. Whatever it was, the stout man stood accused of a major crime against the Bendigo empire: bungling.

Ellery held down an impulse to laugh.

And at last King's counsel came to the end of his argument, and he sat down and patted his papers together into a tight, neat pile. Then he leaned back, crossed his dapper legs, and stared with some interest at the stout man.

"Anything to say?" This was evidently the King's juridical voice, cold, solemn, and above-it-all.

The stout man licked his lips and blinked rapidly, struggling with a great wish to produce sound. But then his lips sagged along the lines of his cheeks, and he lapsed into helplessness.

"Speak up, Norton." The voice was sharper, more personal. "Do you have anything to say?"

Again the stout man struggled, the sag lifting. He was no more successful this time, but his failure ended with a shrug— the weariest, most hopeless shrug Ellery had ever witnessed.

Ellery felt his father's fingers on his arm. He sank back. King made a flicking gesture with his shapely right hand.

The stout man might have been a fly.

The guards took him out, each wrestling an arm. The knees kept buckling, and a step before the door they collapsed altogether.

The trio disappeared.

The splendid office sunned itself. There was a siesta mood over everything. No one said a word.

King Bendigo sprawled on his throne, chin thoughtful, black eyes dreamy.

King's advocate Peabody kept his legs comfortably crossed, one hand on his neat, tight pile of papers. However, his head was cocked.

The rapid-fire motion of Max'l's feeding hand had stopped. The hand was suspended before the mouth.

They were waiting. That was it.

But for what?

A laugh that would shatter this dream—wake everyone up and restore the sanity of the world?

A shot?

Nonsense, absurd. . . .

Anyway, the walls were soundproof—

Ellery jumped.

King Bendigo had risen. Lawyer Peabody uncrossed his legs. Max'l's hand popped to his mouth, dipped for a fresh supply of hulled nuts.

It was over.

Whatever had happened, it was over.

The King was speaking graciously to the lawyer. There was a matter of a tax suit for sixty million dollars pending in the high court of some European country. Bendigo was discussing the incomes of the judges and inquiring for more information of the same personal nature.

Peabody replied busily.

At the door, waiting for his father, Ellery glanced back. The King and his Lord Advocate were seated again, their heads together. They were deep in conversation. The curved wall glowed and the long office was serene. Max was tossing nuts into the air now and balancing under them with his mouth open, like a seal.

Ellery stumbled out.

WEDNESDAY night came, and there was still no word of Abel Bendigo. Peabody, whom Ellery chased for half a day, merely looked blank when asked about Abel's mission to Washington. Karla knew nothing about it.

His talk with Karla left Ellery unhappy.

"It is a long time since I shook at every threat," she said with a toss of her red hair. "I had to make up my mind early that I had married a unique personality, one who would always be the target of something." She smiled her crooked little smile. "Kane is better guarded than the President of the United States. By men at least as devoted and incorruptible."

"Suppose," Ellery said carefully, "suppose, Mrs. Bendigo, we found that your husband's life is being threatened by some one very close to him—"

"Close to him!" Karla threw her head back and laughed.

"Impossible. No one is really close to Kane. Not even Abel is. Not even I am."

Ellery went away dissatisfied by this transparent sophistry. If Karla suspected anything, she was keeping it to herself.

As the night wore on and Thursday approached, Ellery's skin began to itch and he found it difficult to remain in one spot for more than a few minutes. The more nervous he became, the angrier he grew with all of them—with King, for treating the subject of his own death first with amusement, then with contempt, and finally with irritation, as at a minor but persistent infraction of some Company rule; with Abel, for dragging them into the case and then, unaccountably, staying away from them; with Karla, for being candid when candor was meaningless, and inscrutable when candor would have been helpful; with Judah, for being a man who drank brandy from morning to night and smiled vaguely when his bloodshot eye was caught . . . surely one of the most unsatisfying assassins in history.

The Inspector was no help. He spent most of Wednesday grumpily in his bathroom, locked away from the world of Bendigo. He was copying his sketches of the island's restricted installations, filling in details as best he could, and transcribing his notes in a minute shorthand.

THE call came just as the Queens were about to go to bed Wednesday night.

"I understand you've been asking for me, Mr. Queen."

"Asking for you!" It was Abel Bendigo. "The latest note—"

"I've been told about it."

"Has there been another one? There's going to be another one—"

"I'd rather not discuss it over the phone, Mr. Queen."

"But has there?"

"I don't believe so—"

"You don't *believe* so? Don't you realize that tomorrow is the twenty-first? And you've been away—"

"It couldn't be helped. I'll see you in the morning."

"Wait! Can't we talk now? Why don't you come down here for a few minutes, Mr. Bendigo—"

"Sorry. King and I will be up half the night on the matter that took me to Washington. In the morning, Mr. Queen."

"But I've found out—!"

"Oh." There was silence on the wire. Then Abel said, "And what did you find out?"

"I thought you didn't want to discuss it over the phone."

"Who is it?" The twang vibrated the receiver.

"Your brother Judah," said Ellery brutally. "Does that agree with your conclusion?"

There was another silence. Finally, Abel's voice said, "Yes."

"Well, what do my father and I do now, Mr. Bendigo? Go home?"

"No, no," said Abel. "I want you to tell my brother King."

"Tonight?"

"Tomorrow morning, at breakfast. I'll arrange it with Karla. You're to tell him exactly what you've found out, and how. We'll proceed from there, depending on my brother's reaction."

"But—"

But Ellery was left holding the receiver.

ALL night he tossed over the problem of Abel Bendigo's apparent diffidence, and he came with his father to the breakfast table in the private dining room without having solved it. But as he took his seat he suddenly had the answer. Abel, a planner, could plan nothing where his brother King was concerned. King was an imponderable, a factor who would always remain unknown. In a crisis as personal as this, he might fly off in any one of a dozen directions. Or he might fold his royal wings and refuse to fly at all. *We'll proceed from there, depending on my brother's reaction. . . .* This was probably why Abel, who had detected Judah's guilt at once, called for outside confirmation before revealing his knowledge. He could only pile up his ammunition and wait for developments to tell him which way and how much to shoot.

The King was in a sulky mood this morning. He stamped into the dining room and glared at the Queens, not greeting them. His black eyes were underscored by his nightwork; he looked almost seedy, and Ellery suspected that this had something to do with his mood—King Bendigo was not a man to relish strangers seeing him at less than his best.

Abel was there. Max'l. And Judah.

It was Abel unquestionably who had engineered Judah's presence at breakfast—a considerable engineering feat, to judge by Judah's almost normal appearance. In spite of the early hour, the dark little assassin could sit in his chair reasonably straight-backed. His hand shook only a little. He was gulping his second cup of coffee.

And Abel was nervous. Ellery rather enjoyed that. Abel's gray schoolmaster's face was far grayer than usual. He kept touching the nosepiece of his eyeglasses, as if he felt them skidding. All his gestures were jerky and full of caution.

"Something special about today?" King glanced darkly about, his hand arrested in the act of picking up his napkin. "Our troublemakers from New York—and you, Judah! How did you manage to get up so early in the morning?"

Judah's sunken eyes were on the fine hand of his brother. The hand completed the act of picking up the napkin.

An envelope tumbled to the table.

Max'l shouted something so sudden. hat Karla gripped the arms of her chair, going very white. Max'l was on his feet, glaring murderously at the envelope.

"Who done that?" he roared, tearing the napkin from his collar. "Who, who?"

"Sit down, Maxie," King said. He was looking at the envelope thoughtfully. All his sulkiness had disappeared. Suddenly his mouth curved in a brief malicious smile. He picked the envelope up. His name was typed on it: *King Bendigo.* Nothing else. The envelope was sealed.

"Today is Thursday, the twenty-first of June, Mr. Bendigo —that's what's special about it." Ellery was on his feet, too. "May I see that, please?"

King tossed the envelope onto his brother Judah's plate.

"Pass it to the expert, Judah. This is what he's getting paid for."

Judah obeyed in silence.

Ellery took the envelope with care. His father hurried around the table with a knife. Ellery slit the envelope.

"And what does this one say, Mr. Queen?" Karla's tone was too light. She was still pale.

It was the same stationery. The o's were nicked. Another product of Judah Bendigo's Winchester portable.

"What does it say!" Abel's voice cracked.

"Now, Abel," mocked King. "Control yourself."

"It's a duplicate of the last message," said Ellery, "with two differences. A single word has been added, and this time it ends not with a dash but with a period. *You are going to be murdered on Thursday, June 21, at exactly 12:00 o'clock midnight.*"

"Midnight, period," muttered Inspector Queen. "That's it. There won't be any more. There's nothing more for him to say."

"For who to say?" bellowed Max'l, inflating his ape's chest. "I kill him! For who?"

King reached across Judah, seized Max'l's dried-apricot ear, and yanked. Max'l fell back into his chair with a howl. The big man laughed. He seemed to be enjoying himself.

"Kane, let us go away today." Karla's hand was smoothing the damask cloth. "Just the two of us. I know these letters are nothing, but—"

"I can't go away, Karla. Too much to do. But I'll take a raincheck on that. Oh, come! You all look like professional pallbearers. Don't you see how funny it is?"

"King." Abel spoke slowly. "I wish you'd take this seriously. It isn't funny at all. . . . Mr. Queen has something to tell you."

The black eyes turned on Ellery, glittering. "I'm listening."

"I have something to ask you first, Mr. Bendigo." Ellery did not look in Judah's direction. "Where would you normally be at midnight tonight?"

"Finishing the confidential work on the day's agenda."

"But where?"

"Where I always work at that hour. In the Confidential Room."

"That's the room with the heavy steel door, across the hall from your brother Judah's quarters?"

"Yes."

Abel said quickly: "We usually spend an hour or two in there, Mr. Queen, starting at eleven or so. Work we can't leave to the secretaries."

"If Abel is away, I take his place," said Karla.

Her husband grinned at the Queens. "All in the family. Where the big plots are hatched. I'm sure you suspect that."

"Kane, stop making jokes. You're not to work there tonight."

"Oh, nonsense."

"You are not to!"

He looked across at his wife curiously. "You're really concerned, darling."

"If you insist on working there tonight, I insist on working with you."

"On that point I yield," he chuckled, "seeing that Abel's going to be occupied elsewhere, anyway. Now, let's have breakfast, shall we, and forget this childishness?"

The servants, who had been standing by frozen, sprang to life.

"I would like to suggest, Mr. Bendigo—" began Ellery.

"Overruled. Now see here, Queen. I appreciate your devotion to the job, but the confidential work stops for nothing, the idea of murder is ridiculous, and in that room impossible. Sit down and enjoy your breakfast. You, too, Inspector Queen."

But the Queens remained where they were.

"Why impossible, Mr. Bendigo?" asked the Inspector.

"Because the Confidential Room was built for just that purpose. The walls, floor, and ceiling are two feet thick— solid, reinforced concrete. There isn't a window in the place —it's air-conditioned and there's artificial daylight lighting in the walls. There's only one entrance—the door. Only one door, and it's made of safe-door steel. As a matter of fact, the whole room is a safe. So how would anyone get in to kill me?"

King attacked his soft-boiled eggs.

Max'l looked uncertain. Then he sat down and pounded the table. Two servants jumped forward, getting busy.

But Karla said uncomfortably, "The air-conditioning, Kane. Suppose someone got to that. Sending some sort of gas—"

Her husband roared with laughter. "There's the European mind for you! All right, Karla, we'll station guards at the air-conditioning machinery. Anything to wipe that look off your face."

"Mr. Bendigo," said Ellery. "Don't you realize that the person who wrote those letters is not to be laughed away? He knows exactly where you'll be at midnight tonight—in what amounts to the classic sealed room, guarded moreover by trusted armed men. Since he warns us, he must know that that room tonight will be absolutely impregnable. In other words, he chooses the time and place apparently worst for his plan, and he insures by his warning that even farfetched loopholes will be plugged. Doesn't that strike you as queer, to say the least?"

"Certainly," replied the King briskly. "Queer is the word, Queen. He's queer as Napoleon. It just can't be done."

"But it can," said Ellery.

The big man stared. "How?"

"If it were my problem, Mr. Bendigo, I'd simply get you to let me in yourself."

He sat back, smiling. "No one ever gets into that room except a member of my family—" He stopped, the smile disappearing.

The room was very quiet. Even Max'l stopped chewing. Karla was looking intently at Ellery, a crease between her eyes.

"What do you mean?" The voice was harsh.

Ellery glanced at Judah now, across the table from him. Judah was tapping a bottle of Segonzac cognac softly with a forefinger, looking at no one.

"Your brother Abel did some investigating on his own before calling us in," said Ellery. "We've compared conclusions, Mr. Bendigo. They're the same."

"I don't understand. Abel, what's all this?"

Abel's gray face seemed to go grayer.

"Tell him, Mr. Queen."

Ellery said: "I located the typewriter on which all the notes have been typed. I also found the notepaper; it comes from the same place as the typewriter. I nicked the lower-case *o* on the machine, and all *o*'s typed in the two notes since have shown the nicks. This checks the typewriter identification.

"As a further check, I arranged to have the room where the machine is located watched by your guards. The result was conclusive, Mr. Bendigo: During the period in which the fourth note must have been typed, only one person entered and left those rooms—the person who belonged there. Your brother Judah."

King Bendigo turned slowly toward his small, dark brother. Their arms, on the table, almost touched. A flush began to creep over the big man's cheeks.

Max'l was gaping from his master to Judah.

Karla said in a breathless way, "Oh, nonsense, nonsense. This is one of your cognac jokes, Judah, isn't it? Isn't it?"

Judah's hand as he reached for the bottle was remarkably well controlled. He began to uncork the bottle.

"No joke, my dear," he said hollowly. "No joke."

"You mean," began King Bendigo incredulously. Then he began again. "Judah, you mean you wrote those notes? You're threatening to kill me? *You?*"

Judah said: "Yes, O King."

He did it well, Ellery thought, for a man who was so taut you could almost hear the tension in him. Judah raised the bottle of Segonzac high. Then he brought it quickly down to his mouth.

King watched his brother drink. His eyes shimmered with amazement. They went over Judah, the crooked nose, the droop of the bedraggled mustache, the stringy neck, the rise and fall of the Adam's apple. But then Judah lowered the bottle and met his brother's glance, and something passed between them that made King seem to swell.

"At midnight, eh?" he said. "Got it all figured out."

"At midnight," said Judah in a high voice. "At exactly midnight."

"Judah, you're crazy."

"No, no, King. You are."

The big man sat quietly enough. "So you've had it in for me all these years. . . . I admit, Judah, I'd never have thought of you. Has anyone ever given a damn about you but me? Who else would put up with your alcoholic uselessness? The very fact that you've had all the booze you can soak up you owe to me. So you decide to kill me. Are you out of your mind completely? Is there any sense to it, Judah —or should I say Judas?" Judah's pallor deepened. "I'm your brother, damn it! Don't you feel anything? Gratitude? Loyalty?"

"Hatred," said Judah.

"You *hate* me? Why?"

"Because you're no good."

"Because I'm strong," said King Bendigo.

"Because you're weak," said Judah steadily, "weak where it counts." Now, although his face was like a death mask, the eyes behind it kindled and flamed. "There is strength that is weak. The weakness of your strength, brother, is that your strength has no humanity in it."

The big man looked at the little man with eyes dulled over now, clouded and secretive, in a sort of retreat. But his face was ruddy.

"No humanity, O King," said Judah. "What are human beings to you? You deal in corporate commodities—metals, oil, chemicals, munitions, ships. People are so many work-hours to you, such-and-such a rate of depreciation. You house them for the same reason you house your tools. You build hospitals for them for the same reason you build repair shops for your machines. You send their children to school for the same reason you keep your research laboratories going. Every soul on this island is card-indexed. Every soul on this island is watched—while he works, while he sleeps, while he makes love! Do you think I don't know that no one caught in your grinder ever escapes from it? Do you think I don't know what that devil Storm is up to in the laboratory he had you build for him? Or why Akst has disappeared? Or Fingalls, Prescott, Scaniglia, Jarcot, Blum before Akst? Or what's going on in Installation K-14? Or," Judah said in a very clear, high voice, "why?"

Now the flush was leaving the handsome man's face, and the face was settling into grim, contemptuous lines.

"The dignity of the individual, the right to make choices, to exist as a free man—that's been done away with in your empire as a matter of business policy. All the old laws protecting the individual have been scrapped. There's no law you recognize, King, except your own. And in carrying out your laws you're judge, jury, and firing squad. And what kind of laws are they that you create, administer, and execute? Laws to perpetuate your own power."

"It's such a small island," said King Bendigo in a murmur.

"It covers the planet," retorted his scrawny brother. "You needn't act the amused potentate for the benefit of the Queens. That kind of remark is an insult to their intelligence as well as mine. Your power extends in every direction, King. Just as you're cynical about the sovereignty of individuals, you're cynical about the sovereignty of nations. You corrupt prime ministers, overthrow governments, finance political pirates, all in the day's work. All to feed orders to your munitions plants—"

"Ah, I wondered when we'd get to that," said his brother. "The unholy munitions magnate, the international spider— Antichrist with a bomb in each hand. Isn't that the next indictment, Judah?"

Judah made thin fists on the cloth. "You're a plausible rascal, King. You always have been. The twist of truth, the intricate lie, the woolpulling trick—you're a past master of that difficult technique. But it doesn't befog the issue. Your sin isn't that you manufacture munitions. In the world we live in, munitions are unfortunately necessary, and someone has to manufacture them. But to you the implements of war are not a necessary evil, made for the protection of a decent society trying to survive in a wolves' world. They're a means of getting astronomical profits and the power that goes with them."

"The next indictment," said his brother with a show of gravity, "is usually that I create wars."

"No, you don't create wars, King," said Judah Bendigo. "Wars are created by forces far beyond your power, or the power of a thousand men like you. What you do, King, is take advantage of the conditions that create wars. You stoke them, blow on them, help them go up in flame. If a country's torn by dissension, you see to it that the dissension breaks out into open revolt; if two powers, or two groups of powers, are at odds, your agents sabotage the negotiations and work for a shooting war. It doesn't matter to you which side is *right;* right and wrong have no meaning in your dictionary except as they represent conflicts, which mean war, which mean profits. That's where your responsibility lies, King. It's as far as one man's responsibility can go. It's too far!"

Judah's fists danced as he leaned toward his brother. "You're a murderer, King. I don't mean merely the murders you've committed on this island, or the murders your thugs have committed here and there throughout the world in your execution of some policy or deal of the moment. I mean the murders, brother, of which historians keep a statistical record. I mean the war murders, brother. The murders arising out of the misunderstandings and tensions and social and economic stresses which you encourage into wars. You know what you are, King? You're the greatest mass-murderer in history. Oh, yes, I know how melodramatic it sounds, and how you're enjoying my helplessness to keep it from sounding so! But the truth is that millions of human beings have died on battlefields which would never have been except for you. The truth is that millions upon millions of other human beings have been made slaves, stripped of the last rag of their pride and dignity, thrown naked into your furnaces and on your bone piles!"

"Not mine, Judah, not mine," said his brother.

"Yours! And you're not through, King. You've hardly begun. Do you think I'm blind merely because I'm drunk? Do you think I'm deaf just because I shut my ears to your factory whistles? Do you think I don't know what you're planning in those night sessions in your Confidential Room? Too far, King, you go too far."

Judah stopped, his lips quivering. King deliberately edged the bottle of Segonzac closer to him. Judah wet his lips.

"Dangerous talk, Judah," said King gently. "When did you join the Party?"

Judah mumbled: "The smear. How could I be a member of the Party when I believe in the dignity of man?"

"You're against them, Judah?"

"Against them, and against you. You're both cut from the same bolt. The same rotten bolt. Any means to the end. And what end? Nobody knows. But a man can guess!"

"That's typically muddled thinking, Judah. You can't be against them and against me, too. I'm their worst enemy. I'm preparing the West to fight them—"

"That's what you said the last time. And it was true, too. And it's true now. But a twisted truth that turns out to be no truth at all. You're preparing the West to fight them, not for the reason that they're a menace to the free world, but because they happen to be the current antagonist. Ten years from now you'll be preparing the West—or the East, or the North, or the South, or all of them put together!—to fight something or someone else. Maybe the little men from Mars, King! Unless you're stopped in time."

"And who's going to stop me?" murmured King Bendigo. "Not you, Judah."

"Me! Tonight at midnight I'm going to kill you, King. You'll never see tomorrow, and tomorrow the world will be a better place to live in."

King Bendigo burst into laughter. He threw back his handsome head and laughed until the spasm caused him to double up. He put his fists on the table's edge and heaved to his feet. There were actually tears in his eyes.

Judah's chair went over. He scrambled around the corner of the table and sprang at his brother's throat. His hands slipped. He beat with his thin fists on that massive chest. And as his little blows drummed away, he screamed with hate and outrage. For a moment King was surprised; his laughter stopped, his eyes widened. But then he only laughed harder. He made no attempt to defend himself. Judah's fists kept bouncing off him like rubber balls from a brick wall.

Then Max'l was there. With one hand he plucked the shrieking, flailing little man from his master and thrust Judah high in the air, holding him up like a toy. Judah dangled, gagging. The gagging sounds made Max'l grin. He shook Judah as if the little man were made of rags, shook him until his face turned blue and his eyes popped and his tongue stuck out of his mouth.

Karla whimpered and put her hands to her face.

"It's all right, darling," wheezed her husband. "Really it is. Judah doesn't mind punishment. He loves it. Always did. Gets a real kick out of a beating—don't you, Judah?"

Max'l flung the little man halfway across the dining room. Judah struck a wall, thudded to the floor, and lay still.

"Don't you worry," Max'l said, grinning at his master. "I take care of him. After I eat."

And he sat down and seized his fork.

"Don't be more idiotic than nature made you, Max. When the time comes—midnight, did he say?—he'll be blind drunk and about as deadly as an angleworm." King glanced at the heap in the corner. "That's the trouble with democracy, Queen. You're one of the intellectual, liberal, democratic world, aren't you? You never get anywhere. You stick your chin out and happily ask for another crack on the jaw. You poison yourselves into a coma with fancy talk, the way Judah poisons himself with alcohol. All you do is jabber, jabber, jabber while history shoots past you into the future."

"I think we had a little something to do with the orbit of history, Mr. Bendigo," Ellery found himself saying, "not so very long ago."

"You mean I did," chuckled the King, lowering himself into his chair again.

The servants leaped forward as he picked up his napkin. But he waved them away.

"And you, Maxie. You leave Judah alone," he said severely. "He's had a strenuous morning. *Max.*"

The gorilla had leaped from his chair. Judah was stirring. There was blood on Judah's face.

"Sit down."

The gorilla sat down.

"Here, Judah, let me help you—" began Inspector Queen.

Judah raised a hand. Something in the way he did it stopped the Inspector in his tracks.

Judah's brothers looked on, Abel gray as evening, King with no flicker of pity.

Judah crept out of the dining room. They watched him go. His right leg took a long time getting out of the room. But finally it, too, disappeared.

"Karla, my dear," said King briskly. "Karla?"

"Yes. Yes, Kane."

"I'll be at the Home Office all day and most of the evening —I'll have dinner there. You meet me at eleven at the Confidential Room."

"You mean to work tonight, Kane? In spite of—?" Karla stopped.

"Certainly, darling."

"But Judah—his threats—"

"He won't lift a pinkie when the time comes. Believe me, Karla. I know Judah. . . . Yes, Queen? You were going to say something?"

Ellery cleared his throat. "I think, Mr. Bendigo, you tend to underestimate the intellectual, liberal democrat when aroused. I don't know why I say this—it's certainly nothing to me whether you live or die—"

"Or maybe it is," said King Bendigo, smiling.

Ellery stared at him. "All right, maybe it is. Maybe after what I've seen here I'd greet the news of your death with cheers. But not this way, Mr. Bendigo. I'm an antimurder man from way back—was indoctrinated from childhood by the Bible and I happen to believe in democracy. They both teach the ethics of the means, Mr. Bendigo. And murder is the wrong means—"

"You'd like to see me die, but you'll lay your life down to protect mine from violence." King laughed. "That's what's wrong with you people! Could anything be more hopelessly asinine?"

"You really believe that?"

"Certainly."

"Then it would be a waste of your valuable time to discuss it." And Ellery went on in the same painful way, "What I have been trying to say is that your brother Judah not only wants to kill you, Mr. Bendigo, he's made plans about it. So he must have some weapon in mind. Prepared. Does he own a gun?"

"Oh, yes. Pretty good shot, too, even when scuppered. Judah practices sometimes for hours at a time. On a range target, of course," the big man said dryly. "Nothing alive, you understand. Makes him sick. Judah couldn't kill a mouse—he's often said so. Don't be concerned about me, Queen—"

"I'm not. I'm concerned about Judah."

The black eyes narrowed. "I don't get that."

Ellery said slowly, "If he gets blood on his hands, he's lost."

"Why, you're nothing but a psalm-singer," King said impatiently. "You're through here. I'll have you flown out this morning."

"No!" Abel jumped up. He was still shaken. "No, King. I want the Queens here. You're not to send them away—"

"Abel, I'm getting tired of this!"

"I know you," shouted Abel. "You'll put a gun in his hand and dare him to shoot! King, I know Judah, too. You're underestimating him. Let the Queens stay. At least till tomorrow morning."

"Let Spring handle it."

"Not Spring, no. King, you've got to let me handle this my way!"

His brother scowled. But then he shrugged and said, "All right, I suppose I can put up with these long-faced democrats another day. Anything to stop this gabble! Now get out, the lot of you, and let me finish my breakfast."

10

BY WRITTEN ORDER of Abel Bendigo, the Queens were permitted that afternoon to inspect the Confidential Room. Colonel Spring himself, looking a wee bit flustered, unlocked the big steel door. The Colonel, the officer in charge of the household guards, and two armed guards went in with them and watched them as closely as if it were the bullion vault of Fort Knox.

It was a great empty-looking room painted hospital gray. There was only one door, the door through which they had entered. There were no windows at all, the walls themselves glowing with a constant, shadowless light. A frieze of solid-looking material ran around the walls near the high ceiling; this was a porous metal fabric invented by Bendigo engineers to take the place of conventional heating and air-conditioning vents and grilles. "It's a metallic substance that actually breathes," explained Colonel Spring, "and does away with openings." The air in the room was mild, sweet, and fresh.

No pictures, hangings, or decorations of any kind broke the blankness of the walls. The floor was of some springy material, solidly inlaid, that deadened sound. The ceiling was sound-proofed.

In the exact center of the Confidential Room stood a very large metal desk, with a leather swivel chair behind it. There was nothing on the desk but a telephone. A typewriter-desk, its electric typewriter exposed, faced the large desk; this one was equipped with an uncushioned metal chair. Solid banks of steel filing cases lined the walls to a height of five feet.

Above the door, and so in direct view of the occupant of the large desk, there was a functional clock. It consisted of two uncompromising gold hands and twelve unnumbered gold darts, and was imbedded in the wall.

And there was nothing else in the room.

"Who besides the Bendigo family, Colonel, uses this room?" asked Inspector Queen.

"No one."

Ellery said: "Does Judah Bendigo come in here often?"

Colonel Spring cocked a brow at the officer of the guard. The officer said: "Not often, sir. He may wander in for a few minutes sometimes, but he's never here very long."

"When was the last time Mr. Judah visited this room?"

"I'd have to consult the records, sir."

"Consult them."

The officer glanced at Colonel Spring. The Colonel nodded, and the officer went away. He returned shortly with a ledger.

"About six weeks ago was the last time, sir. And a week before that, and three weeks before that."

"Would these records show if at those times he was in this room alone?"

"Yes, sir."

"Was he?"

"No, sir. He never comes in here when the room is unoccupied. He can't get in. No one can but Mr. King and Mr. Abel. They have the only two keys, aside from an emergency key kept in the guardroom in a wall safe. We have to open the room daily for the maids."

"The maids, I take it, clean up under the eye of the guards?"

"*And* the officer on duty, sir."

The Queens wandered about the Confidential Room for a few minutes. Ellery tried a number of filing cases, but most of them were locked. The few that were not locked were empty. In one of the unlocked drawers he found a bottle of Segonzac cognac, and he sighed.

Ellery examined the steel door. It was impregnable.

When they left the room, Colonel Spring tried the door with his own hands and gave the key to the captain of the guard. The officer saluted and took the key to the guardroom.

"Is there anything else I can do, gentlemen?" asked the Colonel, rather plaintively, Ellery thought. "My orders are to put myself completely at your disposal."

"Just the matter of the air-conditioning unit, Colonel," the Inspector said.

"Oh, yes. . . ."

Ellery left them and crossed the hall. He knocked on Judah Bendigo's door. There was no answer. He knocked again. There was still no answer. So he went in.

Max'l was straddling a chair the wrong way, his chin on his hairy hands. Only his eyes moved, following like a watch-dog's the movements of Judah Bendigo's hands. An empty bottle of Segonzac lolled on Judah's desk. Judah was opening a fresh bottle. He had torn away the tax stamp and was just running the blade of a pocketknife around the hard wax seal. He paid no attention to the troglodyte, and he did not look when Ellery came in.

ELLERY spent the rest of the day trying to save Judah Bendigo's soul. But Judah was doomed. He did not resist salvation; he shrugged it down. He was looking more like a corpse than ever—a corpse who had died of violence, for his cheekbone was bruised, swollen, and purple from its encounter with the dining room wall, and a split lip gave his mouth a sneering grin such as Ellery frequently saw at the morgue.

"I'm not enjoying this, Ellery, really I'm not. I don't care for the idea of killing my brother any more than you do. But someone has to do the dirty job, and I'm tired of waiting for the Almighty."

"Once you shed his blood, how do you differ from King, Judah?"

"I'm an executioner. Executioners are among the most re-spectable of public servants."

"Executioners do their work by sanction of law. Self-appointed executioners are simply murderers."

"Law? On Bendigo Island?" Judah permitted his ragged mustache to lift. "Oh, I admit the circumstances are unusual. But that's just the point. There are no sanctions I can evoke here except the decent opinions of mankind, as expressed in a handful of historic documents. The conscience of civilization has appointed me."

At another time—toward dusk—Judah interrupted Ellery to say, simply, "You're wasting your breath. My mind is made up."

It was at this point that it occurred to Ellery that Judah Bendigo was talking like a man who expects to consummate his crime.

"Let me understand you, Judah. Granted the firmness of your resolve, hasn't it sunk home that you've been detected *in advance?* You don't think we're sitting by and letting you execute your plan, whatever it is? Max'l alone in this room with you would be enough to thwart whatever you have in mind. There's going to be no murder, Judah." By this :ime Ellery was talking as if Judah were a child. "We simply can't allow it, you know."

Judah sipped some cognac and smiled. "There's nothing you can do to stop me."

"Oh, come. I'll admit that a man bent on violence may sooner or later find an opening, no matter what precautions are taken. But we know the exact time and place—"

Judah waved a thin white hand. "It doesn't matter."

"What doesn't matter?"

"That you know the time and place. If I cared whether you knew or not, I'd never have written the note."

"You'll do it in spite of the fact that we're forewarned?"

"Oh, yes."

"At that time? In that place?" exclaimed Ellery.

"Midnight tonight. The Confidential Room."

Ellery looked at him. "So that's it. You have another plan entirely. This was all a red herring to foul up the trail."

Judah seemed offended. "Nothing of the sort! I give you my word. That would spoil it. Don't you see that?"

"No."

Judah shrugged and tipped his bottle again.

"Of course, none of this is really necessary," Ellery said, "since you have my personal assurance you won't leave this room tonight and your brother King won't enter it. So I can afford to play games, Judah. Tell me this: You announced the time of the murder, we know the exact place—if you stick to your word about the time—so do you mind telling me by what means you intend to kill your brother?"

"Don't mind at all," said Judah. "I'm going to shoot him."

"With what?"

"With one of my favorite guns."

"Nonsense," said Ellery irritably. "My father and I have searched these rooms twice today, and neither of us is exactly a novice at this sort of thing. Including, if you'll recall, a very thorough body-search. There is no gun on these premises, and no ammunition of any kind."

"Sorry. There's a fully loaded gun right under your nose."

"Here? Now?"

"It's not six feet from where you're standing."

Ellery looked around rather wildly. But then he caught himself and grinned. "I must watch that trick of yours. It's unsettling."

"No trick. I mean it."

Ellery stopped grinning. "I consider this downright nasty of you, Judah. Now, on the off chance that you may be telling the truth, I've got to search the place all over again."

"I'll save you the trouble. I don't mind telling you where the gun is. It won't make any difference."

It won't make any difference. . . . "Where is it, Judah?" Ellery asked in a kindly voice.

"In Max'l's pocket, where I slipped it when you started searching."

Max'l jerked erect. He began to paw at his coat pocket. Ellery ran over, flung his hand aside, and explored the pocket himself. It was crowded with pieces of candy, nuts, and other objects Ellery's fingers could not identify; but among the sticky odds and ends there was a hard cold something. He drew it out.

Max'l glared at it.

It was a rather silly-looking automatic pistol. It was so snubnosed it could be concealed in a man's hand, for the barrel was only about one inch long—the entire length of the

weapon was scarcely four inches. It was a German Walther
of .25 caliber. For all its womanish size, Ellery knew it for a
deadly little weapon, and this one had a used look. The ivory
inlays on the stock were rubbed and yellow with handling,
and the right side of the grip was chipped—a triangular bit of
the ivory was missing from the lower right corner.

Judah was gazing at it fondly. "Beauty, isn't it?"

The automatic was fully loaded. Ellery emptied the magazine and chamber, dropped the little Walther into his pocket,
and went to the door. By the time he had unlocked and
opened it, Inspector Queen blocked the doorway.

"What's the matter, Ellery?"

"I've extracted Judah's teeth." Ellery put the cartridges in
his father's hand. "Hold on to these for me."

"Where the devil—Maybe he's got more!"

"If he has, they're not in there. But I'll look again."

Ellery relocked the door and regarded Judah thoughtfully.
Why had he disclosed where the gun was? Was it a trick designed to head off still another search which would turn up a
second gun—the gun Judah had intended to use from the beginning?

Ellery said to Max'l, "Watch him," which was quite unnecessary, and searched Judah's two rooms and bath again.
Judah kept drinking with every appearance of indifference.
He made no protest when Ellery insisted on another body-
search. Afterwards, he redressed and reached for the bottle
again.

There was no other gun, not a single cartridge.

Ellery sat down facing the thin little figure and looked it
over searchingly. The man was either insane or so fogged
with alcohol that he could no longer distinguish between
fancy and reality. For practical purposes it really did not matter which. If the German automatic was the weapon he had
meant to use, its teeth were drawn; Judah would not and
could not leave the room; and it had been arranged between
the Queens, with Abel Bendigo's unqualified consent, that
King Bendigo would be prevented by force, if necessary, from
crossing the threshold of Judah's quarters.

There was simply no way for the dedicated assassin to kill the tyrant. And if Judah's antics masked a plan whereby some bribed or hired killer was to attempt the murder, that was taken care of, too.

AT exactly eleven o'clock that night King and Karla Bendigo appeared in the corridor. Six guards surrounded them. Karla was pale, but her husband was smiling.

"Well, well," he said to the Inspector. "And are you gentlemen enjoying yourselves?"

"Don't joke about it, Kane," begged Karla. "Nothing is going to happen, but . . . don't joke about it."

He squeezed her shoulder affectionately and produced a key from a tiny gold case attached to his trousers by a gold chain. Inspector Queen glanced about: two guards were at Judah Bendigo's door across the corridor, one of them with his hand on the doorknob, gripping it tightly. On the other side of that door, the Inspector knew, Judah was guarded by Max'l and Ellery. Even so, he was taking no chances.

"One minute, Mr. Bendigo." King had unlocked the massive door and Karla was about to precede him into the Confidential Room. "I have to ask you to let me search this room before you step inside."

The Inspector was already in the doorway, barring the way.

King stared. "I was told you searched it this afternoon."

"That was this afternoon, Mr. Bendigo." The Inspector did not move.

"All right!" King stepped back peevishly. Three guards managed to slip between him and the doorway. They stood there shoulder to shoulder. Something about the maneuver restored the magnate's good humor. "What's he had you men doing today, rehearsing? You did that like a line of chorus girls!"

The room was exactly as the Inspector had left it during the afternoon. Nevertheless he prowled about, glancing everywhere—at the filing cases, the desks, the chairs, the floor, the walls, the ceiling.

"Mr. Bendigo, I want your permission to look in these desks and filing cases."

"Denied," came the brusque answer.

"I've got to insist, Mr. Bendigo."

"Insist?"

"Mr. Bendigo." The Inspector came to the doorway. "I've been given a serious responsibility by your brother, Abel. If you refuse to let me handle this as I think it ought to be handled, I have your brother's permission to keep you from entering this room—by force, if necessary. Mr. Abel wanted your consent to my searching those drawers and cases, but he recognizes the necessity for it. Do you want to see his personal authorization?"

The black eyes engulfed him. "Abel knows that no one outside my family—no one!—is allowed to see the contents of those drawers."

"I promise not to read a single paper, Mr. Bendigo. What I'm looking for is a possible booby trap or time bomb. A glance in a drawer will tell me that."

King Bendigo did not reply for several moments.

"Kane. Do whatever they say. Please." Karla's voice sounded as if her tongue were stiff.

He shrugged and unhooked the little gold case from the end of his chain. "This key unlocks the file drawers. This one the drawers of my desk. The drawers of the small desk are not locked."

The Inspector took the two keys. "Would you permit me to shut this door while I search?"

"Certainly not!"

"Then I must ask you and Mrs. Bendigo to step aside, out of range of the doorway. These three guards," the Inspector added with a certain bitterness, "can keep watching *me*."

He searched thoroughly.

When he came out into the corridor he said, "One thing more, Mr. Bendigo. Is there a concealed compartment of any kind in that room, or a concealed door, or a panel, or a passageway, or anything of that sort? Anything of that sort whatsoever?"

"No." The big man was fuming at the delay.

The Inspector handed him the two keys. "Then it's all right for you to go in."

When the master of the Bendigo empire had entered the Confidential Room followed by his wife, and the great door had swung shut, Inspector Queen tried the door. But it had locked automatically; he could not budge it.

He set his back against the door and said to one of the guards, "Do you have a cigaret?" Ellery's father resorted to cigarets only in times of great stress. For the first time it had occurred to the Inspector that he had just risked being blown into his component parts to save the life of a man whose death under other circumstances would have caused him no more, perhaps, than a mild humanitarian regret.

JUDAH was well into his current bottle of Segonzac, and by 11:20 P.M. it was almost empty and he had settled down to serious drinking. He had politely inquired if he might play some music, and when Ellery, before consenting, re-examined the record-player, Judah shook his head dolefully as if in sorrow at the suspicious nature of man.

"Don't go near those albums," said Ellery. "I'll get what you want."

"Do you suspect my music?" exclaimed Judah.

"You can't have a weapon concealed in those albums," retorted Ellery, "but there might be a cartridge tucked away in one of them that I somehow missed. You sit just where you are, impaled by Max'l's glittering eye. I'll handle your music. What would you like to hear?"

"You would suspect Mozart. Mozart!"

"In a situation like this, Judah, I'd suspect Orpheus. Mozart?"

"The Finale of the C-Major symphony—there, the Forty-first. There's nothing as grand in human expression except parts of Shakespeare and the most inspired flights of Bach."

"Window dressing," muttered Ellery, perhaps unjustly; and for a few minutes he listened with grudging pleasure to *l'Orchestre de la Suisse Romande* under the baton of Ansermet.

Judah grudged nothing. He sprawled in the chair behind his desk, a snifter between his palms, eyes wide and shining.

Mozart was in full swing when Ellery glanced at his watch and saw that it was 11:32. He nodded at Max'l, who was as impervious to the counterpoint as a Gila monster, went quietly to the door, and unlocked it. Before pulling it open, he glanced back at Judah. Judah was smiling.

At the sound of the door the Inspector came quickly across the corridor. He blocked the opening with his back, still watching the door of the Confidential Room.

"Everything all right, Dad?"

"Yes."

"King and Karla still in there?"

"The door hasn't been open since they went in."

Ellery nodded. He was not surprised to see Abel Bendigo across the hall, standing among the guards before the locked room. Abel glanced at Ellery anxiously and came over to join them.

"I couldn't work. It's ridiculous, but I couldn't. How has Judah been, Mr. Queen?"

"He's hard to figure out. Tell me, Mr. Bendigo—does your brother Judah have any history of mental disturbance?"

Abel said: "Because he's threatened to kill King?"

"No. Because even though he knows we're aware of his intentions, he still talks as if he's going to do it."

"He can't, can he?" Abel said it quickly.

"Impossible. But it's a word he apparently doesn't recognize."

"Judah has always been a little peculiar. Of course, his drinking . . ."

"How far back does his alcoholism go?"

"A good many years. Do you think I ought to talk to him, Mr. Queen?"

"No."

Abel nodded. He went back across the hall.

"He didn't answer the question," remarked the Inspector.

Ellery shrugged and shut the door. He turned the key and put it back in his pocket.

WHEN the symphony was over, Ellery put the records away. He turned from the album shelves to find Judah regarding his empty glass. The would-be fratricide picked up the cognac bottle and tilted it. Nothing came out. He grasped both arms of his chair, raising himself.

"Where are you going?" asked Ellery.

"Get another bottle."

"Stay there. I'll get it for you."

Ellery went behind the Bechstein and took a new bottle of Segonzac from the case on top of the pile. Judah was fumbling in his pockets. Finally he produced his pocketknife.

"I'll open it for you."

Ellery took the knife from him, slit the tax stamp, and scraped the hardened seal off the bottle's mouth. The knife had a corkscrew attachment; with it Ellery drew the cork. He placed the bottle on the desk beside the empty glass.

"I think," he murmured, "I'll borrow this, Judah."

Judah followed his knife in its course to Ellery's trouser pocket.

Then he picked up the bottle.

Ellery glanced at his watch.

11:46.

AT 11:53 Ellery said to Max'l: "Get in front of him. I'll be right back."

Max'l got up and went to the desk, facing Judah seated behind it. The great back blocked Judah out.

Ellery unlocked the door, slipped outside, relocked the door from the corridor.

His father, Abel Bendigo, and the guards had not changed position.

"Still in there?"

"Still in there, son."

"The door hasn't been opened at all?"

"No."

"Let's check."

Ellery rapped.

"But Judah . . ." Abel glanced across the corridor.

"Max is standing over him, the door's locked, and the key's in my pocket.—Mr. Bendigo!" Ellery rapped again.

After a moment the lock turned over. The guards stiffened. The door opened and King Bendigo towered there. He was in his shirt sleeves. At the secretarial desk, Karla twisted about, looking toward the door a little blankly.

"Well?" snapped the big man.

"Just making sure everything's all right, Mr. Bendigo."

"I'm still here." He noticed Abel. "Abel? Finish with those people so early?"

"I'll wind it up in the morning." Abel was tight-lipped. "Go in, King. Go back in."

"Oh—!" The disgusted exclamation was lost in the slam of the door. The Inspector tried it. Locked.

Ellery looked at his watch again.

11:56:30.

"He's not to open that door again until well after midnight," he said. He ran across the hall.

WHEN Ellery relocked Judah's door from inside, Max'l backed away from the desk and padded to the door to set his shoulders against it.

"What did he do, Max?"

Max'l grinned.

"I drank cognac," said Judah dreamily. He raised the snifter.

Ellery went around the desk and stood over him.

11:57:20.

"Time's a-ticking, Judah," he murmured. He wondered how Judah was going to handle the moment of supreme reality, when he was face to face at last with the stroke of midnight.

He kept looking down at the slight figure in the chair. In spite of himself, Ellery felt his muscles tighten.

Two minutes to midnight.

Judah glanced at the watch on his thin wrist and set the empty glass down.

And turned in his chair, looking up at Ellery.

"Will you please be good enough," he said, "to give me my Walther?"

"This?" Ellery took the little automatic out of his pocket. "I'm afraid there isn't much you can do with it, Judah."

Judah presented his upturned palm.

There was nothing to be read in his eyes. The light Ellery saw in them might be mockery, but he was more inclined to ascribe it to cognac. Unless . . .

Because he was what he was, Ellery examined the Walther, which had not left his pocket since he had removed its ammunition.

The automatic, of course, was empty. Nevertheless, Ellery examined it even more closely than before. It might be a trick gun. It might, somehow, conceal a bullet, and a pressure somewhere might discharge it. Ellery had never heard of a gun like that, but it was possible.

Not in this case, however. This was an orthodox German Walther. Ellery had handled dozens of them. It was an orthodox German Walther and it was not loaded.

He dropped the little automatic into Judah's hand.

He could not help feeling an embarrassed pity as Judah transferred the empty gun to his right hand and took a firm grip on the stock, his forefinger curled at the trigger. Judah was intent now, making small economical movements, as if what he was about to do was of the greatest importance and required the utmost in concentration.

He pushed downward with his left hand on the desk top and got to his feet.

Ellery's glance never left those hands.

Now Judah raised his left forearm. He stared down at the second hand of his wristwatch.

Thirty seconds.

His right hand, with the empty gun, was in plain view. There was nothing he could do with it, no sleight-of-hand, not a trick, not a bluff, not an anything. And if he could? If, by an unreasonable miracle, he could materialize a cartridge and load the gun with it with Ellery at his elbow, what could he do with it? Shoot Ellery? Hypnotize Max'l? And if he got out into the corridor, what then? A locked door of safe steel. A hallful of armed, alert men. And even then, no key.

Fifteen seconds.

What was he waiting for?

Judah raised the Walther.

Max'l moved convulsively, and Ellery almost sprang. He had to check his own reflex. Max'l uttered a growly chuckle, rather horrible to hear, and relaxed against the door again.

It was too stupid. There was nothing Judah could do with that empty little gun, nothing. Too, an obscure curiosity stayed Ellery. There was nothing Judah could do, and yet he was preparing to do something. What?

Seven seconds.

Judah's right arm came up until it was straight out before him. He was apparently taking aim at something, getting his sight set for a shot he couldn't possibly fire. A shot he couldn't possibly fire at a wall he couldn't possibly penetrate.

Five seconds.

A theoretical extension of Judah's right arm with the Walther at the end of it would make a line through the wall of his study, across the corridor, through the wall of the Confidential Room, into the approximate center of that room and—perhaps—the torso of a seated man.

Three seconds.

Judah was "aiming" at his brother King.

He was mad.

Two seconds.

Judah watched his upheld wrist.

One second.

And now, Judah?

At the tick of midnight, Judah's finger squeezed the trigger.

HAD the little Walther flamed and bucked at that instant Ellery could not have been so astounded. A gun that went off in spite of the impossibility of a gun's going off would at the least have made reasonable the unreasonable play that went before. It would have been a physical miracle, but it would have given Judah's actions the dignity of logic.

The little Walther, however, neither flamed nor bucked. It merely went *click!* and was quiet again. No roar reverberated through the room, no hole appeared in the wall, no voice cried out.

Ellery squinted at the man.

He was incredible, this Judah. He was not acting like a man who had just pulled the trigger of a gun that could not and did not go off. He was acting like a man who had seen the flame and felt the buck and heard the roar and the cry. He was acting like a man who had successfully fired a shot.

Judah lowered the Walther slowly and with great care put it down on his desk.

Then he sank into the chair and reached for the bottle of Segonzac. He uncorked it slowly, slowly poured several ounces of cognac, slowly and steadily drank, the bottle still gripped in his left hand. Then he flung bottle and glass aside and, as they crashed to the floor, he put his face down on the desk and wept.

Ellery found himself going over the facts indignantly. No bullet in the gun. A wall, a corridor, then another wall two feet thick made of reinforced concrete. And a man safely beyond it. Safely. Unless . . . unless . . .

Impossible. *Impossible.*

Ellery heard a harsh voice, hardly recognizable as his own. "You act as if you shot your brother."

"I did."

The words were sobby. Thick with grief.

"As if you really killed him, I mean."

He didn't understand. He couldn't have said—

"I did."

So he had said it. Ellery passed his hand over his mouth. The man *was* insane.

"You did what, Judah?"

"King is dead."

"Did you hear what he said?" Ellery glanced bitterly across at Max'l.

Max'l tapped his temple, grinning.

Ellery took hold of Judah's shoulder in a burst of annoyance and pulled him upright, holding him against the back of the chair.

Crying, all right.

He let go. Judah stopped crying to bite his lower lip with his uneven, stained teeth. He fumbled for something in his back pocket. His hand reappeared with a handkerchief. He blew his nose into it and relaxed, sighing.

"They can do what they want with me," he said in a high monotone. "But I had to do it. You don't know what he was. What he was planning. I had to stop him. I had to."

Ellery picked up the Walther. Glared at it.

He tossed it back on the desk and strode across the room. He said stridently to Max'l, "Get out of my way."

He unlocked the door.

The corridor was at peace. The Inspector and Abel Bendigo were leaning against the door of the Confidential Room, talking in lively voices. The guards lounged in visible relief.

"Oh, Ellery." The Inspector looked around. "Well, that's that.—What's the matter? You're pale as a ghost."

"Is Judah all right?" asked Abel quickly.

"Yes." Ellery gripped his father's arm. "Did . . . anything happen?"

"Happen? Not a thing, son."

"You didn't hear . . . anything?"

"What?"

"Well . . . a shot."

"Of course not."

"Nobody's gone in or out of the Room?"

"No."

"The door's remained shut—locked?"

"Certainly." His father stared at him.

Abel, the guards . . .

Ellery felt like a fool. He was furious with Judah Bendigo. Not merely a lunatic—a malicious lunatic. Still . . .

He stepped up to the big steel door, looked at it.

The men around him watched him, puzzled.

Ellery knocked.

After a moment he knocked again, harder.

Nothing happened.

"There's no use standing there waiting," said a tired voice.

Ellery whirled. Judah had come out into the corridor. Max'l had both of Judah's arms locked behind his back. Max'l was grinning.

"What does he mean?" asked the Inspector, nettled.

Ellery began to pound on the steel door with both fists. "Mr. Bendigo! Are you all right?"

There was no answer. Ellery tried to turn the knob. It remained immovable.

"Mr. Bendigo!" shouted Ellery. "Unlock this door!"

Abel Bendigo was cracking his knuckles and muttering. "He would go into his high-and-mighty act. But why doesn't Karla . . . ?"

"Get me a key, somebody!"

"Key?" Abel started. "Here. Here, Mr. Queen. Oh, why doesn't he—? He'll roar, but . . . Here!"

Ellery snatched the gold case from Abel. It was a duplicate of King's. He jabbed the key in the lock, twisted, jerked, heaved. . . .

Karla was lying on the floor beside her husband's desk. Her eyes were shut.

King Bendigo was seated in the leather swivel chair behind his desk, and his eyes were open.

But the way he sat and the way he looked made Ellery's blood stop running.

Bendigo was slumped in the chair off the perpendicular, one shirt-sleeved arm between his knees and the other dangling overside.

His head lolled back on his shoulder and his mouth was open, too.

The white silk of his shirt, on the left breast, showed a stain roughly circular in shape, and in color bright red.

In the center of the red circle there was a small, black bullet hole.

11

THE FIRST THING Ellery did had nothing to do with miracles at all. He turned to Abel Bendigo and said, "Do you want Colonel Spring in on this?"

He was barring the doorway, arms and legs spread. Unbelieving eyes stared over his shoulders into the room.

"Mr. Bendigo." He tapped Abel's arm and repeated the question.

"No. My God, no." Abel came to life. "Don't let the guards in! Just—"

Ellery pulled Abel in. He pulled Judah in; Max'l came along as if he were on the end of a line. He pulled his father in.

He shut the door in the faces of the guards.

He tried the door. Locked. Automatically.

Ellery went over to the man in the chair. Inspector Queen dropped on his knees beside Karla. The brothers remained near the door, almost touching. Judah looked exhausted; he leaned against a filing case. Abel kept mumbling something to himself. Max'l was stunned; there was no ferocity left in him. His breathing deposited flecks of spittle on his lips. He kept staring at the quiet figure in the chair with awe.

The Inspector looked up. "She didn't get it."

"What is it?"

"A faint, I guess. I can't find any wound or contusion."

Ellery reached for the telephone on King Bendigo's desk. When the operator answered, he said, "Dr. Storm. Emergency."

The Inspector glanced from Ellery to the body in the chair. Then he lifted Karla very carefully and carried her over to the secretarial chair behind the typewriter-desk and laid her over the chair face down. He took off his coat and wrapped it about her. He raised her legs, keeping her head low.

"Dr. Storm?" said Ellery. "This is Queen. King Bendigo has been shot. Serious chest wound, near the heart. He's not dead. Bring everything you'll need—you may not be able to move him for a while." He hung up.

"Not dead!" Abel took a step forward.

"Please don't touch him, Mr. Bendigo. We can't do a thing until Dr. Storm gets here."

Abel's face was pocked with perspiration. He kept swallowing and glancing at his brother Judah.

Where before Judah had seemed spent, as at a task executed at great physical cost, now—with the news that he had not killed successfully after all—he was dazed. His eyes mirrored some shock Ellery could not quite make out. Ellery was in no mental condition to draw a bead on subtleties, but he had the feeling that Judah had shot his bolt.

"Max." Ellery touched the massive arm. "Watch Judah."

Max'l wiped his lips on his sleeve. He turned to Judah. His head sank into his shoulders and he took a step toward the dark man.

"No, Max, no," Ellery said patiently. "You're not to touch him. Just make sure he doesn't go near King."

Karla moaned, rolling her head. The Inspector began to slap her cheeks. After a moment he sat her up.

She did not cry. The blood, which had rushed to her head, receded swiftly, leaving her face whiter than before. She stared across the desks at the slumped figure.

"He's not dead, Mrs. Bendigo," said the Inspector. "We're waiting for Dr. Storm. Relax, now. Take deep breaths."

What he said apparently had no meaning for her. The man in the chair looked dead.

The door was pounded. Ellery, on his hands and knees peering under the big metal desk, sprang to his feet and raced to the door.

"I'll open it!" he said to Abel Bendigo. "Keep away, please."

He opened the door. Dr. Storm rushed by him. The corridor was crowded with guards and people of the Residence staff. A hospital emergency table was pushed through the doorway by a white-coated man, and a portable sterilizer was wheeled

up by another. But Ellery refused to allow the attendants to
cross the threshold. Other things were handed in; the Inspector took them while Ellery stood guard. Elbowing his way
:hrough the jam came Colonel Spring. He shouted, "Wait,
don't shut that door!" Ellery said to Abel Bendigo over his
shoulder, "You'd better tell him yourself." From behind Ellery,
Abel shook his head at the charging Colonel. "No one else,
Colonel, no one else." Ellery shut the door in Spring's set green
face.

He knew the door locked automatically, but he tried it anyway.

"You men. Help me get him onto the table." There was
nothing in Dr. Storm's voice but preoccupation. The sterilizer
was going. The contents of his kit were spread out on the desk.

Under the doctor's direction they transferred the wounded
man from the chair to the hospital table. His heavy body
seemed without life.

"What's the prognosis, Doctor?"

Storm waved them away. He was preparing a hypodermic.

Ellery took the small metal chair from the secretarial desk
to a corner of the room, and the Inspector led Karla to it. She
went submissively. She sat down, her eyes on the still figure of
her husband and Dr. Storm's fingers. Max'l stood over Judah
in the other corner of the room, on the same side. Neither
man moved.

"Mrs. Bendigo," the Inspector said. He touched her. "Mrs.
Bendigo?"

She started.

"Who shot him?"

"I do not know." Suddenly she began to cry, without lowering her face or putting her hands to it. They did nothing.
After a while she stopped.

"Well, who came into the room, Mrs. Bendigo?" asked
Ellery.

"No one."

Abel was going about the room gathering up papers—
from the secretarial desk, from the floor where they had been
thrown by Dr. Storm in clearing the top of King's desk. There

was something pitiful about the action, a mechanical gathering up of the secrets of a man who might never put them to use . . . the good and faithful servant going through the motions of preserving order in a house from which all reason for order had passed away. Abel stacked the documents in precise piles, transferring them to filing cases which he opened with a key and relocked afterwards. He seemed grateful for having something to do.

"No one passed through that door, Mrs. Bendigo?" Ellery kept looking around the room, his glance baffled and tormented.

"No one, Mr. Queen."

"Neither in nor out?"

"No one."

"Was there a phone call?"

"No."

"Did either you or your husband make a call?"

"No."

"No interruptions of any kind, then."

"Just one."

"When was that?" Ellery's eyes came around quickly.

"At a few minutes to midnight, Mr. Queen, when you rapped on the door."

"Oh, yes." Ellery was disappointed. "And that was the only interruption? You're sure?"

"Yes."

"Ellery," said his father patiently, "we've gone all through that. Abel and I were outside the door—"

Ellery's glance took up the search again. "And then what happened, Mrs. Bendigo?"

"It recalled the whole dreadful thing to me, but only for a moment." Karla glanced at the hospital table again, quickly shut her eyes. "When Kane closed the door and returned to his desk, he immediately resumed work on his papers. I was at the other desk, going over some reports for him. My back was to the door, where the clock is, so I had no idea what time it was . . . that the time was so close . . ."

Her voice trailed. They waited.

"I had to concentrate on what I was doing. I forgot . . . again. The next thing I knew the clock was chiming—"

"Chiming?" Ellery's glance went to the golden hands set into the wall above the door. "That clock?"

"Yes. It chimes the hours. I looked up and around. The chimes had just begun. The clock was striking twelve. And I remembered again."

"What happened?" And now Ellery gave her his whole attention.

"I turned from the clock to look at Kane, wondering if the chiming of midnight would recall it to him, too." Karla opened her eyes; she looked once more across to the man on the table, with the pudgy figure in white working over him. And she went on rapidly: "But he was immersed in what he was doing. He had dismissed the whole affair as beneath his notice. Oh, if only he had felt a little fear—just a little! Instead, he sat there behind his desk in his shirt sleeves making notes on the margin of a confidential report. Then—it happened."

"What?"

"He was killed. Wounded."

"How?" exclaimed the Inspector.

"One moment, Dad. The clock was still chiming, Mrs. Bendigo?"

"Yes.—How? I do not know. One instant he was sitting there writing, the next his body . . . jerked with great violence and he fell back in his chair. I saw a . . . I saw a hole, a black hole, in his breast and a red stain spreading . . ." Her mouth worked uselessly. "No, I am all right . . . if only I can be of help . . . I do not pretend to understand it . . . I rushed around my desk to the side of his, with no thought but to take him in my arms . . . it had happened so suddenly I had no feeling of death—merely that he needed my help . . . I put out my hand to touch him, and that is all I remember until Inspector Queen revived me. I must have fainted as my hand went out."

"Listen to me carefully, Mrs. Bendigo." Ellery leaned over her chair, his face close to hers. "I want you to think before you answer, and I want you to answer with absolute fidelity to *fact*. Are you listening?"

"Yes?" Her face was tilted anxiously.

"Did you hear a shot?"

"No."

"You didn't think first," Ellery said gently. "You're ill and upset, a great deal has happened in a few minutes.—Think. Think back to that moment. You are sitting, facing your husband, who is at his desk. One instant he's writing away. The next his body jerks and falls back and a black hole and stain appear on his shirt. Obviously he was shot. Someone fired a gun at him. Wasn't the jerk of his body accompanied by a *sound?* Of *some* sort? Maybe it wasn't a loud report. Maybe it was a sharp crack. Even a pop. Even a metallic click. Wasn't there a click?"

"I remember no sound at all."

"Did you smell anything at that moment, Mrs. Bendigo? Like something burning?"

She shook her head. "If something burned at that moment, I did not smell it."

"Smoke," said the Inspector. "Did you see any smoke, Mrs. Bendigo?"

"Nothing."

"But that can't be!"

Ellery put his hand on his father's arm. "You see, of course, that someone must have been in this room with you and your husband, Mrs. Bendigo. *Must* have been. Couldn't someone have been hiding here without your knowledge?"

"But that can't be," said the Inspector again, testily. Ellery touched his arm again.

"I don't see how," said Karla vacantly. "I had just looked around at the clock, as I have told you. I would have to have seen him had he been somewhere behind me. There is no place in this room to hide, as you can see. Besides, how would someone have got in?" She shook her head. "I do not understand it. I can only tell you what happened."

Ellery straightened. He took his father's left hand and held his own by its side.

Their wristwatches agreed.

Both men automatically glanced up at the clock above the door.

The clock, their watches, synchronized perfectly.

So they turned back to each other in a total embarrassment of the imagination. Ellery had already told his father the fantastic story of Judah's actions in his study.

Karla's testimony only compounded the fantasy.

At precisely the moment Judah had aimed his empty pistol in the direction of his brother King—with two thick walls and a corridor full of men between them—and squeezed his powerless trigger . . . at that precise moment, in spite of men and walls and locked doors and no ammunition, King Bendigo had slumped back with a bullet in his breast!

JUDAH was saying, "I need a drink. Tell him to take his hands off me. I want a drink."

Abel said, "I'll take care of him, Max."

Max gave up his hold. Judah moved out of his corner, rubbing his arm with a grimace. Max moved after him.

"You'll have to wait for your drink." Ellery came over quickly. "You can't leave this room."

Judah went by him. He paused before the filing cases, licking his lips, squinting, forehead tightened in thought. Then he sprang at one of the cases, and he pulled. The steel drawer gave and, with a little cry of triumph, he groped inside. His hand came out with a bottle of Segonzac. He began to fumble in his pockets.

"I'd forgotten about that," said Ellery dryly, "but apparently where your hidden treasures are concerned, Judah, you have the memory of a map."

"My knife! You took it!" Judah's hands twitched.

"I'll open it for you." Ellery produced Judah's pocketknife. He cut the tax stamp and seal off the top of the bottle, and removed the cork with the corkscrew.

Judah seized the bottle. His Adam's apple rose and fell. A little color began to stain his sallow cheeks.

"That's enough now, Judah—enough!" muttered his brother Abel.

Judah lowered the bottle from his lips. His eyes were still glassy, but the glass had a sparkle. He held the bottle out. "Anyone for a nip?" he asked gaily.

When no one answered, he moved back to his corner and let himself slide to the floor. He took another drink on the way down and set the bottle of cognac on the floor beside him.

"There, all tidy," said Judah. "Don't let me keep you gentlemen. Go about your business."

"Judah." Ellery sounded comradely. "Who did shoot King?"

"I did," said Judah. "You saw me do it." He brought his knees up suddenly to wrap his thin arms about them. Hugging himself.

"Judah!" Abel sounded ill.

"I said I'd kill him at midnight, and I did it." Judah rocked a little.

"He's not dead," said the Inspector, looking down.

Judah kept rocking. "A detail," he said obscurely, waving his hand. "Principle's the same." His hand fell on the bottle. He raised the bottle to his mouth again.

They turned away from him. All except Max'l, whose hands were opening and closing within inches of Judah's throat.

Judah paid no attention.

DR. STORM said, "Our great man is going to live. What are bullets to the gods? Here, who wants this?"

He spoke without stopping his work, offering his hand sidewise. Inspector Queen took a wad of bloodstained cotton from the hand. On the cotton lay a bullet.

Ellery joined him quickly as Abel and Karla came timidly over to the desk and stared across at the man on the hospital table. Karla turned away at once.

"Back, stand back," said Dr. Storm. He was unrolling some bandages. "You're not sterile—none of you is. Neither am I, for that matter. The great Storm—country sawbones! Poor Lister is rotating rapidly in his grave."

"He's still unconscious," said Abel softly.

"Of course, Abel. I didn't say he could jump off the table and do a handstand. He's had a narrow squeak, this emperor of ours, and he's still a mighty sick emperor. But he'll make it, he'll make it. Constitution of Wotan. In a little while I'll have him moved down to the hospital. Get out of my way, Abel. You, too, Mr. Queen. What are *you* sniffing at?"

"I want," said Ellery, "to see his wound."

"Well, there it is. Haven't you ever seen a bullet wound before, or do you solve your cases in a vacuum?" The stout little doctor worked swiftly.

"It's a real wound," said Ellery, "isn't it?" He stooped and picked up the shirt. Storm had cut it from the King's body. "And no powder marks."

"Oh, move back!"

"PERFECT," said Inspector Queen. They were staring down at the bullet on the stained cotton in his palm. "Not a bit deformed. Did you spot a shell anywhere, Ellery?"

"No," said Ellery.

"If this came from an automatic, the shell should be here."

"Yes," said Ellery, "but it isn't."

The Inspector enveloped the bullet in cotton. He went over to the typewriter-desk and opened drawers until he found an unused envelope. He tucked the cotton wad into the envelope and sealed the envelope and put it into his inside breast pocket.

"Let's get over there," he said mildly, "out of the way."

They went to an unoccupied corner. Ellery wedged himself into the corner and his father turned his back on the room.

"But it isn't," said the Inspector. "All right, mastermind, let's look at this thing like a couple of Missouri mule traders instead of two yokels billygoogling at a shell game."

"Go ahead," said Ellery. "How does the mule shape up?"

"It's a mule," murmured his father, "not a damned mirage. Get that into your skull and keep it there. Judah says he shot King. Judah is lying through his alcoholic teeth. I don't know what his point is, or even if he has a point, but the thing's impossible. The bullet Storm extracted from King's chest didn't get there by osmosis or the mumbling of three sacred words. It was *in* King's chest and Storm took it out of King's chest— I saw him do it, and he wasn't pulling a Houdini when he did

it, either. He really dug it out. That means the bullet was part
of a cartridge that was fired from a gun. Whose gun? Which
gun? Fired where?"

Ellery said nothing. The Inspector ran the edge of his forefinger over his mustache, savagely.

"Not Judah's, my son. Or at least it certainly wasn't the
gun in Judah's mitt at the dot of midnight across the hall in
that apartment of his. That gun, according to your own story,
was empty—you'd unloaded it yourself and you gave me the
cartridges. Judah didn't have another cartridge—you searched
his quarters a couple of times—and even if he had, you examined his Walther a few seconds before midnight and it was
still empty. You didn't take your eyes off it, you say, from
that second on. He pulled the trigger and there was a click.
The gun didn't go off, it shot nothing. It couldn't. That takes
care of Mr. Judah Bendigo. He ought to be in an asylum."

"Go on," said Ellery.

"So it was another gun that went off. Fired from where?
From outside the Confidential Room? Let's see. The walls of
this room are reinforced concrete two feet thick. Hole bored
through beforehand? Where is it on these bare walls? I haven't
spotted it and, while we'll do a thorough check, you know and
I know we won't find such a hole. How could it have been
bored without the guards, on duty twenty-four hours a day a
few yards away, hearing it? The door? Closed and locked, and
it's solid steel. No opening of any kind except the keyhole,
which is far too small and narrow to fire a bullet through; besides, the interior lock mechanism would stop it. No window.
No transom. No peephole. No secret passageways or secret
compartments or secret anything, according to King himself.
The air-conditioning and heating business running around the
walls up there at the ceiling? Some sort of specially designed
metal fabric, Colonel Spring said, that 'breathes.' Look at it—
solid mesh. And not a hole visible in it anywhere. Besides, a
shot from up there would make an impossible angle."

"Your conclusion is—"

"The only conclusion that makes sense. The shot was fired
from inside this room. And who was in this room? King Ben-

digo and his wife—and you didn't see any powder marks on his shirt, did you?"

Ellery stared at Karla Bendigo over his father's shoulder.

"But of course," murmured the Inspector, "you've known that all along."

"Yes," said Ellery. "But tell me: Where is the gun?"

"In this room."

"Where in this room?"

"I don't know where. But it's here."

"I've been over the room, Dad."

"Not the way it ought to be gone over," said his father tartly. "Not the way it's *going* to be gone over. . . . No, it's not *on* her. Where would she hide a gun in that gown she's wearing? Besides, when I carried her over to the chair and went to work on her in that phony faint she pulled, I made sure. I don't like to take liberties with another man's wife, but what can you do? It's here, Ellery. It's got to be. Nobody's left the room. All we have to do is find it. Let's get started."

"All right," said Ellery, pushing away from his corner. "'Let's."

He said it without the least conviction.

THEY searched the room three times. The third time they divided it into sections and went at it by the inch. They got the key to the filing cases from Abel and they examined every drawer. They cleared each one, case by case, of suspicion of concealing a secret compartment. They went through every cubic inch of the interior of both desks, and they went over the desk legs and frames for hollow spaces. They climbed to the tops of the filing cases and fingered every inch of the walls. Ellery set the metal chair on the cases and went over the metallic frieze at the ceiling, following it all around the room. He examined the clock with special care. They determined the immovability of the cases, which were permanently attached to the walls. They took the two desk chairs apart. They dismantled the telephone. They probed the typewriter. They even examined the hospital table with the unconscious man

on it, the sterilizer, Dr. Storm's medical bag, and the other
equipment that had been brought in after midnight.

There was no gun. There was no shell.

"It's on one of them," said the Inspector through his den-
ture. He raised his voice. "We're going to do a body-search.
On everybody. I'm sorry, Mrs. Bendigo, but that includes you,
too. And the first thing I'm going to ask you to do is take your
hair down. . . . You can console yourself with the thought
that I'm an old man who thinks life's greatest thrill is that
first cup of coffee in the morning. Unless you people would
like to call us off—here and now?"

Abel Bendigo said quietly, "I want to know about this. Start
with me, Inspector."

The Inspector searched Abel, Karla, and Max. Ellery
searched Judah, Dr. Storm, and the man on the table. Ellery
spent a great deal of time over the man on the table. He even
contemplated the possibility of the bandages on that big torso
as a place of concealment. But that possibility was an impossibility; a glance told him that. Dr. Storm hovered over him
like an angry bantam.

"Careful! Oh, you idiot—No! If he dies, my fine fellow,
you're a murderer. What do I care about somebody's gun!"

The gun was on none of them. Neither was the shell. Any
shell.

The Inspector was bewildered. Ellery was grim. Neither said
anything.

Abel began to pace.

Karla stood by the hospital table, her makeup smeared,
her hair tangled, just touching her husband's marble hand.
Once she stroked his hair. Judah squatted in his corner sipping cognac peacefully; his glassy eyes were dull again. Max'l's
great shoulders had developed a droop.

Dr. Storm prepared another hypodermic.

The Queens stood by, watching.

Abel was working up to something. He kept glaring at
Judah as he paced, apparently struggling with unfamiliar emo-
tions and losing the struggle. Finally he lost control.

He sprang forward and seized Judah by the collar. The attack was unexpected, and Judah came up like a cork, clutching his bottle frantically. His teeth were gleaming, and for a horrible moment Ellery thought he was laughing.

"You drunken maniac," Abel whispered. "How did you do it? I know that brain of yours—that diseased, dissatisfied brain! We were always too ordinary for you. You always hated us. Why didn't you try to kill me, too? How did you do it!"

Judah put the bottle to his lips, eyes popping from the pressure on his neck. Abel snatched the bottle from him. "You're not drinking any more tonight—ever, if I can help it! Did you really think you were going to be allowed to get away with this? What do you suppose King will do when he gets on his feet again?"

Judah glugged. His brother hurled him back against the cases. Judah slid to the floor and looked up.

He *was* laughing.

THEY searched everyone again before each left the room. Dr. Storm. King Bendigo, still unconscious on the table. Judah, lurching and grinning to himself. Max'l. Karla. Abel . . .

The Inspector did the searching and Ellery passed them out. One by one, so that there was no possibility of a trick. The Inspector also made a final search of the equipment that went out.

There was no gun. No shell.

"I don't understand it," said Abel, the last to leave. "And I've got to find out. My brother will want to know. . . . I give you gentlemen full power. I'm telling Colonel Spring that in anything connected with this business he and his entire security force are under your orders." He glanced at the bottle in his hand, and his lips thinned. "Don't worry about Judah. I'll see that he gets no further opportunity to do anyone any harm."

He strode out, and Ellery made sure the door was locked. Then he turned around. "Inspector Queen, I presume . . ."

"Very funny," said his father bitterly. "'Now what?"

"Now we *really* search," said Ellery.

FORTY-FIVE minutes later they faced each other across King Bendigo's desk.

"It's not here," said Ellery.

"Impossible," said his father. "Impossible!"

"How was King shot? From outside this room?"

"Impossible!"

"From inside this room?"

"Impossible!"

"Impossible," nodded Ellery. "Impossible from outside and impossible from inside—there's positively no gun in this room."

The Inspector was silent.

After a moment, Ellery said: "Ourselves."

"What?"

"Search yourself, Dad!"

They searched themselves.

They searched each other.

No gun. No shell.

Ellery raised his right foot and deliberately kicked King Bendigo's desk. "Let's get out of here!"

THEY slammed the door of the Confidential Room and Ellery tried it for the last time.

It was locked.

There was no sign of Colonel Spring. Colonel Spring evidently preferred to transfer his authority *in absentia.*

"Captain!"

The captain of the guards hurried up. "Yes, sir."

"I want some sealing wax and a candle."

"Yes, sir."

When they were brought, Ellery lit the candle, melted some of the wax, and smeared it thickly over the keyhole of the steel door. He waited a moment. Then he pressed his signet ring into the wax directly over the keyhole.

"Put a guard before this door day and night on three-hour tricks. That seal isn't to be touched. If I find the seal broken—"

"Yes, sir!"

"I believe there's a reserve key to the Confidential Room kept at the guard station up here? I want it."

They walked down the corridor and waited for the key to be brought. A guard was already stationed at the door of the Confidential Room.

"You have the other two keys, Dad, haven't you?"

The Inspector nodded. Ellery handed him the third key. The Inspector tucked it carefully away in one of his trouser pockets.

"We'd better get some sleep."

The Inspector started for the elevator. But then he stopped, looking back. "Aren't you coming?"

Ellery was standing where his father had left him. There was a queer expression on his face.

"Now what?" snarled the Inspector, stamping back.

"That bullet Storm extracted from King's chest," Ellery said slowly. "What caliber would you say it is?"

"Small. Probably .25."

"Yes," said Ellery. "And Judah's gun is a .25."

"Oh, come on to bed." The Inspector turned away.

But Ellery seized him by the arm. "I know it's insane," he cried.

"Ellery——" began his father.

"I'm going to check."

"Damn it!" The Inspector stamped after him.

THERE was a guard at Judah's door, too. He saluted as the Queens came up.

"Who put you here?" grunted the Inspector.

"Mr. Abel Bendigo, sir. Personal orders."

"Judah Bendigo's in his rooms?"

"Yes, sir."

Ellery went in. The Inspector went past him to the door of Judah's bedroom. The room vibrated with snores. The Inspector switched on the lights. Judah was lying on his back, mouth open. The room reeked; he had been sick.

The Inspector turned the lights off and shut the door.

"Got it?"

Ellery had his hand over the little Walther. It was on the

desk, where he had tossed it after Judah's exhibition of murder-by-magic at midnight.

"Now what? What are you staring at?"

Ellery pointed with his other hand.

On the rug, behind Judah's desk, lay a cartridge shell.

The Inspector pounced on it. Out of his pocket he brought one of the unexploded cartridges Ellery had taken from Judah's Walther before midnight and handed over for safekeeping.

"It's a shell from the same make and caliber of cartridge. The same."

"He didn't fire it," Ellery said. "It never went off. No shell came out when he went through that hocus-pocus. The gun was empty, I tell you. It's a trick, part of the same trick."

"Let's see that gun!"

Ellery handed it to his father. The Inspector examined the German automatic with its ivory-inlaid stock and the triangular nick in the corner of the base. He shook his head.

"It's sheer lunacy," said Ellery, "but do you know what you and I are going to do before we go to bed?"

The Inspector nodded numbly.

They left the room without words, the Inspector carrying the gun, Ellery carrying the shell. Once the Inspector tapped his breast pocket, where the bulge was of the envelope containing the cotton-wrapped bullet from King Bendigo's body.

At the guard station Ellery said to the officer in charge, "I want a fast car with a driver. Get your ballistics man, whoever and wherever he is, out of bed and have him meet Inspector Queen and me at the ballistics lab, wherever that is, in ten minutes!"

THEY never did learn the name of the ballistics man. And they could never afterward recall what he looked like. The very laboratory in which they passed through the final episode of the nightmare remained a watery blur to them. Once during the next hour and a half the Inspector remarked that it was the finest ballistics laboratory he had ever seen. Later, he denied having said it, on the ground that he hadn't really seen anything. Ellery could not argue the point, as the machinery of his memory seemed to have stopped operating, as well as all his other long-functioning equipment.

The shock was too great. They hovered over the ballistics man, watching him work over the shell and the bullet and the little Walther—firing comparison shots, washing, ammoniating, magnifying—watching him angrily, jealously, hopefully, guarding against a trick, anticipating more magic, smoking like expectant fathers, even laughing at the absurdity of their own antics.

The shock was too great.

They saw the results themselves. It was not necessary for the ballistics man to point out what he pointed out, nevertheless, in the most technical detail—firing-pin marks, extractor and ejector traces, marks from the breech block. This was all about the shell they had picked up from the floor of Judah's study. And they studied the near-fatal bullet and the test bullet in the comparison microscope, eying the fused images of the two bullets unbelievingly. They insisted on photographic corroboration and the ballistics man produced it in "rolled photographs" showing the whole circumference of the bullet on a single plate. They peered and compared and discussed and argued, and when it was all over they faced the paralyzing conclusion:

The bullet Dr. Storm had dug out of King Bendigo's chest had been fired from the gun Judah Bendigo had aimed emptily at his brother with two impenetrable walls and a lot of air space crowded with hard-muscled men in the way.

It was impossible.

Yet it was a fact.

12

JULY CAME—the first, the Fourth.

There was a ceremony of sorts before the Home Office, with the American flag raised beside the black Bendigo standard and a short speech by Abel Bendigo. But this was for the benefit of the Honorable James Walbridge Monahew, unofficial representative of the United States to The Bodigen Company—a courtesy such as the sovereign power extends to a friendly government. Present were Cleets of Great Britain and Cassebeer of France. There was a cocktail party afterwards in the Board Room, which neither Ellery nor his father was invited to attend. They learned later that several toasts were drunk—to the health of the absent King Bendigo, the President of the United States, the King of England, and the President of the Republic of France, in that order.

Bendigo was still confined to the hospital wing at the Residence, under twenty-four-hour guard. Ambiguous bulletins posted by Dr. Storm gave the impression of a rapid recovery. By July fifth the patient was reported sitting up. Still, no visitors were permitted except his wife and his brother Abel. Max'l was not classified as a visitor; he never left the sickroom, feeding there three times a day and bedding down on a cot within arm's reach of his divinity.

Karla spent most of her days in the hospital. The Queens saw little of her except at dinner, when she would chat in a strained, preocccupied way about everything but the subject uppermost in their minds. Abel they saw rarely; with the King helpless in bed, the Prime Minister was a busy man.

Judah was the surprise. For the first week after the attempted assassination he was confined to his quarters under guard, and the six cases of Segonzac cognac behind his Bechstein grand were removed at Abel Bendigo's order. But Judah kept mellow. His apartment was searched repeatedly, and a bottle or two was found occasionally in a rather obvious hiding-place; the guards suspected him of trying to keep them happy. The chief source of his supply they never located. For a few days it was a game which Judah showed every evidence of enjoying in his sardonic fashion. After his confinement was lifted and he was given freedom of the Residence, with the exception of the hospital wing, all attempts to keep him sober were abandoned. It would have taken a general of logistics commanding an army corps of Carrie Nations to track down half his secret caches.

The Queens wondered grimly about Judah's release, and they spent several days seeking an explanation. Finally they succeeded in ambushing Abel. It was late one night, as he entered the Residence bound for bed.

"Honestly, gentlemen, I haven't been avoiding you. With King down, there's been no time to breathe." Abel looked grayer than usual and his narrow shoulders sagged with fatigue. "What's on your mind?"

"Lots of things," said Ellery, "but a good place to start would be: Why did you order Judah's release?"

Abel sighed. "I should have explained that. Do you mind if we sit down? . . . One of the critical things that's been occupying me—perhaps the most critical—is keeping the real story of what happened on the night of June twenty-first from getting out. You'll have noticed that Mr. Monahew and Sir Cardigan and Monsieur Cassebeer are under the impression that King is indisposed because of influenza. If it became known that he was the victim of an assassination attempt that nearly succeeded, the news would cause the most serious repercussions. Throughout the world. Our affairs are normally very delicate, gentlemen, and they're so spread out that—as a great European statesman remarked only the other day—let King Bendigo stand in a draft and the whole world sneezes."

Abel smiled faintly, but the Queens remained grim.

"What's that got to do with your brother Judah?" asked the Inspector.

"The gentlemen from the United States, Great Britain, and France are very astute. If Judah were kept out of sight for any length of time, they would start speculating. They might put two and two together—King's sudden 'illness,' Judah's sudden disappearance." Abel shook his head. "It's safer this way. Judah can't possibly get to King. And he's being watched closely without seeming to be."

The Queens said nothing for a while.

Then the Inspector said: "Another thing, Mr. Bendigo. We've been trying to see Dr. Storm's patient without being permitted within a hundred yards of his bed. There are some questions we'd like to ask him. How about arranging a visit to his bedside?"

"Dr. Storm won't allow it. My brother's still a very sick man, he says."

"We understand *you* see him daily."

"For just a few minutes. To relieve his mind about pending matters; he frets a good deal. That's all, really."

Ellery said quietly: "Have you asked him anything about the shooting?"

"Of course. He's been no help at all. And I can't press him. Storm says he must not be excited."

"But he must have said something. He was shot in the breast. How can you be shot in the breast at close range without seeing who's shooting you?"

Abel said earnestly: "Exactly what I asked King, knowing it's the one thing you'd want answered. But he says he can't remember anything happening except that he woke up in the hospital." Abel rose. "Is there anything else, gentlemen?"

"Yes," said Ellery. "The most important question of all."

"Well, well?" said Abel, a trifle impatiently.

"What are we doing here?"

Abel stared his illegible, unavoidable stare. They could see his features smooth out as if under a hot iron. When he spoke, he was the Prime Minister. "I hired you to confirm my own findings about the authorship of the letters. You did so. I then asked you to stay on to help in a delicate family situation. Which isn't settled yet."

"You want us to keep going, Mr. Bendigo?" There was nothing to be read in Ellery's face, either.

"Most certainly I do. Especially during the next few weeks. When King is allowed out of bed we'll have the whole problem of Judah on our backs again. I can't keep him under lock and key—"

"Why not?" demanded the Inspector. "With King back on his feet, anything you do with Judah won't be noticed."

The Prime Minister vanished. Abel sat down again, shaking his head, his glasses twinkling a little. "I don't blame you. It must all seem very strange to you. The truth is, what we have most to contend with is not so much Judah as King himself. Contrary to my expectations, King won't allow Judah to be locked up. He has his weaknesses, you know. Courage to the point of foolhardiness is one of them. Tremendous pride is another. To lock Judah up, according to King's code, would be a personal defeat. I realize that now. And then the family relationship . . . I'm sure I don't have to go on. . . . Of course, there's still the matter of the way Judah did it. That bothers me, Mr. Queen, bothers me enormously. And King. We can't make head or tail of it. Have you made any progress at all?"

Ellery shifted to the other foot. "You can hardly progress, Mr. Bendigo, when you're caught between the irresistible force and the immovable object. The facts say the attack on your brother was a physical impossibility—and yet, here he is with a bullet hole near his heart. Did you find time to read our report on the ballistics tests?"

"Incredible," murmured Abel.

"Exactly. Not to be believed. And yet there's no room for doubt. That the bullet dug out of your brother's chest was fired from Judah's gun when Judah's gun couldn't possibly, under the ironclad circumstances, have fired it, is a scientific fact. It's something new under the sun, as far as my father and I are concerned."

"And that bothers *you*. Of course. A man of your training, your exceptional talents, Mr. Queen . . . No offense, Inspector." Abel smiled. "You and I are in the same class—good, solid plug-horses. But the pace of the thoroughbred—" He shook his head as he rose again. "You keep on it, Mr. Queen. I know if anyone can make sense out of it, you're the man."

It was only when the private Bendigo elevator had closed on Abel's smallish figure, the narrow bland face, the broad disturbing brow, that the Queens found themselves totting up the items of their conversation with him. And reaching the sum total of zero.

As usual, Abel had really not answered anything.

THEY were at breakfast in their suite the next morning when Abel phoned.

"I got to thinking last night, as I was getting ready for bed," Abel's twang said, "about our talk, Mr. Queen. It seems to me Dr. Storm is being overcautious. King is really getting along very well. And I see no reason why you should have to rely on secondhand answers to your questions when you can get them directly from King. I've arranged with Dr. Storm for you and Inspector Queen to visit my brother at eleven o'clock this morning. Storm gives you only a few minutes—"

"That's all we want," Ellery said quickly. "Thank you!" But when he hung up he did not speak quickly at all. "Abel's arranged for us to see King this morning, Dad. It's his way of telling us he knows we were skeptical or dissatisfied with his report of what King said about the shooting. I wonder what it means."

"I wonder what anything means!"

They were admitted to the hospital wing without question, and a guard escorted them to the door of King Bendigo's room. As they walked up the beautiful corridor they met Immanuel Peabody. The lawyer had just emerged from the royal sickroom with a briefcase under his arm, and he hurried past them with a frown and a wave of the hand. "The White Rabbit," muttered Ellery. " 'Oh, my ears and whiskers, how late it's getting!' "

"I wonder where *he* was when Judah pulled his miracle," grunted his father. "And what the devil he carries in that briefcase!"

Then they were admitted to the presence.

The King looked very well, as his brother had remarked. He was thinner and his complexion had paled, but his black eyes were as lively as ever and there was scarcely a trace of weakness in his gestures.

And Max'l was eating nuts again, in a chair beside his master's bed.

Dr. Storm stood Napoleonically before one of the windows, his back to them. Without turning he snapped, "Five minutes."

"Fire away," said the King. He wore white silk pajamas. The crown surmounting the two linked globes was embroidered in metallic gold thread on the breast through which his brother's bullet had gone.

"First," said Inspector Queen. "Do you remember the clock's chiming midnight, Mr. Bendigo?"

"Vaguely. I was absorbed in what I was doing, but it seems to me I remember the chimes."

"All twelve of them?" asked the Inspector.

"No idea."

"At that moment—when you heard the midnight chimes— you were sitting at your desk?"

"Yes."

"In what position, Mr. Bendigo? I mean, taking the front edge of the desk as a line of reference, were you sitting squarely to it? Facing left? Facing right? How?"

"Squarely. I was leaning over, writing."

"Looking down, of course?"

"Naturally."

"When you heard the shot—"

"I didn't hear the shot, Inspector Queen."

"Oh, I see. There was no shot?"

The man in the bed said dryly, "So that's the way you fellows do it. Yes, of course there was a shot."

"Why do you say that, Mr. Bendigo?"

"There must have been. There's nothing imaginary about the bullet hole in my chest."

"You didn't hear the shot. Did you *see* anything? A flash? A sudden movement? Even something you can't identify?"

"I saw nothing, Inspector."

"Did you smell anything unusual?"

"No."

"One moment you were writing, the next you were unconscious. Is that it, Mr. Bendigo?"

"Yes.—Queen. You haven't opened your mouth. Don't you have a question to ask?"

"Yes," said Ellery. "How do *you* think it was done, Mr. Bendigo?"

"I don't know," said the King grimly. "Isn't that your department?"

"I'm not running it too well. The facts and the results are totally contradictory. We were hoping you'd recall something that would give us a clue to what happened. Ordinarily, the fact that you didn't hear, see, or smell anything at the moment you were shot might simply mean that you blacked out instantaneously from a near-fatal wound. But Mrs. Bendigo didn't hear, see, or smell the shot, either, and she wasn't wounded—in fact, she was conscious long enough to see you slump back in your chair with the point of the bullet's entry visible and the blood oozing out to stain your shirt around the bullet hole. So your testimony, Mr. Bendigo, only tends to confirm your wife's and confuse matters further.—All right, Doctor, we're leaving."

Four weeks to the night after the attempt on King Bendigo's life, Ellery made the decision which changed the course of their investigation and turned it at last into a channel with a discernible port.

He and his father were parked in one of the Residence cars. They had driven off into the soft summer night after dinner that evening in an attempt to escape from the headsplitting maze in which they were trapped. Ellery drove absently, and it was with some surprise that he found himself emerging from the camouflage belt of woods surrounding the island. He pulled over to the raw edge of the cliffs and turned off his motor. At their feet lay the harbor of Bendigo Island, twinkling with a thousand lights and even at this hour the scene of an insectlike activity. In the bay formed by the embrace of the harbor's arms lay a great number of vessels, and they could see, lying athwart the narrow entrance to the bay, the riding lights and big guns of the heavy cruiser *Bendigo*, King Bendigo's "yacht."

"Seems like ten years since that first day, when Abel made the airport car turn sharp inland the minute we caught a glimpse of the harbor," remarked the Inspector after a few moments. "I wonder why they've stopped tailing us and shooing us away from the hush-hush installations. It's weeks since I've even seen the Bobbsey Twins."

"The who?" Ellery automatically fingered the Walther in his pocket. He had been carrying Judah's little gun about with him ever since the night of June twenty-first.

"The colored-shirt boys."

"Oh, they're in the States somewhere on an assignment."

"That's where I'd like to be, gol ding it. I can't take much more of this, son, Washington or no Washington."

"King's being discharged from the hospital this Saturday, according to the grapevine."

"Maybe Judah'll put the hex on him and he'll turn into gold or something," the Inspector said hopefully. "Anything for a little action!"

They were silent for a long time.

"Dad."

"What, son?"

"I'm leaving here."

"So am I, if I live that long," said his father gloomily. Then he turned to stare. "You're *what?*"

"Leaving."

"When?"

"Tomorrow morning."

"Suits me," said the Inspector with celerity. "By golly, let's go back right now and start packing."

"Not you, Dad. Just me. You'll have to stay."

"Of all the dirty, lowdown tricks," exclaimed his father. "What's the idea?"

"Well . . ."

"What do you have to cover up, your reputation? With me holding the potsy? Why do *I* have to stay? I mean, *why* do I have to stay? I've got as much in my spy notes as I can hope to get, and the oilskin pouch has given my belly a permanent itch. It's *your* end that's not finished—remember?"

"One of us has to keep a line open here, Dad. And an eye on Judah. There's something I've got to look into."

The Inspector eyed him. "You've got something?"

"No," mumbled Ellery. "No, I've got nothing. But a hunch, that is. When there's nothing else to latch onto, a hunch can look mighty comforting."

After a moment his father sank back and looked glumly down at the lights of the harbor. "Well, give my regards to Broadway."

"I'm not going to Broadway."

"You're not? Where you going?"

"To Wrightsville."

"Wrightsville!"

"I made up my mind this afternoon, while you were dunking in the pool. I meandered into the gardens and ran across Judah doing a Ferdinand. He was lying under a royal poinciana waving a peacock flower under his crooked nose and sipping guess-what. We had a long chat, Judah and I. He was unusually voluble."

"What's all this got to do with Wrightsville?"

"Judah says that's where he, King, and Abel were born."

"You're kidding!"

"That's what he told me. And enough more about their boyhood there to make me damned curious."

"The big boy was *born* there?"

Ellery shifted in his seat. "It gave me a queer lift, Dad. You know how Wrightsville's mixed in my life in recent years. I've become a little superstitious on the subject. I suppose it's inane —after all, the Bendigos are Americans by birth . . . they had to be born somewhere in the United States . . . and Abel's

twang never came out of anything but a New England nose.
Still, learning it was my old Wrightsville jabbed me in the
seat of the pants. The moment Judah uttered the magic word—
he *is* a magician!—I knew I'd have to run up there for a
session with the town. Because the secret's probably buried
there, just waiting to be dug up. The way Wrightsville secrets
have a way of doing."

Ellery looked out to the dark sea.

"What secret?" demanded his father petulantly.

"*The* secret." Ellery shrugged. "The secret of what makes
these people tick. Of how this case came to happen, Dad. I'm
no longer obsessed with the answer to how Judah pulled that
marvelous flimflam. We'll get to that in due course. . . . Up
there in Wrightsville something's waiting to be discovered
about Kane, Abel, and Judah Bendigo that's going to restore
my self-respect. I feel it in my bones and, by God, I'm flying
there tomorrow morning!"

13

THE LAST THING Ellery saw was his father on the roof
of the observation building waving his hat under a flapping
Bendigo flag. The steward pulled and fastened the last black
blind, and Bendigo Island disappeared. This time Ellery did
not mind. He was thinking of people, not places.

The big trimotor took off.

There were three other passengers—Immanuel Peabody,
with the inevitable briefcase; an eagle-nosed man in a wing
collar and blue polka-dot foulard tie; and an old woman with
a Magyar face and badly stained fingers who was wearing a
silly-looking Paris hat. Peabody hurried into a compartment,
already unbuckling the straps of his briefcase, and he remained invisible until the plane—its windows free again—

circled Gravelly Point for a landing at the National Airport in Washington. The old woman in the hat chain-smoked Turkish cigarets in a long gold holder and read a magazine throughout the trip. When she set it down to eat her lunch Ellery saw that it was not a copy of *Vogue* but a highly technical scientific journal in the German language, published, he knew, in Lausanne. Immediately the old woman in the silly hat ceased to be an old woman in a silly hat and became— he now recalled those Magyar features—one of the world's most famous research chemists. The man in the wing collar he never did identify. Neither attempted to speak to him, but all through the trip Ellery was afraid one or both of them would. He was relieved when they got off the plane with Peabody at Washington.

The people Ellery was turning over in his mind were the Bendigos, particularly Abel. He had rather neglected Abel, he thought, but he could not quite settle on why this should seem a serious oversight. Abel's attitude throughout the affair had been in the tradition of high politics, a puzzling mixture of the right words and the wrong actions. Like the camouflaged shore batteries of Bendigo Island, Abel effaced himself against his background; like them, he concealed a powerful potential. But a powerful potential for what?

And always Ellery came back to the question he had asked himself from the beginning: Why had Abel brought him into the case at all? It was a question as remarkably lacking in answerability as the riddle of the little gun that could not possibly have fired the shot, and yet had.

Ellery's jaw shifted. There was an answer; all he had to do was find it. And as the plane flew farther north, he had the curious feeling that he was approaching the answer at the exact m.p.h. shown on the pilot's instruments.

It was midafternoon when the big black and gold Bendigo ship set Ellery down at Wrightsville Airport. He waved to the pilot and copilot and hurried up the steps of the administration building lugging his bag.

Outside, the taxi man was someone he didn't know, a smartly capped youngster with red-apple cheeks. The cab was a new one, bright yellow, with black-and-white-striped trim and a meter.

Gone are the Wrightsville owner-driven cabs of yesteryear, the dusty Chevvy and Ford black sedans with the zone maps showing the quarter, half-dollar, and seventy-five-cent trip areas, and drivers like Ed Hotchkiss, who called John F. Wright by his Christian name, and Whitey Pedersen, who had started hacking back in the horse-and-buggy days, when the stone base of the Jezreel Wright monument in the Square (which was round) actually watered the buggy and surrey horses of the farmers-come-to-town instead of being planted to geraniums, as now, by the ladies of the Keep-Wrightsville-Beautiful Committee of the Civic Betterment Club.

"Where to?" asked the youngster with a smile.

Wrightsville Airport lies in the valley running north by west between the Twin Hills-Bald Mountain section and the foot-hills of the great Mahoganies. North Hill Drive is almost due south; it's quite a climb, the road running southeast up the hump past the eastern terminus of "The Hill" (Hill Drive) and the western terminus of Twin-Hill-in-the-Beeches. Hill Drive is not to be confused with North Hill Drive, where the "new" millionaires have their estates. "The Hill" is the residential section of the real thing, the bluestocking families who go all the way back to the 1700s—the Wrights, the Bluefields, the Livingstons, the Granjons, the F. Henry Minikins. Twin-Hill-in-the-Beeches is the town's newest "good" development (not the smartest; Skytop Road facing Bald Mountain farther north is the smartest). It's full of fine, bright, sort of modern homes, though, built by well-to-do business people like the MacLeans ("Dunc MacLean—Fine Liquors," on the Square next door to the Hollis Hotel; Dunc gets all the hotel trade), people who couldn't crash any of the Hill Drive properties for all the cash in Hallam Luck's vaults at the Public Trust Company. And don't think the MacLeans and their crowd don't know it; they don't even try!

"The Hollis," said Ellery, leaning back. The mere sound of the name made him feel as if he had come home.

ELLERY checked in at the Hollis Hotel, and when he checked out sixteen days later he paid a bill for $122.25, $80.00 of which was for rental of his room. Laundry and pressing took up most of the balance. He ate one meal in the main dining room, but he found it so full of the thunder of organizational ladies and business-group lunchers that he never went back.

High Village hadn't changed much. About the only difference in the Square was that the old Bluefield Store on the north arc, where Upper Dade comes down from North Hill Drive, was gone, replaced by a fluorescent beauty of a shop with a brand-new purple neon sign outside saying *It's Topp's For T-V.* There were a few other changes, more minor than that, but those were chiefly on Wright Street, which had always been a "dead spot" for business.

Death had been there in the past year or so—Andy Birobatyan of the florist shop in the Professional Building on Washington Street was among the departed, Ellery sorrowed to learn. The flower business Andy had built up with his one arm (he had left the other in the Argonne Forest in 1918) was being run by his two-armed son Avdo, and not half so well, according to report. Ellery was inclined to salt this rumor, as Avdo was the one who had eloped with Virgie Poffenberger, Dr. Emil Poffenberger's daughter, and made a go of it, too, though it ruined his father-in-law's social standing, caused Dr. Poffenberger's "resignation" from the Country Club, and subsequently the sale of his dental practice and his removal to Boston. And Ma Upham of Upham House had died of a stroke and her Revolutionary-type hostel had been sold to a Providence syndicate, causing a D.A.R. boycott and a series of fiery editorials in the *Record.*

Ellery spent his first evening and all of the next day lining up his sights: looking up old friends, greeting acquaintances, strolling along familiar streets, catching up on the gossip, and generally enjoying himself. It was not until he had been in Wrightsville for thirty-six hours that he realized why his enjoyment was so thorough. It was not merely the re-experience of old times in a place he loved; it was that he had just left a place he detested, called Bendigo Island, with its electrified fences and swarming guards and secret police with blank faces and robotized employees and its soft, curiously rotten, air. This, on the other hand, was Wrightsville, U.S.A., where people lived, worked, and died in an atmosphere of independence and decency and a man never had reason to look back over his shoulder. This air, even mill-laden, could be breathed.

It made Ellery all the more inquisitive about the Bendigos.

On the second morning after his arrival he went to work in earnest. His object was to get a biographical picture of King Bendigo and his brothers Abel and Judah from conception, if possible, with the emphasis on King.

He consulted town records, he hunted up Wrightsvillians strange to him, he spent long hours in the morgue of the Wrightsville *Record* and the reference room of the Carnegie Library on State Street. He hired a Driv-Ur-Self car at Homer Findlay's garage down at Plum Street in Low Village and he made numerous trips—Slocum Township, Fyfield, Connhaven, even to little Fidelity, in whose dilapidated cemetery he had an old grave marker to hunt up. Once he flew to Maine.

Especially helpful was Francis "Spec" O'Bannon, who was still in Wrightsville running Malvina Prentiss's *Record* (Malvina, the eternal Rosalind Russell, retired from newspaper publishing when she married O'Bannon but retained her maiden name!); O'Bannon kept the *Record* morgue copiously supplied with bourbon while Ellery was dug in there. And, of course, there was Chief of Police Dakin, who was beginning to look more like Abe Lincoln's mummy than Abe Lincoln; and Hermione Wright, who had never looked more radiant; and Emmeline DuPré, the Town Crier, who practically bayed for an entire afternoon; and many others.

Ellery had two whole weeks of it, digging up the pieces, jigsawing them; crosschecking the testimony, establishing the facts, integrating them with world events, and finally arranging them in roughly chronological order. At the end he had a picture of "the oldest Bendigo boy" and his brothers which, kaleidoscopic as it was, delineated them with photographic brutality.

Excerpts from E.Q.'s Notes

DR. PIERCE MINIKIN:

(Dr. Pierce Minikin is 86, retired from practice. Semi-invalid, cared for by Miz Baker, old Phinny's widow, since Phinny died and the *Record* lost the best pressman it ever will have. Dr. Pierce is great-uncle to F. Henry Minikin, but two branches not on speaking terms for over a generation. Dr. Minikin has very small income from some Low Village property. Still lives in Colonial Minikin house on Minikin Rd. between Lincoln and Slocum Sts. In bad shape, needs painting, etc. Dated 1743, squeezed between Volunteer Fire Dept. and Slocum Garage, backyard overlooks Van Horn Lumber Yard. Old fellow a tartar with frosty twinkle and sharp tongue. Physically feeble, mentally very alert. We had several wonderful visits.)

"King" Bendigo? My dear young fellow, I knew that great man when he was mud in his father's eye. Brought all three Bendigo boys into the world. From what I've heard, I owe the world an apology. . . .

His father? Well, I don't suppose anybody remembers Bill Bendigo in Wrightsville except a few old hasbeens like me. I liked Bill fine. Of course he wasn't respectable—didn't come from a high-toned family, didn't go to church, was a regular heller—but that didn't cut any ice with me, I liked my men hard and my women patients to bear down, haha! Bill was hard. Hard drinker, hard feeder, hard boss—he was a building contractor, built that block of flats over on Congress Street near the Marshes they're just getting round to tearing down—and a hard lover? Boys at the Hollis bar used to call him Wild Bill. There's many a story I could tell you about . . .

Well, no, can't say I do. No, not Italian, that's on their mother's side. Don't know how they got the name Bendigo, except that Wild Bill's people were Anglo-Saxon. Came over from England around 1850. . . .

Big man, six foot three, a yard wide, and a pair of hands on him could bend a crowbar. Champion wrestler of the Green. The Green? That's before it was named Memorial Park. Boys used to grapple there Saturday afternoons. Nobody ever pinned Bill Bendigo. They used to come from all over the County to try. Handsome devil, too, Bill was—blue-eyed, with dark curly hair and lots of it on his chest. If you didn't know about the English, you'd have said Black Irish. . . .

The lover part. Well, now, I didn't know *all* Bill's secrets! But when he fell in real love it was all the way. Worshiped the ground Dusolina walked on. Little Low Village girl from an Italian family. Can't remember her maiden name to save my life. Yes, I do. Cantini, that's what it was. Her father'd been a track walker for the railroad, killed by an express train in '91. No, '92. Left a big brood, and his wife was a religious fanatic. Dusolina—Bill called her Lena—fell just as hard in love as Bill, and they had to elope because Mrs. Cantini threatened to kill her if she married a Protestant. Dusolina did, anyway; they were married by Orrin Lloyd, he was Town Clerk before Amos Bluefield. Orrin Lloyd was the brother of Israel Lloyd, who owned the lumber yard then— grandfather of Frank Lloyd who owned the *Record* up to a few years ago . . . Where was I?

Yes. Well, I was the Bendigo family doctor and when Duso- lina got pregnant I took care of her. She had a hard time, died a few days later. Child was a great big boy, weighed almost thirteen pounds, I recollect that clearly. That was Bill's first son—your great man. Bill took little Dusolina's death hard, the way he took everything. Didn't blame me, thank the Lord—if he had, he'd have crippled me. He blamed the baby. Unbelievable, isn't it? Said the baby was a natural- born killer! And Bill said there was only one name for a natural-born killer, and that was Cain, like in the Bible. And Cain was what he had me register the baby in the Town Hall records. Only child I ever delivered by that name. That was

THE KING IS DEAD

161

in 1897, young man, fifty-four years ago, and I remember it
as if it were yesterday . . .

SARA HINCHLEY:

(Of the Junction Hinchleys. Trained nurse. Miss Sara is
arthritic, getting anile, lives in the Connhaven Home for
the Aged, private institution, where I saw her. Supported
by her nephew, Lyman Hinchley, the insurance broker
of Wrightsville. Was Jessica Fox's day nurse during J.F.'s
fatal illness in 1932.)

That's right, sir, Nellie Hinchley was my mother. She died
in . . . in . . . I don't remember. Except for my brother Will—
that was my nephew Lyman's father—and myself, none of
my mother's children lived. They all died in infancy, and she
had seven. We were very poor, so my mother did wet-nursing,
as they called it in those days. She always had a lot of milk,
and after she lost one she would . . .

Dr. Minikin told you that? Well, of course, she wet-nursed
so many, and I was just a girl. . . . Oh, that one! Let's see,
now . . . Mr. Bendigo's wife died delivering his first child . . .
yes . . . and Mama wet-nursed the baby for a year. He had a
queer name . . . I don't remember. . . . But she did use to say he
was the hardest she ever nursed. He'd just about suck the life
out of her. What *was* his name? . . . Cain? Cain . . . Well,
maybe it was. I don't remember things as good as I used to.
. . . I think Mama stopped when Mr. Bendigo got married
again. Or was that with the Newbold child? . . .

ADELAIDE PEAGUE:

(One of Cain's earliest living grade-school teachers. Now
71, retired on pension, keeps house for Millard Peague,
her first cousin, of the locksmith shop at Crosstown and
Foaming. Brisk and very bright, with a jaw like a plow-
share.)

I most certainly do, Mr. Queen! I'm not one to bow and
scrape and forget the way it *used* to be just because a pupil of
mine becomes *famous*, although frankly I don't know what

he's famous for except that if he's anything like the way he *was* . . .

No, not the Piney Road school that Elizabeth Schoonmaker taught. The one I taught in is still standing, though of course it's not a schoolhouse any more, it's the D.A.R. headquarters. . . .

He was an impossible child. In those days we taught the first four grades in the same room. The boys were hellions, and if a teacher didn't go about armed with a brass-edged ruler she didn't last a term. . . . Cain Bendigo was the worst, the *worst*. He was the ringleader in every bit of mischief, and some of the things he did I simply cannot repeat. I'll bet he remembers *me*, though. Or his knuckles do. . . .

Yes, I suppose his name had something to do with it, although I'm not one of these advanced people who test everything by psychology. He *did* hate to have me call on him, and now that I think of it, it was probably because of course I had to use his name. Did you ever hear the like? He did take a lot of joshing because his name was Cain, and any time one of the other boys ragged him about it there was a fist fight. He was big and strong for his age and he would fight at the drop of a hat. In the four years I taught him he licked every blessed boy in school, just about, and some of the girls, too! There was no nonsense about chivalry in *that* child. . . .

Oh, he stopped them making fun of it, yes. Toward the end of the fourth grade—when Opal Marbery inherited him, thank goodness!—no, she's been dead for many years— toward the end, as I say, while he was still having plenty of fights, they weren't about his name. But he and I had a feud over it to the bitter end. I always felt that it was a very unfair thing for a child to do. After all, I couldn't help his name being Cain, could I? I had to call the little devil *something*. . . .

URIAH SCOTT ("U.S.") WHEELER:

(68, principal of Fyfield Gunnery School. Kin to the Wheelers of Hill Drive. Kept referring to his family's hero, Murdock Wheeler, Wrightsville's last surviving vet of the G.A.R., who died in 1939, as if the old fellow had

been General Grant himself. Was Cain's teacher at the
Gunnery School in 1911, when Cain was 14.)

My dear Mr. Queen, on the contrary I consider it an honor.
I have always allowed myself to brag that I had a little
something to do with shaping the character, and therefore the
destiny, of Mr. Bendigo. Although I've lived in Fyfield ever
since coming to teach at Gunnery in 1908 as a very young man,
I have always retained a soft spot in my heart for the town of
my birth, and Mr. Bendigo is without doubt Wrightsville's
greatest living citizen. It's high time indeed that someone like
yourself collated the facts of his early life among us humble
folk for posterity. . . .

Yes, of course, about his name. Excellent point of character! His father enrolled him at Gunnery as Cain Bendigo—
C-a-i-n—as nasty a trick to play on a future great man as I've
ever heard of, haha! We used to joke about it in the Faculty
Room. But he soon changed all that. A mere boy, sir, in a
school in which discipline has always been preached and prac-
ticed as a cardinal virtue. My kinsman, Murdock Wheeler,
who did distinguished service for our country in the Civil
War, used to say . . .

He changed it! Just like that. One day he marched into the
Administration Office and *demanded* that the spelling of his
name be changed on the school's roster from C-a-i-n to
K-a-n-e. He had already begun heading his papers in his various classes with his first name in the revised spelling. He was
confined to quarters for three days for his disrespectful tone
and attitude. When he returned to classes, he immediately
marched into the Administration Office and made the identical
demand—in, I might add, haha, the identical tone! He was
again punished, more severely this time. Nevertheless as soon
as he was released, there he was again. His father was summoned to Fyfield. Mr. Bendigo Senior, on hearing what had
occurred, forbade the school authorities to alter the spelling
of his son's name. The boy listened in silence. When he came
to my class that very day, his first action was to head a paper
"K-a-n-e Bendigo." It made a very pretty problem for us!—

and I must confess it was a problem we never solved. He
never wrote his name "C-a-i-n" again, to the best of my
knowledge. And when he was graduated and saw that the
name on his diploma was spelled "C-a-i-n"—the school had
no choice, you see—he marched into Principal Estey's office,
tore the diploma in quarters before Dr. Estey's nose, flung the
pieces on the desk, and marched out again! . . .

CAIAPHAS TRUSLOW:

> (Town Clerk. 'Aphas succeeded Amos Bluefield as Clerk
> after old Bluefield's death on Columbus Day eve in 1940.
> 'Aphas helpful throughout.)

Yep, here it is, Mr. Queen. *William M. Bendigo and Ellen
Foster Wentworth, June 2, 1898.* My father knew Mr. Ben-
digo well. And Ellen Wentworth was the sister of old Arthur
Wentworth, who was attorney for John F. Wright's father.
The Wentworths were one of the real old families. All dead
now. . . .

Well, yes, except for the two younger Bendigo brothers, but
they don't count, now, do they? . . .

About this marriage, that was Mr. Bendigo's second. His
first was . . .

They were married in the First Congregational Church on
West Livesey Street. Reason I know is I was a choir boy at
the ceremony. Way I heard it, Ellen Wentworth insisted on
a church wedding just because her folks were against the
match. She had a lot of spunk for a girl in those days. Wasn't
a soul there—not a soul in the pews, not even her family!
No, there was one—Nellie Hinchley, who was holding Mr.
Bendigo's first child by his first wife on her lap. . . .

Old Mr. Blanchard was pastor then—no, no, he's been
dead and gone for forty-two years—and he was so fussed he
messed up the service. Mr. Bendigo got so riled at poor old
Mr. Blanchard he puffed up to twice his size just holding himself in—and he looked like a mighty big man to us kids! . . .

DR. PIERCE MINIKIN:

. . . delivered the second boy, too. Different mother this
time, one of the Wentworths. Ellen, her name was. Not as
pretty as Dusolina. Dusolina was little and dark and had a
face shaped like a valentine and big black eyes. Ellen was
blonde and blue-eyed and on the skimpy side—looked a little
bloodless. But she had breeding, that girl. And money, of
course. Leave it to Bill Bendigo to pick up a bargain. There
were lots of men from good families in Wrightsville tried to
shine up to Ellen. But she wanted love. And I reckon she got
it, haha! . . .

Oh, Bill was wild the second time, too. Not because the
mother of the child died, though Ellen never was very strong
and soon after developed the heart condition that in a few
years made her a semi-invalid. It was because for his second
child he'd made up his mind to have a girl. And damned if the
baby didn't outsmart him this time, too! Turned out to be a
boy again. Bill never did get over that. If he hated young Cain
for being a mother-killer, he had nothing but contempt for
the second boy for not turning out to be a girl. Wouldn't spit on
him. These days a doctor would send a man like Bill to a
psychiatrist, I guess. Those days all you could do was take a
buggy whip to him, only Bill was too big. So when he said to
me, "Doc Pierce, my wife has birthed a sneaky little demon
who spent nine months in the womb figuring out how to cross
me up, and there's only one name for a baby like that. You go
down to Town Clerk Orrin Lloyd and you register this child's
name as Judas Bendigo," I tell you, young fellow, I was hor-
rified. Said I wouldn't do any such thing and he could damned
well put that curse on his own child himself. And he did. Bill
Bendigo had a cruel sense of humor, and he was cruelest when
he was mad. . . .

Don't know how he squared it with Ellen. She found out
pretty early in married life that there was only one boss in
Bill Bendigo's house. Of course, having a heart condition . . .
Often wondered what became of Bill's second boy. Imagine
naming a boy Judas! . . .

MILLICENT BROOKS CHALANSKI:

(69, aunt of Manager Brooks of the Hollis Hotel. Married Harry Chalanski of Low Village. Chalanski was
Polish immigrant boy whom M.B. tutored in English,
fell in love with, helped through State U. Their son is
young Judson Chalanski who succeeded Phil Hendrix as
Prosecutor of Wright County, when Hendrix went to
Congress. One of the happiest *mésalliances* in Wrightsville!)

No, I will *not* call him Judas. I taught that poor child on
and off for four years when Adelaide Peague and I alternated
with the lower grades in the old Ridge Road school, and I
could never see him without a tug at my heart. He was a frail
little boy with very beautiful eyes that looked straight through
you. One of the quietest children I've ever taught, the soul of
patience. His eyes were always sad, and I don't wonder. He
wanted to play with the other children, wanted it desperately,
but there's always one child the others pick on, and Judah
was that one. I was convinced it was because of his name.
The other children never let him forget it. You know how
mean young children can be. I could see him cringe every time
the hated name was flung at him in the play yard, cringe and
turn away. He never fought like the other boys. He would just
go very pale when he was taunted about being a "traitor"
and a "coward," go pale and then walk away. His brother
Cain, who was older, fought a lot of his battles, and it was
Cain who protected him from the parochial school boys when
they walked home from school.

. . . told his father what I thought of a man who'd give a
child a name like that, while his mother sat by wrapped in
lap rugs, not saying a word. Mr. Bendigo just laughed. "Judas
is his name," he said to me, "and Judas it's going to stay."
But I'd seen the look in Mrs. Bendigo's face, and that was all
I needed. The next day I took the boy aside during recess
and I said to him, "Would you like to have a new name?" His
pinched little face lit up like a Christmas tree. "Oh, yes!" he
cried. But then his face fell. "But my father wouldn't let me."

"Your father doesn't have to know anything about it," I said. "Anyway, we don't have to change it much, just one letter, so that if he does see the new name on a report or something, he'll think it's simply a mistake. From now on, dear, we'll just drop the *s* and put an *h* in its place, and you'll be *Judah* Bendigo. Do you know what 'Judah' means? It means someone who is praised. It's a fine name, and a famous one, too, from the Bible." The child was so overcome he was unable to speak. He looked at me with his big, sad eyes, then his lips began to tremble and before I knew it he was in my arms, sobbing. . . .

It didn't take the other children long. Just about one term. I called on him by his new name as frequently as I dared. By the next year they were all calling him Judah, even his brother Cain. I don't know how Mr. Bendigo took it, and I didn't care. He was going through a lot of business troubles at that time, his wife was sick—I suppose he was too busy to make an issue of it. . . .

DR. PIERCE MINIKIN:

Let's see, remarried in '98—the second boy was born in '99, which makes him two years younger than Cain Bendigo. The third boy was born five years after the second, which would be 1904. My Lord, Abel's forty-seven! . . .

Don't know, can't say, but I'll guess. My guess is the third one was an accident. I know I'd warned Bill about his wife's health, and taking it easy, but Bill being what he was . . .

No, I don't know why he named the third one Abel. Figured he'd keep his Biblical string running, I guess. I do remember he had no more interest in Abel than in the other two. Just had nothing to do with them. And Ellen was getting sicker, and after a while she developed a chronic whine, which was exactly what those three boys could have done without. The truth is the Bendigo boys grew up without any real love or affection, and whatever's happened to them is no surprise to me whatsoever, young fellow, *what*soever. . . .

MARTHA E. COOLYE:

(67, Principal of Wrightsville High School.)

I'm not really *that* ancient, Mr. Queen. I was very, very young when I taught Cain Bendigo in the upper grades. . . .

Student is hardly the word. I don't believe he stuck his nose into a book ever in his life. Certainly not while *I* taught him. I don't know how that boy got by. . . .

Cain's forte was violence. If there was a fight at recess, you could be sure Cain Bendigo was at the bottom of the heap. If a window was broken, you checked up on Cain first. If one of the girls came to you in tears exhibiting a braid which had been dipped in an inkwell, you knew in advance who had done the dipping. If you turned to the blackboard in class and jumped at a B-B shot on your backside, you looked for the peashooter in Cain's desk. . . .

He led the boys in everything. Except, of course, scholarship. He was ringleader of the worst boys in school. I was always having to haul him down to Mrs. Brindsley's office to be disciplined. . . .

Athletics? Well, of course, we didn't have organized athletics in the lower grade schools in those days the way we have them today. But there was one game Cain Bendigo excelled at while *I* was his teacher, and that was the game of hookey. . . . No, I didn't say hockey, Mr. Queen. He was the champion hookey player of the school! . . .

CHARLES G. EVINS:

(Director, Wrightsville Y.M.C.A.)

My father, George Evins, was truant officer for the town between 1900 and 1917. He never forgot Cain Bendigo. Used to call him "my best customer." He called the Bendigo boys "The Three Musketeers," which was funny, because Abel, the youngest, was only seven when Cain graduated from grade school. I remember myself how Cain would go off with Judah and Abel after school to fool around in the Marshes, and that was unusual for a boy in the eighth grade—he and I graduated

together. Usually we big boys kicked the little kids aside. Cain
was the first to do the kicking, except where his little brother
Abel was concerned. He fought a lot of bloody battles over
Judah and Abel. Way I've figured it out, it was Cain's way of
getting back at his father. He hated his father with a burning
hatred, and anything his father was against, he was for. Of
course, he led the younger boys around by the nose, but they
never minded. To Judah and Abel Cain was God, and whatever he said went. . . .

I've often wondered how Cain Bendigo turned out. I know
he's supposed to be a multimillionaire and all that, but I mean
as a man. Even as a boy he was a contradiction. . . .

WRIGHTSVILLE *Record*, July 20, 1911:

> (In 1911 the Wrightsville *Record* was published only
> once a week, on Thursdays.)

Wrightsville buzzed this week over a deed of heroism done
by a 14-year-old boy.

Cain Bendigo, eldest son of William M. Bendigo, well-
known High Village building contractor, risked his life last
Saturday to save his brother Abel, 7, from drowning while the
two boys and their other brother, Judah, 12, were on a tramp
through the woods in Twin Hills.

According to the young hero's account, they had gone to
the rocky pool at the foot of Granjon Falls, which is a favorite "swimming hole" of Wrightsville's younger element. The
7-year-old boy, who does not know how to swim, was sitting
at the edge of the pool watching his brothers when he somehow fell into the water, struck a jagged rock, and was borne
unconscious by the fast current toward the rapids at the foot
of the Falls. Cain, who was on shore, saw little Abel being
swept away to certain destruction. Showing rare presence of
mind for a lad of 14, Cain did not try to swim after Abel.
Instead he raced alongshore and plunged in to meet his
brother's body rushing towards him. In rough water and
fighting the strong current, Cain managed to struggle ashore

with the little boy and, exhausted as he himself was, he
worked over Abel until Abel regained consciousness.

Cain and Judah then carried Abel down Indian Trail to
Shingle Street, where the three boys were picked up by Ivor
Crosby, farmer, who was driving his team to Hill Valley. Mr.
Crosby raced the boys back to town. Medical treatment was
administered by Dr. Pierce Minikin of Minikin Rd., the
Bendigo family physician. Mr. Minikin said Cain did a fine
job of resuscitation. Abel was taken home shortly thereafter,
little the worse for his experience.

Cain Bendigo was graduated from Ridge Rd. Grade School
this June. . . .

SAMUEL R. LIVINGSTON:

(84, Wrightsville's elder statesman. Dean of the "Hill"
Livingstons and all his life a power in local politics. In
1911 he was in his 6th year as First Selectman.)

The medal was ordered from a Boston house and it was a
month getting here. We had the ceremony on the steps of the
Town Hall. Everybody came out for it—it was like Fourth of
July. They packed the Green solid and overflowed into the
Square. Course, I'd picked a Saturday for it, when everybody
was in town anyway, but the boy deserved it, he surely did. . . .

That Cain Bendigo, he stood up straight as a soldier when
I pinned the medal on him. The crowd called for a speech,
which I thought was pretty rough on a boy of fourteen, but
it didn't feaze him one bit. He said he thanked everybody in
Wrightsville for the medal, but he didn't feel he really deserved
it—anybody would have done the same. That made a real hit
with the townspeople, I'm here to tell you, and I said to myself then and there, "Sam Livingston, that boy is going places."
And he surely did! . . .

WRIGHTSVILLE *Record*, August 17, 1911:

. . . as follows: 24-jewel Waltham open-face watch with
black silk fob, presented with the compliments of Curtis
Manadnock, High Village Jeweler. A Kollege Klothes brand

suit with new style accessories presented with the compliments of Gowdy & Son Clothing Store, The Square. Wright & Ditson tennis racquet, with press, New York Department Store. Ten-volume set of *The Photographic History of the Civil War,* Semicentennial Memorial Edition, just published by The Review of Reviews Co., New York, presented with the compliments of Marcus Aikin Book Shop, Jezreel Lane. Good-natured hilarity greeted the announcement that Upham's Ice Cream Parlor on Washington St., High Village, would present the young hero with a full month's supply of Upham's Banana Splits Supreme at the rate of one per day. An Iver Johnson bicycle, presented with the compliments of . . .

(From the 1911 Files of Fyfield Gunnery School.)

C O P Y

FYFIELD GUNNERY SCHOOL

August 15, 1911

Mr. Cain Bendigo
Wrightsville

DEAR MR. BENDIGO:

It gives me the greatest pleasure to inform you that, for manifesting the high qualities of manly character which are prerequisite to matriculation in Fyfield Gunnery School, the Scholarship Board at a special meeting has voted to present you with a full four-year tuition scholarship, to take effect at the opening of the Fall Term next month.

If you will present yourself with your parent or guardian during Registration Week, September 8-15, with proof that you have duly completed your grade school requirements as prescribed by the laws of the State, arrangements for your immediate enrollment at Gunnery will be concluded.

With warmest good wishes, I remain,

Yours very truly,

(Signed) MELROSE F. ESTEY
Principal

MFE/DV

BEN DANZIG:

(54, prop. High Village Rental Library and Sundries.)

Cain Bendigo was certainly the big squeeze in Wrightsville
the rest of that summer before he went off to Gunnery. I remember the rush he got from the girls, and it made the rest of
us boys, who'd graduated from the Ridge school with him
and were going on to just Wrightsville High, kind of jealous.
But there was one kid in town who'd have got down on his
hands and knees and licked Cain's shoes if Cain had let him,
and that was his little brother Abel. I never saw such worship.
Why, that kid just followed Cain around all over like a
puppy. . . .

Judah? Well . . .

EMMELINE DUPRÉ:

(52, better known as the Town Crier. Teaches dancing
and dramatics to the youth of the Hill gentry.)

Where was Judah during the accident? Why didn't *he* help
save Abel's life? Those were the burning questions of the day,
Mr. Queen. There was one boy in our class—I was in Judah's
class, so I'm in a position to discuss this *intelligently*—this
boy, his name was Eddie Weevil, rather a nasty boy as I recall,
it wasn't long before he was being seen down in Polly Street
and that sort of thing, but he did say he'd seen it, and after all
even a chronic liar can tell the truth some time, don't you
agree, Mr. Queen? Well, Eddie was going around telling the
boys in the seventh grade—that was just after Cain went off
to Gunnery—that he'd been up around Granjon Falls that
day and just happened to witness the whole incident. Eddie
Weevil said Judah didn't do *anything*. Didn't even *try*. The
pure craven. Eddie said Judah was *closer* to Abel than Cain
and could have fished him out easily if he'd had half the
spunk of a ground hog, but that he ran away and cried like a
baby and let Cain do the whole thing all by himself. . . .

Well, yes, he *was* asked that, but Eddie said the reason he
didn't come forward with his story at the time was he didn't

want to get Judah Bendigo in trouble. Of course, I don't know, the Weevil boy may have made the whole thing up just to call attention to himself, but it *was* funny, don't you think, that Judah didn't have a word to say about his part in the rescue, and Cain didn't either? . . .

REVEREND ALAN BRINDSLEY:

(52, Rector, First Congregational Church on West Livesey St.)

I occupied the seat next to Judah Bendigo in the seventh grade. I think I was probably the only boy in the class Judah trusted. He never said much about himself, though, even to me. I do know that he suffered horribly during the first few months after the rescue incident. Somehow the rumor spread that he had funked the chance to save his little brother and had run away instead of helping, or something of the sort. Even if it had been true, it was unfair to condemn a twelve-year-old boy as a coward, as if physical bravery were the highest good. Not all of us have what it takes to be a hero, Mr. Queen, and I'm not sure it would be a good thing if we had. Judah was a highly intelligent, sensitive boy who'd been branded from birth with surely the wickedest name ever given a child, I mean his given name, which was Judas. . . .

It got to the point where it was too much for me to bear. Some of the boys began to call him "coward" to his face, rough him up in front of the girls, dare him to fight, challenge him to "swimming" races—you can imagine. Judah merely hung his head. He never replied. He never struck back. I used to beg him to come away, but he would stand there until they were through, and only then would he turn his back. I realize now what courage—what truly great courage —this must have taken. . . .

DR. PIERCE MINIKIN:

Judah as a boy was what the fancy fellows these days would call a masochist. He enjoyed punishment. . . .

REVEREND ALAN BRINDSLEY:

It subsided eventually. It took about six months, I'd say.
Then the whole thing was forgotten. By everyone, I'm sure,
but Judah. I'm sure he remembers that Golgotha to this day.
You say you've seen him recently. Does he brood? Is he
lonely still? What's happened to him? I always detected something Christlike in Judah. I was sure he would leave the world
a little better than he had found it. . . .

WRIGHTSVILLE *Record*, November 28, 1912:

BENDIGO'S 4 TOUCHDOWNS
CRUSH HIGH 27–0

WRIGHTSVILLE *Record*, June 12, 1913:

BENDIGO'S HOMER IN 9TH
BEATS SLOCUM 6–5

WRIGHTSVILLE *Record*, April 30, 1914:

GUNNERY TAKES TRACK–FIELD
MEET WITH 53 POINTS

———

Big Ben Breaks 3 Marks,
Scores 29 Points

WRIGHTSVILLE *Record*, February 11, 1915:

KANE BENDIGO KO'S JETHROE IN 4TH

———

Gunnery Star Takes State
Junior Light-Heavy Title

"DOC" DOWD:

(76, Director of Athletics at Fyfield Gunnery School
1905-1938; retired, now living in Bannock.)

Kane Bendigo was the finest all-round athlete produced by

Gunnery in the thirty-three years I directed the school's athletics. . . .

PRINCIPAL WHEELER (OF FYFIELD GUNNERY):

I'm sure my memory can't be that much off, Mr. Queen. . . . I'm astonished. Graduated forty-ninth in a class of sixty-three! I could have sworn the records would show he stood far, far higher than that. Of course, Gunnery's scholastic standards have always been extremely stringent. . . .

WRIGHTSVILLE *Record*, July 1, 1915:

SEN. HUNTER CONSIDERING WRIGHTSVILLE APPOINTEE TO U.S. MILITARY ACADEMY

If Kane Bendigo Named, Will Be First Wrightsville West Pointer Since Clarence T. Wright in '78

DR. PIERCE MINIKIN:

There was a lot of pressure put on Bob Hunter to name the boy, I remember. He wanted to, too—it would have been good politics, because Bob was always weak in Wright County. But in the end he had to say no. The boy's marks just wouldn't stand up. And, as Bob told me himself, he couldn't let Bendigo take the entrance examinations because if he failed that would be a nice big Senatorial black eye. So he gave it that year to a boy from up Latham way. . . .

Kane was furious, deathly mad. I was in the Bendigo house on a professional call to his stepmother when the news came. His face got black, I tell you. The only way he showed his disappointment in *action* was pretty mild, I thought, considering that look on his face. He kicked the cat through one of the stained-glass side windows of the vestibule. That cat never was the same again, haha! . . .

WRIGHTSVILLE *Record,* July 29, 1915:

KANE BENDIGO TO ATTEND
MERRIMAC U. THIS FALL

CHET ("IRON MAN") FOGG:

(By long-distance phone to his home in Leesburg, Va.
Fogg was football coach at Merrimac University from
1913 to 1942, when he retired.)

I never made any bones about it, and I don't today. Kane
Bendigo put Merrimac U. on the college athletic map. He was
real big-time, the kind of athlete a coach dreams about. He
was as good as Jim Thorpe any day. There wasn't anything
Kane couldn't do, and do better than anybody else. He ran
wild in the backfield the two seasons he played Varsity. He
played baseball like Frank Merriwell—or was it Dick?—
anyway, whichever one was Superman, that's the one he
played like. He made track records that still stand. He was a
natural-born boxer, and he slugged his way to the state college
heavyweight championship—and if he'd ever gone into his
senior year, my money would have been on him to take the
national. No college wrestler ever took a fall over him, though
that's one he used to say he owed to his old man—the only
thing, he'd say, he did owe "the old bastard." And if you'll
look it up, you'll find that in 1918 he was named by *Collier's*
magazine the most promising all-round college athlete in the
U.S., even though by that time he was in the Army. . . .

That's right. He left to enlist in the middle of his junior
year—around Christmas of 1917, I think it was. . . .

WRIGHTSVILLE *Record,* October 10, 1918:

KANF BENDIGO WINS NATION'S
HIGHEST MILITARY AWARD

———

Wrightsville Hero of Saint-Mihiel Gets
Congressional Medal of Honor

WRIGHTSVILLE *Record*, September 4, 1919:

WAR HERO FETED;
ANNOUNCES PLANS

———

Kane Bendigo, Wrightsville's Congressional Medal of Honor hero of the late conflict, was given a roaring welcome today when he returned to the city of his birth after being mustered out of the U.S. Army. . . .

After the reception, Mr. Bendigo granted an exclusive interview to the *Record*. Queried as to his postwar plans, Mr. Bendigo said: "I have had all sorts of offers to go back to college, and a dozen pro offers in various fields of athletics, but I am through with that stuff. I am going into business, where I can make some real money. I saw too many young fellows die in France to waste any part of my life on rah-rah stuff or working for somebody else. When my father was killed last year in that construction accident, he left a sizable estate. Most of it is in my stepmother's name, but she and my brothers have agreed to let me handle the money and I know just what to do with it. I am going into business for myself. I have something all lined up. . . ."

Excerpts from E.Q.'s Digest

Between January 1920 and November 1923 K. B. had four business failures. He went into the manufacture of sports equipment in Wrightsville and at the same time tried to run his father's contracting business. Result: Both went into bankruptcy. His next venture was to take over a factory that manufactured metal containers. He ran this into the ground in a little over a year, filing a petition in bankruptcy in January of 1922. He then negotiated a deal whereby he took over the Wrightsville Machine Shop in Low Village for the manufacture of light machinery. By November of 1923 this had flopped, too. His main trouble, as I was able to piece it together, seems to have been that he always bit off more than he could chew. He constantly made grandiose plans, over-extended himself, and fell flat on his face. What he did have, as evidenced by the record, was the ability to charm hard-boiled New England monied people into loosening up. . . .

Note historic parallel: About the time Kane Bendigo was broke and discredited, apparently a total failure, a man in Germany named Hitler was lying wounded in prison as the result of the collapse of his ambitious Beer Putsch march on Munich. Both were at the nadir of their careers. . . .

Abel had had a brilliant scholastic record, and at 17 (Sept. 1921) entered Harvard on a scholarship. He quit college at the end of his junior year (June 1924). Note that between November of 1923 and June of 1924, Kane was licking his commercial wounds. But he wasn't entirely idle, he was back at his old charm routine. He must have been, because coincidentally with Abel's leaving Harvard to join him in Wrights-ville, we find Kane starting a new enterprise with the financial backing of such a goulash as John F. Wright, Richard Glannis, Sr., the then-young Diedrich Van Horn, and old Mrs. Granjon. Kane took over an abandoned factory on the outskirts of town and went into the manufacture of shell-casings for the U.S. Navy. Abel went in with him. . . .

At this time Judah was in Paris studying music at the Conservatoire. . . .

Mrs. Bendigo, mother of Judah and Abel and stepmother of Kane, died in 1925. . . .

. . . prospered from the start. The small plant mushroomed into a large plant, the large plant became two large plants. The expansion was incredibly quick. Apparently Abel's native business brilliance exactly complemented Kane's charm, drive, and unbounded ambition. They went more and more deeply into the field of munitions. The further they expanded, the smaller dwindled the group which had financed them. One after another Kane bought out his original backers. At this time the company was known as The Bendigo Arms Company (it was in the early 30s that the company name was quietly changed to Bodigen), and Kane was apparently determined

to give himself exclusivity in fact as well as in title. There is
reason to believe that Kane did not gain total control without
a struggle, as the profits and dividends were beginning to be
considerable. Talked with old Judge Martin, Samuel R. Livingston, one of the Granjon sons, and with Wolfert Van Horn.
The Judge recalls John F. Wright's battle only vaguely, and
Livingston was mysterious. Van Horn cagey but transparent.
Convinced me that Kane brought lots of pressure to bear and
used methods the victims never talked about as a matter of
pride. Considering Wolfert Van Horn's own business reputation, this shows genius of the lowest order. . . .

By 1928 all the inside outsiders were outside looking in,
and the Bendigos owned all the shares in the parent company,
which now had six immense plants in operation. . . .

October 29, 1929, was the turning point. On the ruins of
the stock market Kane Bendigo built his fabulous fortune.
He had sold out all his holdings early in October, at the peak
highs, after buying everything in sight on dangerous margin
at the lows. The crash made him a multimillionaire. Just how
much he made cannot be determined; there is reason to believe his profits ran to the hundreds of millions of dollars.
This was the effective beginning of the Bendigo empire. Kane
was 32. Abel was 25!!!!! . . .

They began expanding immediately. Bought out a very
large munitions company. In rapid succession several smaller
ones. These plus what they already had became the nucleus
of the gigantic overall organization, of which The Bodigen
Arms Company today is only a part. . . .

In the summer of 1930 the Bendigos left Wrightsville. It
had become like a whale trying to maneuver in a pond. They
had to get to where they could move around. They built a
whole city in southern Illinois, an industrial city of 100,000
population. Their main offices were in New York. They
began to open branches in foreign countries. . . .

Some of the original Bendigo plants are still operating in
Wrightsville, although the ownership is so tangled up it would
take an army of experts to work its way through. . . .

There is no evidence that either Kane or Abel Bendigo has

set foot in Wrightsville since that day. Dr. Minikin, who recalls the old days with far greater clarity than the recent past, "thinks" Judah was back during the mid-30s for a few days, alone, but I have found no one who remembers having seen him, and a search of the register records of the Hollis, Upham House, and the Kelton for that period has not turned up his name. . . . William M. Bendigo's grave in the little Fidelity cemetery is untended, overgrown, and almost obliterated. Ellen Wentworth Bendigo is buried in the Wentworth family plot in the Wrightsville cemetery. . . .

June 22, 1930: Government of Bolivia overthrown.
Aug. 22–27, 1930: Peruvian government ditto.
Sept. 6, 1930: Argentine government ditto.
Oct. 24, 1930: Brazilian government ditto.

ITEM: Between January and June of 1930 all plants of The Bodigen Arms Co. (year name-change effected) worked on double shift. Sales almost exclusively South American.

NOTE: It is clear, in the light of this and certain other evidence, that Bendigo provided the explosive force which blew up four South American governments within five months. . . .

NOTE: Bendigo did not *cause* the revolutions. He merely made them possible. . . .

NOTE: Obviously, these were King Bendigo's practice sessions, trying out his muscles. Small stuff—in one of the insurrections there were a mere 3000 casualties. . . .

Jan. 2, 1931: Panama Republic overthrown.
Mar. 1, 1931: A second overthrow of the Peru government.
July 24, 1931: By-by existing régime of Chile.
Oct. 26, 1931: Ditto Paraguay.
Dec. 3, 1931: Ditto Salvador.

NOTE: Five more tests of power. What might be called the buildup of the body beautiful, with biceps and chest expanding rapidly. But this is mere gym work, with setups; he's about ready to step out into the big time. . . .

IN 1932 we find peaceful consolidation, improvement, and
further expansion. The organization is unwieldy. There is
weeding out of personnel all along the line. Companies are
merged, finances consolidated and redistributed, soft spots
strengthened, production streamlined, new industries absorbed.
The speed of K. B.'s empire building is stupendous; there is
only one precedent in modern times, and it stumbles by comparison. This is the kind of industrial story that could never
be invented in fiction. No one would believe it. . . .

June 4, 1932: Another revolution in Chile.

This was apparently the result of an error in calculation, or
overzealousness on the part of some Company supersalesman.
It was immediately remedied by . . .

Jan. 30, 1933: Adolf Hitler named Chancellor of Germany.

The global phase, to which the other was the merest pre-
liminary, begins here.

FINDING Capt. Mike Bellodgia has been a stroke of greatest
good luck. The famous round-the-world flyer was put under
contract by K. B. toward the end of 1932. He had one job—
to fly King Bendigo. He was King's personal chief pilot for
almost 13 years—until, in fact, a bit after the end of World
War II, when Bendigo was persuaded that Bellodgia was getting too old to be trusted with his precious passenger.

Bellodgia is still bitter about it, probably the real reason
why he allowed me to take a look at his diaries, although we
both pretended he believed my story that I was there in the
interests of posterity. I flew up to Maine, where he now lives,
and spent several days with him. He lives very handsomely, I
must say—Bendigo was generous with him to the point of
prodigality, and Bellodgia is financially secure for the remain-
der of his days. Bellodgia remarks dryly that he earned it; he
says that never once in 13 years of flying Bendigo all over
the world did he have to make a forced landing or develop
serious engine trouble.

Capt. Bellodgia's diaries are really not diaries at all but
personal logs. He doesn't seem to realize what he has, and I
have not enlightened him.

By juxtaposing Bellodgia's record of King Bendigo's flights,
destinations, dates, and lengths of stay with historical events, it
has been possible to place Bendigo pretty accurately in his
true perspective between Hitler's ascension to power in Germany and the end of World War II. . . .

*   *   *

IN 1933 the Reichstag voted absolute power to Hitler. The
following day a German newspaper which had been the most
powerful pro-Nazi propaganda organ was sold to a German.
It had been owned by Kane Bendigo for two years. The conclusion is evident: With Hitler's position secure, Bendigo no
longer needed the newspaper. . . .

On Oct. 14, 1933, Germany quit the League of Nations and
withdrew from the Disarmament Conference. On Oct. 12, 13,
and 14 of that year Bendigo was in Berlin, spending most of
his time at the Chancellery. He flew back to his New York
headquarters on the night of Oct. 14. . . .

On Apr. 27, 1934, an antiwar pact—previously agreed on
at the Pan-American Conference in Montevideo—was signed
in Buenos Aires by the U.S. and certain Central and South
American countries; Mexico and others had signed on Oct.
10, 1933. The record of Bendigo's air trips at this time is
illuminating; they tripled in number. The Bendigo munitions
works now spread to South America and Europe, were working around the clock. The Bodigen Arms Company, then, in
the midst of peace talks and pacts was playing the world
short. . . .

On June 15, 1934, the U.S. Senate ratified the Geneva Con-
vention for the supervision of international trade in arms, ammunition, and implements of war. Bendigo was not in Washington, D.C. at any time during June 1934. . . .

On Aug. 1, 1934, he flew back to Berlin. He remained there
for nearly 3 weeks, until Aug. 20. During those 3 weeks
President von Hindenburg died and the offices of President
and Chancellor were consolidated in the single office of Leader-

Chancellor. One of Der Fuehrer's first acts in his new official capacity was to decorate Herr Kane Bendigo in a strictly private ceremony. The next day Bendigo left Berlin. . . .

On Jan. 10, 1935, Italy resumed fighting in Ethiopia. Between 1934 and the middle of 1936 the Company made huge shipments to Italy. . . .

On Mar. 16, 1935, Hitler broke the Versailles Treaty, ordered conscription in Germany, and began expansion of the German Army. Only one month before, the Company had acquired four more giant plants in widely scattered locations. In Mar. 1935 these were running at full capacity. . . .

On June 5, 1936, Léon Blum, leader of the Socialist Party in France, formed the first Popular Front ministry. Within six weeks a far-reaching program of social reform was introduced, including (July 17) nationalization of the munitions industry. Bendigo was in and out of France frequently between the end of July 1936 and June 1937, when the Blum cabinet was forced to resign. Contiguity of additional Bendigo visits to France with significant dates—November, when the Cagoulards were frustrated in their revolutionary plot against the Republic; Mar. 1938, when the Chautemps government fell; Mar.–Apr. 1938, when Blum's second ministry failed, to give way to the cabinet of Édouard Daladier—indicates that Bendigo from the very beginning worked to defeat the Popular Front and its social and nationalization program. . . .

In 1937 the Japanese renewed fighting in China, Hitler repudiated German war guilt, Italy withdrew from the League, civil war raged even more violently in Spain. The Bodigen Arms Company in 1937 enjoyed its greatest year to that time. . . .

On Mar. 11, 1938, Hitler's troops crossed the Austrian frontier. Sept. 29–30, 1938—Munich. Mr. Kane Bendigo, the ordinarily tireless, was "forced" to desert the arduous cares of business for a "rest." He took a one-month vacation. The month: Sept. 1938. The place: A small hotel in Pfaffenhofen. Pfaffenhofen is some 50 kilometers from Munich. . . .

In Mar. 1939 the Spanish war ended. In a private ceremony

in Madrid, El Caudillo decorated Señor Kane Bendigo for un-
named reasons. . . .

Czech Bohemia and Moravia . . . Memel . . . Lithuania . . .
Albania . . .

Aug. 1939: Bendigo's connection with the events leading up
to the diplomatic revolution which shook the world, the Nazi-
Soviet non-aggression pact, remains obscure. Certain entries in
Bellodgia's diaries are strongly suggestive. That it was to
Bendigo's advantage to see the Soviet power temporarily neu-
tralized so that Hitler might feel free to invade Poland and
risk British and French declarations of war is childishly evident. K. B. had several sessions with Hitler and von Ribben-
trop in early August, and there is reason to believe that he
had a meeting with, or was present at a conference which was
attended by, Molotov. . . .

Sept. 1, 1939: Poland. On Sept. 3 Prime Minister Chamberlain announced in Parliament that a state of war existed between Great Britain and Germany: "Hitler can be stopped
only by force."

King Bendigo could have told Mr. Chamberlain that some
time before. . . .

THE picture is monotonous and unmistakable. It clearly shows
this man riding the rollers of history. It must be emphasized
again that Bendigo does not cause events; he insinuates himself into their midst and diverts them to his purposes.

It is of no interest to him whether a Hitler comes to power,
or a Stalin; he has done business with both. His dealings with
the Soviet have been far more obscure than those with the
Nazis, but only because there is virtually no data on them
available. That they have been considerable and far-reaching
is not to be doubted.

Bendigo is completely above loyalties or duties, isms or
ologies. Patriotism to him is a device, not an ideal. His politics
are fluid; they flow in every direction at once. . . .

A Few Further Excerpts from the Notes

In the bombing of Rennes in 1940, 4500 persons were

killed. Bancroft Wells, the philanthropist, heading a committee of distinguished people, formally asked Mr. Kane Bendigo
to act as honorary chairman of an international committee
dedicated to the future restoration of the historic cathedral.
Mr. Kane Bendigo accepted with an indignant speech de-
nouncing "the barbaric practices of the enemies of civilization. . . ."

On May 10, 1941, London suffered its worst air raid of the
war—1436 lives lost. King Bendigo left London in his private
plane on May 9. *Inevitable speculation: Did he have advance
information? . . .*

Dec. 7, 1941: Capt. Bellodgia records a rare item. For the
one and only time in his long association with King Bendigo,
Bellodgia was privileged to see the great man howling drunk.
"He kept beating his chest like Tarzan in the movies—it was
positively embarrassing. Also kind of out of place, I thought,
seeing that Pres. Roosevelt had only just announced the Jap
attack on Pearl Harbor. . . ."

I was curious to see—purely as a point of character—exactly
when and under what circumstances he met, wooed, and married Karla. The four-day period of their courtship in Paris
provided the clue, and Karla had intimated that it was just
after the war . . . I worked it out. They met in Paris on July
25, 1946, and they were married on July 29. On July 29,
1946, the first peace conference of World War II began—in
Paris.

Between busy seasons, as it were.

14

THE INSPECTOR embraced him without shame.

"I thought you were never coming back, son."

"Dad—"

"Wait till we get in the car. I purposely drove down to the field so we could have a few minutes alone." When they were in the little Residence car, he said, "Well?"

"First," said Ellery, "how is King?"

"Up and about, and as far as I can see he's good as new. Storm won't let him do more than a couple of hours' work a day, so he's taking mild exercise and spending a lot of time with Karla. What have you got?"

"The whole story."

His father scowled. "Isn't that ducky."

"You don't seem pleased!"

"Why should I be? Because you've got the whole story of what they did as kids in Wrightsville? How does that help us get off this damned reef?"

"The whole story," said Ellery, "of the attempted murder. What's behind it . . . and what, I think, is ahead of it."

And Ellery started the car.

"Wait!" cried his father.

"Do you know where King is now?"

"When I left, he and Karla and that Max were lying around the outdoor pool. But Ellery—"

"Then I'd better hurry."

"What are you going to *do?*"

"Look for something first. Something," muttered Ellery, "I don't expect to find."

ELLERY lingered outside the Residence long enough to ascertain that the royal couple was still basking on the bank of the outdoor pool. He did not go near the pool; he investigated from behind a bird-of-paradise bush in the gardens, and the Bendigos remained unaware of his presence. He could see Max'l's furred body and bullet head rolling around in the water. Karla was stretched out on a beach pad; her skin, usually so fair, was red-gold, as if she had been spending her days in the sun. King dozed in a deck chair. He was in light slacks, but he had removed his shirt and Ellery saw the puckered scar of the wound against his dark skin. The wound looked entirely healed.

They took the private elevator to the Bendigo apartments.

The captain of the guard saluted and then shook hands. "We heard you were expected back, sir. There's no one in just now but Mr. Judah."

"I'll want to see him in a few minutes. . . . I notice the seal on the Confidential Room, Captain, is broken."

"Yes, sir," said the officer uneasily.

"King himself broke the seal, Ellery. He was angry, and it was all we could do to convince him that these men weren't at fault but were just following orders. I had to give the boss man back his key."

Ellery shrugged and went directly to King's suite, his father following eagerly.

"This is it, I think."

They stepped into King Bendigo's wardrobe room.

"Shut the door, Dad." Ellery looked around.

The Inspector shut the door and leaned against it. "Now what?"

"Now, we take inventory," said Ellery. "You watch and make sure I don't overlook any closet, drawer, or shelf. This has to be thorough." He approached the first closet to the left of the entrance and slid back its door. "Suits . . . suits . . . and more suits. Morning, afternoon, evening, formal, informal, semiformal . . ."

"Am I supposed to take notes?" asked his father.

"Mental notes . . . And so forth. But all suits. Next." Ellery opened another closet, ran his hand along the racks. "Coats

Topcoats, overcoats, greatcoats, fur coats, storm coats, rain-coats—What's up here? Hat department. Fedoras, Homburgs, derbies, silk toppers, golf caps, hunting caps, yachting caps, et cetera, et cetera. . . ."

"What a man."

"Isn't he."

"I meant you," said his father.

"Ah, the shoe department. From patent leathers to hunting boots. Ever see anything like this outside a store? Dressing gowns . . . bathrobes . . . smoking jackets . . . *And* the sports division! Sports jackets, shooting jackets, slacks, ski outfits, yachting suits, riding clothes, gym clothes, wrestling tights, tennis whites—"

"Is there anything he's missed?" said the Inspector. "He couldn't wear half these things out if he lived to be as old as I feel right now."

"Shirts, hundreds of shirts, for every occasion. . . . Under-wear . . . pajamas—whew! . . . socks . . . collars . . . and look at these ties! . . . Handkerchiefs . . . sweaters . . . mufflers . . . gloves . . . everything in wholesale lots—"

"And I'm not getting any younger," muttered the Inspector.

"Belts, suspenders, garters, spats, cuff links, collar buttons, studs, tiepins, tie clasps, key chains . . . and wallets. Dad, will you look in this drawer? I wonder what this is made of. If this isn't elephant hide—"

"You missed that one," said his father.

"Which? Oh . . . Walking sticks. About a hundred, wouldn't you say, Dad? And if this isn't a sword-cane, I'll . . . There you are. Sword-cane, too."

"Umbrella rack."

"And the drawer under it . . . Rubbers. Overshoes. Hip boots—have I left anything out?" Ellery went over to the wall beside his father and pressed a button. "We'll make sure."

"I suppose," sighed his father, "you know what you're do-ing. Because I don't."

There was a precise knock behind his back. The Inspector opened the door. A thin man in black stood there.

"Yes, sir?" The voice sounded unused.

"Are you the King's valet?" asked Ellery.

"Yes, sir. I must ask you, sir—"

"Do the contents of this room represent Mr. Bendigo's entire wardrobe?"

"On Bendigo Island—yes, sir. Sir, this room is—"

"There's no other place in or out of the Residence where his personal garments are kept?"

"Not on the island, sir. A similar wardrobe room exists in each residence maintained by Mr. Bendigo. There is one in New York City, one in Bodigen, Illinois, one in Paris—"

"Thank you," said Ellery; and when the valet lingered, he said, "That's all." The valet backed away reluctantly.

"That was all I wanted to know," Ellery said as they made their way to Judah Bendigo's quarters.

"That King has the biggest personal wardrobe this side of the Milky Way, and that it's all in that room?"

"That he has the biggest personal wardrobe this side of the Milky Way," said Ellery, "with one very odd exception."

The Inspector stopped short. "You mean there's somebody has a *bigger* one?"

"I mean there's something missing."

"Missing! From *there?*"

"What I was looking for, Dad, is not in that room. Not one of them. But we'll make sure."

JUDAH was at his Bechstein playing a Bach prelude. There was an open bottle of Segonzac on the piano, and an empty glass.

Blue Shirt rose quietly from a chair and Brown Shirt turned from the window as the Queens came in. Judah paid no attention. Rather remarkably, he did not slouch at the piano. He sat well back on the bench, his back straight, his shallow chest out, head thrown back, hands playing from the wrists in beautiful, dancelike rhythms. His eyes were open and staring out across the strings at some vista visible only to himself. There was a frown on his forehead.

He came to the end of the prelude. With the last chord his

hands dropped, his back and chest collapsed, his head came forward, and he reached for the bottle of cognac.

"You should play Bach more often," said Ellery.

Judah turned, startled. Then he jumped up and hurried forward with every appearance of pleasure. "You're back," he exclaimed. "I've missed you. Maybe there's something you can do about these two barbarians—I've talked to your father about it, but he merely looked wise. Do you know what this one wants me to play? Offenbach!" Judah had the bottle and glass in his hands and he began to pour himself a drink. "Where have you been, Ellery? No one would tell me."

"Wrightsville."

Judah dropped the glass. The bottle remained in his hand, but only by a sort of instinct. He looked down at the rug, foolishly.

Blue Shirt began to pick up the pieces.

"Wrightsville." Judah laughed; it sounded more like the croak of a blackbird. "And how is dear old Wrightsville?"

"Judah, I want you to come with us."

"Wrightsville?"

"The outdoor pool."

Brown Shirt said from his window, "Mr. Judah is confined to his apartment, Mr. Queen."

"I'm unconfining him. I'll take the responsibility."

"We'll have to come with him, sir."

"No."

"Then I'm sorry, sir. We have our orders from the King himself. No one else can countermand them."

"He kind of surprised Abel, I think," murmured Inspector Queen. "He doesn't seem to want any more holes in his hide than he has already, in spite of what Abel told us."

Ellery went to Judah's desk. He said into the telephone, "This is Ellery Queen. Connect me with Abel Bendigo. Wherever he is, whatever he's doing."

The connection was made quickly. Ellery said, "No, from Judah's apartment, Mr. Bendigo. Where are you now?"

"At the Home Office." Abel sounded curious. "I was beginning to think you'd walked out on us."

"If I did, I'm back in again with both feet."

"Oh?"

"Mr. Bendigo, I want to take Judah from his quarters, without a guard. It's a private matter. I understand your brother King himself ordered Judah confined. Will you take these men off the hook?"

Abel was silent. Then he said, "Let me talk to one of them."

Ellery held out the phone to Brown Shirt. Brown Shirt said, "Yes, Mr. Abel?" After a moment, he said, "But Mr. Abel, the King himself—" and stopped. Then he said again, "But Mr. Abel—" and stopped again and said nothing at all for sixty seconds. At last he said, "Yes, sir," in a worried voice, and he handed the receiver back to Ellery. He nodded to Blue Shirt, who was frowning. The two plainclothesmen went quietly out.

"Thus spake Zarathustra," murmured Judah. "And now do we move toward Armageddon?" He put the mouth of the bottle to his lips and threw his head far back.

"One other thing, Mr. Bendigo," Ellery was saying into the phone, his eyes on Judah. "Please meet us at the outdoor pool immediately."

Again Abel was silent. Then his Yankee voice said, "I'll be right over."

KARLA was looking frightened again, and King black at the sight of his brother Judah. Max'l swooped through the water and was out of the pool like a seal.

Ellery stepped before Judah. "It's all right, Max," he said, smiling.

"Max." At his master's tone the almost naked beast came to heel. He kept glowering over Ellery's shoulder at the thin little man with the green bottle. "So you're back," King Bendigo said grimly. "You're an annoying customer, Queen. How did you persuade the guards to turn my brother over to you?"

"Abel gave the order at my request."

The big man sat very still in the deck chair. "Where is Abel?"

"He'll be here in a minute. . . . Here he comes now."

The slightly tubby figure of the Prime Minister appeared, hurrying through the gardens toward them. The group at the pool waited in silence. Karla had sat up. Now she reached for a robe and threw it about her, as if she were suddenly cold. Her red hair kept glittering in the sun nervously. Judah took another pull from his bottle.

"I got here fast as I could—" panted Abel.

"Abel, I don't understand." His brother's voice was arctic. "You knew my order. What has this fellow done, hypnotized you?"

Abel stooped over his brother's chair, saying something in an earnest whisper. But King's cold face did not soften. He kept looking at Ellery as he listened.

"I still don't understand, Abel."

Abel straightened. And a curious thing occurred. As he straightened he seemed to grow tall, and as he grew tall his bland bankerish face seemed to thin, until it looked almost gaunt. It was now as rigid as the face of his brother.

The brothers stared at each other for some time.

Suddenly King Bendigo sprang from his chair. He was trembling. "I'll clear this up later," he exclaimed. "Right now I want to know what *you're* up to, Queen. You went away, now you're back. What did you find out?"

"Everything."

"Everything about what?"

"About what matters, Mr. Bendigo."

"I'm not impressed. What about the bullet I stopped? That's what I'm interested in, Queen, and I want it without frills—in business English. If you can't tell me how the trick was done, pack your bag, take your father, and get the hell off my island. I'm sick of seeing your faces around here."

"I'll be happy to tell you about the murder attempt, Mr. Bendigo." Ellery walked over to the edge of the pool. He stood there, his right hand in his jacket pocket, looking down at the water. Karla was staring up at him; once she glanced at her husband. Abel was no longer looking at his brother; he watched Ellery closely.

Judah clutched his bottle and surveyed them all with unusual warmth.

The Inspector edged back. He felt a certain joy. He stopped very near Max.

Ellery turned to King, bringing his hand from his pocket as he did so. The little Walther nestled in his palm.

"This is the weapon, Mr. Bendigo," Ellery said, "which your brother Judah aimed at you through two walls. The problem is curious. I testify myself that when Judah raised the gun it contained no cartridges. When he squeezed the trigger, there was no shot. Still, the ballistics tests proved that the bullet Dr. Storm dug out of your chest had been fired from this gun and no other. Would you mind examining it, please?"

The big man had been listening stonily, but with attention. Now he strode to the edge of the pool and put out his hand for the automatic.

Ellery's right hand moved to meet it. King Bendigo stepped closer, and with a sweep of the left arm Ellery struck him a heavy blow at the side of the neck and toppled him over the edge into the pool. The King landed with a cry that was smothered in a great splash.

Ellery immediately wheeled. The Walther in his hand was now gripped at the stock and his finger was curled about the trigger.

"You're not to help him," he said. "I loaded this gun fifteen minutes ago."

Behind Max, the Inspector said, "One move and I blow a hole clear through to your gut."

Max stood still. His brutal face was convulsed.

Abel was making stiff little gestures toward the pool. Judah kept looking at Ellery. And Karla swayed on her knees, reaching.

"Mrs. Bendigo, I must ask you," said Ellery, looking at the men, "to get away from the edge."

"Son." The Inspector sounded urgent.

"Cover them, Dad."

His father stepped back; there was a Police Positive in his hand.

Ellery turned to the pool again. Bendigo was flailing the water with his arms, bellowing and strangling. He went under, immediately reappeared, and immediately began to sink again.

Ellery flung himself on the pool's edge and reached far out. He caught the sinking man's hair, but somehow his quarry got away. He grabbed at a clutching hand. This time he held on, and a moment later he had pulled the big man out of the pool onto the shore.

King lay on his stomach, gagging.

Ellery stood over him. The Walther dangled. He made no attempt to touch Bendigo again.

After a while the big man pushed himself to an all-fours position. He was breathing awkwardly. He struggled to his feet, turned around.

He was unrecognizable. The hair that had given way in Ellery's hand was floating in the pool; all that was left on the magnate's head was a dank black fringe. And something had happened to his face. The vigorous cheeks had become hollow, and the strong mouth had changed its shape and outline. Little wrinkles radiated from their corners. The flesh of his neck was suddenly pouchy.

But the change was more than a matter of a lost toupee and dentures. Something far more vital had gone out of him. The black fires in his eyes had been quenched; the proud confidence that had kept his belly in and his shoulders square had been soaked and rotted out of him. Now he was a sagging and drooping as well as a bald and lined old man.

A beaten and a broken old man.

He did not look at them. His wife made an involuntary movement toward him, full of pity, but then she checked herself.

He stumbled off the camouflaged apron of the pool and made his way through them in a ploddy shuffle, difficult to watch. His long arms bobbed and swayed with his shambling progress, mere appendages. He left a thin trail of water which under the hot sun began at once to dry.

They watched him move through the gardens to the rear entrance of the Residence. He did not once look up or back.

Finally he disappeared.

Max'l cried out and plunged away and through the garden, trampling flowers and making frantic gestures to the Residence.

Karla got to her feet. She seemed strangely calm. And she went to Abel Bendigo and stood close by him.

And Judah Bendigo went to both of them.

After a moment, as if one of them had spoken, the three turned and went side by side at a good pace around the garden and one of the five arms of the Residence and so out of the Queens' sight.

"WILL you tell me," said Inspector Queen, "will you tell me what *any* of this means?"

Ellery was eying the toupee, floating like a black crab in the pool. "You know, Dad, I had no idea he wore a toupee. Or false teeth. He looked a thousand years old."

The Inspector hefted his Police Positive. "If you don't open up," he said, "so help me Hannah—"

Ellery laughed. "Not here," he said. "Suppose I take you for a ride."

15

THEY WALKED through the great hall of the Residence to the courtyard. There was a disturbing clatter and buzz all about. It seemed to come from everywhere. Servants and minor flunkies bustled about, doors banged, guards ran here and there. Outside, where they had left the Residence car, there was a traffic jam. An armed PRPD man was trying to untangle it; he was shouting for help. Finally the tangle was unsnarled and vehicles began to move through the gates. There were a great many trucks. On the road outside other trucks and cars struggled toward the Residence, bumper to bumper.

The Inspector stuck his head out of the car window. "Look at the sky!"

It was alive with aircraft. They were all big ones—transports, trimotored passenger planes. Curiously, as many seemed to be coming in as taking off. The island shook under their thunder.

"What's happening!"

"Maybe the King has declared himself a war," said Ellery, inching the car forward. "This has all the earmarks of a mobilization which has been thoroughly worked out in advance, with everything ready to roll at the touch of a button."

"The way he's feeling right now, he couldn't declare a dividend. Turn off this road if you want to get somewhere. This is worse than the Merritt Parkway on Labor Day."

Just past the belt of woods surrounding the Residence, Ellery found a side lane, scarcely wider than a bridle path, which was free of traffic. He swung into it. A truck driver shouted enviously after him.

"I think this comes out near the cliffs somewhere," said the Inspector. "Near the harbor."

"Sounds like just the place for a quiet talk."

A few minutes later they were parked on the edge of the cliffs. The harbor lay below them.

The sight confounded them. The bay was clogged with ships of all lengths and tonnages. The cruiser *Bendigo* had withdrawn from the neck of the bay; it was anchored some distance at sea, near a light cruiser which the Queens had not seen before. Launches darted and skipped about loaded with passengers. The turrets of several big submarines were surfacing. The docks were piled high with crated goods; they were being loaded at a furious tempo into the holds. The roads leading down from the interior of the island looked like ant trails. And from the entire harbor area rose a confused roar that increased in volume with each moment.

"Whatever they're doing," said the Inspector wonderingly, "they sure had everything ready. What's come over this place? Did you have anything to do with this?"

"No," said Ellery slowly. "No, I don't see how I could have." He shook his head. "Well, do you want to see what I brought back from Wrightsville?"

"Brought back?"

Ellery reached over to the back seat of the car. He opened the suitcase he had carried off the plane that morning. A bulky Manila envelope lay on his haberdashery. He took this and sat back.

"This is what I was doing in Wrightsville," he said, unclasping the envelope. "You'd better read it. To the end."

It was a thick manuscript, and the Inspector took it with a glance at the harbor. But he read slowly, without looking up.

While his father read, Ellery watched the harbor. A fleet of seaplanes had landed in the bay to add to the mess. They were taking on passengers. Before the Inspector had finished they took off, making their runs along a narrow channel cleared by a squad of fast launches, evidently of the harbor traffic police.

When the Inspector had put down the last page, he stared incredulously at the frantic activity below them. "I hadn't realized the extent of his power. . . . I suppose," he said suddenly, "this is all on the level?"

"Every word of it, Dad."

"It's hard for a schmo like me to believe. It's too . . . colossal. But, son." The Inspector eyed the manuscript Ellery was stuffing back into the envelope. "You said—"

"I know what I said," Ellery interrupted fiercely. He tossed the envelope behind him. "And I say it again. What's been happening on this island in purgatory is all in that envelope. Not the details, not the little techniques of circumstance and plot! But the backgrounds, the reasons."

Ellery took Judah's little Walther out of his pocket. He pointed it absently through the windshield at the heavy cruiser. And pulled the trigger. The Inspector ducked. But nothing happened. The gun was empty after all.

"Take the problem of Judah's miracle," Ellery said. "It was really no problem at all. What made it a problem was not its impossibility, but the positions of the people involved in it.

Those were the impossibilities—until you knew the story that began in 1897, the story that exposed the people for what they were and are . . . the story that's in the envelope. Then the people were no longer impossibilities and the human problem —the big problem—was solved."

The Inspector said nothing. He did not understand, but he knew that soon he would. It had happened a hundred times before, in just this way. Still, for the hundredth time, he wondered.

"The physical aspects of Judah's miracle first," Ellery said, toying with the Walther. "It was such a very simple miracle. A man points an empty gun at a solid wall, and two rooms away, across a corridor filled with men, with another and even thicker wall intervening, another man slumps back with a bullet in his breast.

"An empty gun can't shoot a bullet. But even if it could, no bullet could have entered the other room from outside. So Judah didn't shoot King. No one shot King—" the Inspector started—"from *outside* the Confidential Room. It was materially impossible. But King *was* shot while in that room. I'd seen him, with my own eyes, unwounded, only three and a half minutes before the shot. So had you. We'd seen him close that door, automatically causing it to lock, and you yourself swore that the door was not opened again until we went in together after midnight. And that was the only way in or out of the room. Conclusion: King was shot from inside the room. He must have been. There's no other possibility."

"Except," remarked his father, "that that was impossible, too."

"There's no other possibility," repeated Ellery. "Therefore the appearance of impossibility is an illusion. He was shot from *inside* the room. That being the fact, only one person could have shot him. There were only two persons in that room, and there is no possibility from the circumstances that there could have been more than two, less than two, or two different ones. The two persons who entered that room, who remained in that room, and whom we found in that room were King and Karla. King could not possibly have shot himself;

there were no powder marks on his shirt. Therefore Karla shot him."

The Inspector said, "But Karla had no gun."

"Another illusion. Why did we assume that Karla had no gun? Because we couldn't find one. But Karla did shoot him. Therefore our search was at fault. Karla *must* have had a gun, and since it couldn't possibly have left the room by the time we entered it to find King unconscious from his wound, then it was still in the room when we entered."

"And the door was immediately shut," retorted his father, "and no one was allowed to leave while we searched, and we searched everything and everyone there, and before anyone was passed out through the door we made another body-search, and before anything was passed out through the door we searched it, too, and still we didn't find the gun. Now that's really an impossibility, Ellery. That's what hung me up. If the gun had to be in that room, why didn't we find it?"

"Because we didn't look in the place where it was hidden."

"We looked in *every*thing!"

"We couldn't have. We must have neglected one thing."

The Inspector mumbled, "Whatever it was . . . Too bad King broke the seal you put on the door. By this time it's been removed from the room."

"It was removed from the room before I sealed the door."

"Now that," cried his father, "*is* impossible! Not a thing was taken out—before you sealed the lock—that we didn't search!"

"I'd have sworn, too, that we searched everything that passed out before we locked and sealed the room. But later I remembered that there was one thing we let go through that we clearly, definitely did not search."

"We searched every human being that passed through that doorway," said the Inspector angrily, "including the wounded man himself. We searched the hospital table he went out on. We searched Dr. Storm's medical kit and every last article of equipment he'd brought in. Do you admit that?"

"Yes."

"Then what are you talking about?" The Inspector waved his arms. "Nothing else went out!"

"One other thing went out. And that thing we didn't search. Therefore it was in that thing that the gun left the room."

"*What* thing!"

"The bottle of Segonzac cognac Judah took out of the filing case while we were all in the room after the shooting."

INSPECTOR QUEEN was dazed. "The gun went out hidden *in a bottle of cognac? A gun? In a bottle?* Are you out of your ever-loving mind? I suppose he just eased it down through the neck of the bottle—trigger guard, stock, and all! What's the matter with you? Besides, that was a brand-new bottle. You yourself sliced off the government tax label and the wax seal and removed the cork with a corkscrew!"

"So I did," said Ellery. "And that's what bamboozled me, as it was planned to do. But you can wriggle from yesterday to doomsday, and the fact stands: There must have been a gun in that room, the gun must have left the room, the only thing that left the room without being searched was Judah's bottle of cognac, therefore it was in Judah's bottle of cognac that the gun left. If we accept that fact, as we must—"

"Accept it!" muttered his father. "How can I accept an impossibility? You weaseled out of two impossibilities only to get yourself . . . bottled up, God help us, in a third!"

"If you accept the fact, then the bottle as a carrier can't be impossible, it must be possible. How can a bottle conceal a gun? Well, let's have a look at a Segonzac bottle." Ellery reached over again to his suitcase and brought out one of the familiar bottles. "I took this sample along on the trip to keep reminding me of my fatheadedness. Since the Segonzac bottles are uniform in shape and size, this one will serve as a model for the one Judah had stashed away in the Confidential Room.

"True, it has a conventional neck—in fact, the neck is on the slender side. So the gun couldn't have been inserted through the mouth and neck, as you so reasonably pointed out. *But it has a broad base—the Segonzac bottles are bell-shaped.* And this Walther .25 that fired the shot—according to the ballistics tests—is how big? It isn't big at all. On the contrary, it's absurdly small. The barrel is only an inch long. *The total length of the gun is scarcely four inches.* Add to the bottle's broad bottom and the tiny size of the weapon the felicitous fact that the Segonzac bottles are also a very dark green in color—*so dark as to be opaque*—and the impossibility melts away, leaving a simple answer."

Ellery tossed the bottle aside. "The bottle Judah took out of the filing case in the Confidential Room that night was specially made, Dad. It had a false bottom. The false bottom must have been lined with cotton, or felt, or some other sound-deadening material. The false bottom in a bottle of opaque glass would easily conceal the Walther from our eyes, and the lining of the compartment would prevent any clink, as the bottle was held or moved, from betraying its contents to our ears. All this in a bottle with a faked government tax stamp, professionally corked and sealed, and the illusion was set."

The Inspector said, "She shot him—he got the bottle out of the drawer. . . . Karla and Judah were in this together!"

Ellery nodded, his eyes on the frenzied harbor scene below. "Each had a part to play, worked out in advance. Judah wrote and sent the threatening letters and with considerable histrionic talent staged and played the scene in which he solemnly aimed and fired an empty gun . . . a gun whose existence and whereabouts he was careful to point out to me beforehand. And in the Confidential Room, where the shooting was to take place, Karla pulled the trigger of the actual murder gun—and in her nervousness bungled the job—hid the gun in the false bottom of the prepared bottle, put the bottle back in the filing case, and then 'fainted.' They were accomplices, all right—"

"Just a minute," said his father. "King was shot with Judah's gun—the gun you took off Judah's desk after the shooting—the gun you're holding right now. That's a fact proved by ballistics tests. But this gun was in Judah's study! How could Karla have shot King with a gun that wasn't in the Confidential Room at any time?"

"Go back to the actual shooting of King," replied Ellery.

"Karla has fired the shot at her preoccupied husband, who is wounded and unconscious before he can see who shot him. Karla then hides the murder gun in the false bottom of the bottle. After we all enter the room, Judah removes the bottle from the drawer, allows me to open it for him—daring touch, that—drinks from it—and subsequently the bottle is taken *out* of the room under our eyes.

"Remember, you and I stayed behind, after the others left, to make a last search for the gun which was no longer there. This gave the person who'd taken it out of the room in the bottle the opportunity to cross the corridor, enter Judah's study, shut the door, take the murder gun out of the false bottom of the bottle, remove any remaining cartridges from the gun . . . and then place *that* gun, the one which had shot King in the other room, on Judah's desk for us to find later! The gun which I had seen Judah pretend to fire at midnight—the always-empty gun—was then taken away. By the time you and I searched the Confidential Room for the last time, locked and sealed the door, and went to Judah's study, the switch had long since been made. The gun I picked up from Judah's desk was no longer the one I had seen Judah pretend to fire in that hocus-pocus at midnight—*it was now the gun Karla had fired at King in the other room.*"

"Identical guns . . ."

"In outer appearance only. It was easy enough to get hold of a pair of guns of the same make, type, and caliber, and deliberately to chip similar slivers of ivory out of the inlays of both stocks. But they couldn't fool ballistics so far as the interior mechanisms of the two guns were concerned, and they knew we'd make the lab tests. That's why there had to be two guns that looked alike: so that a switch could be made after the shooting, putting the murder gun where the dummy gun had been and thereby completing the illusion of a single gun and consequently an impossible crime."

"But why?" cried the Inspector. "Why did they want it to look like an impossible crime?"

"Because an impossible crime, a crime that 'couldn't' have happened, even though a man was shot in the impossible proc-

ess," said Ellery dryly, "would protect the criminals from de-
tection, or at least from prosecution. If the gun we found outside the room was demonstrably the gun that had been fired
at King *inside* the room—when the gun that had been fired
inside the room couldn't possibly have got out!—then neither
Judah outside nor Karla inside could be tagged for the job.
You could suspect and theorize, but unless you could demon-
strate how it was done, they were safe."

Ellery was tapping the wheel with the little gun, frowning at
the activity below them. "I wonder," he began, "if King *is*
mobilizing—"

But his father was not listening. "Karla put the gun in the
bottle, Judah took the bottle out of the drawer. . . . I don't
seem to recall *Judah's* taking that bottle out of the room. Or
Karla, either. It was—"

He glanced at Ellery in bewilderment.

"It was Abel," said Ellery absently. "Abel, who went out of
character to lose his temper, grab Judah by the collar, make
a hammy, emotional speech . . . snatch the bottle of Segonzac
out of Judah's hand, *and leave the room with it.* So it was
Abel who crossed the corridor and switched the guns in
Judah's study. Yes, Abel was in the plot, too, Dad. And now
you see why Abel brought us here and has kept us here on
what seemed a trivial assignment. Our function was purely
and simply to witness the 'impossible' crime—as representa-
tives of the world outside—so that we could testify later to
the facts which seem to clear Judah and Karla."

16

INSPECTOR QUEEN was silent.

"They were all in it," said Ellery, still frowning at the harbor. "Judah, Karla, Abel. The wife and both brothers. Con-

spiring to kill the great King—an assassination in the approved historical tradition. Abel, the leader, the other two acting under his orders."

"Yes," said the Inspector, "it would have to be Abel who led them. Judah's a feeler, and Karla wouldn't be able to conceive such a plan. But Abel's a thinker."

Ellery nodded. "And a brilliant one. A man who's always been run by his head. Who's run his brother King."

"What?" said his father.

"We had proof of that the first hour we were on the island, Dad, if we'd only had the sense to see it. Abel parked us in the reception room while he went into King's office. We overheard what went on in there. . . . Mr. Minister of War of the South American accent got King roaring mad; he almost wrecked a delicate deal. And then King stopped roaring to say, 'Yes, Abel. What is it?' and Abel either whispered to him or passed him a note. Immediately King Bendigo became a very smooth article. He handled Mr. Minister of War exactly right, and Mr. Minister of War walked out with two yachts in his pocket and the Guerrerra works belonging to Bodigen Arms was safe.

"And a few minutes later King ran into trouble again, with the very smooth Monsieur the Minister of Defense. Monsieur the Minister of Defense is a stone; he demands to be flown back. 'What, Abel?' says King, and after a whispered confabulation with Abel, King again pulls off a successful deal and another arms contract is saved for the Company. When Abel is silent, King blusters and blunders. When Abel whispers, King becomes the negotiator supreme."

Ellery stared at the seething bay. "Think back to my notes, Dad. Between 1919 and 1924 Kane Bendigo—flying solo, as it were—cracks up three times. And that's not counting his father's old, established business, which Kane's run into the ground in record time. Then, backed by a Wrightsville group hypnotized by his personality, he starts his first munitions plant and suddenly he's off to the races. Did he start that business alone? Oh, no. Abel has left college to join him—Abel, at the age of twenty! And King's ridden high, wide, and handsome ever since, and Abel's never left his side.

"King knows what he wants. He's always known that. But while he can set the goals, he can't plan and execute the moves needed to reach them. It's Abel who's done the practical work, who's performed industrial miracles behind the plausible, glittering façade of King. Without Abel, King would have been a man with grandiose ideas who couldn't have run a successful newsstand. With Abel, he's become the most powerful man in the world."

The Inspector was shaking his head. "And still it doesn't make sense to me, Ellery. I can see how Karla and Judah would turn on King. Karla's a decent sort, for all her background. She found out the truth about the man she married, what a power-mad lunatic he is—maybe found out a lot about his plans we don't know. Judah's a disappointed artist, a man with a deep feeling about people, and he considers his brother the biggest mass-murderer in history—isn't that what he said? And both Judah and Karla stuck on this nightmare of an island, stewing in the fumes from those damned munitions and atomic plants . . .

"I see those two fine. But Abel's been an active partner in this thing for twenty-seven years, Ellery! You say yourself he's the one who's made it possible. You might say he plotted King's death because of personal ambition. But I don't see that. A man like Abel always prefers the background. He gets a kick out of pulling the wires and hiding in the shadow of his front man.

"And those notes of yours. . . . You can't doubt, from reading them, that Abel's worshiped his brother Kane ever since they were boys in Wrightsville. Ever since Kane saved his life in that swimming hole when Abel was seven years old." The Inspector shook his head again. "It doesn't go down, Ellery. It doesn't wash."

"It goes down, and it washes," said Ellery. "Just because of that life-saving incident."

"How do you mean?" His father stared.

"Remember the day in the gym, when King found Judah's

fourth letter in one of his boxing gloves and got so irritated he slipped on the tiles at the edge of the indoor pool and fell in?"

"Yes?"

"Didn't that strike you as awfully queer, Dad? His sinking, floundering, spluttering? His having to be pulled out of the water? The incident stuck in my mind. It bothered me.

"Then in Wrightsville," said Ellery, "I learned the details of his athletic prowess as a youth. He was an all-round athlete, participated in almost every sport. Football. Baseball. Boxing. Wrestling. Track. Field. But never once did I run across his name in connection with swimming."

"But—" his father began in perplexity.

"Today I took inventory of his wardrobe. There are dozens, scores of every conceivable article of male apparel. Except one, which should have been there—judging from the quantities of everything else—by the dozen or the score, too. *Yet there was not a single pair of swimming trunks, not a single bathing suit or swimming accessory.*"

"That's why you knocked him into the pool!"

"As a last check," Ellery nodded. "And he almost drowned. He would have drowned if I hadn't pulled him out. That's what's behind Abel's motive, Dad: *King can't swim.*"

"But . . . that silver cup awarded to 'Kane Bendigo' for water polo! Did you ever try playing water polo without knowing how to swim? He *must* be able to swim!"

"The 'Kane Bendigo' was re-engraved. Karla even explained that his original name was C-a-i-n and that he had changed it to K-a-n-e, and since he'd won the water polo trophy under his original name, he'd had the cup changed to read K-a-n-e later. She specifically told us that *he* had told her that. . . . Dad, we've seen the proof twice since we got to Bendigo Island that the man doesn't know how to swim. So he lied to his wife about the reason for the re-engraving on that trophy. It couldn't have been his. It had been awarded to someone else, and he'd had the name re-engraved not from Cain to Kane, but from someone else's name to Kane!

"This man with the false hair and the false teeth and the false front has been living another lie. For forty years. Because if King can't swim now, he couldn't swim in 1911. *Once he's learned, no one ever forgets how to swim.*

"Then it wasn't King who jumped into that mountain stream and saved seven-year-old Abel from drowning that day in the hills above Wrightsville. Who could it have been? Only the three brothers were involved, and Abel was the victim. So it could only have been Judah who rescued Abel. We know Judah can swim—we saw him do it in the indoor pool the day King accidentally fell in."

"Judah saved Abel's life," said the Inspector softly, *"and King took the credit."*

Ellery nodded over the flame of a match. He puffed and tossed the match out his window. "There's the explanation in a phrase. The record shows that, even as a boy of fourteen, Kane had a domineering, unscrupulous character. Because Judah was a timid, sensitive boy, younger and physically weaker, and could be bullied into keeping his mouth shut, Kane deliberately stole the credit for Abel's rescue from Judah. Accepted a medal for it—even made an amazing little speech about it, you'll recall, saying modestly that he didn't really 'deserve' the medal, 'anybody' would have done the same! And Kane—as King—has taken the credit, stolen the spotlight, been the big shot ever since. In everything. That single incident, way back in 1911 in what was then one-horse Wrightsville, illuminates each of the three Bendigo brothers.

"Take King. Deep inside, he's afraid. He must have been, he must still be, deathly afraid of the water—a boy who excelled in so many different sports and yet didn't participate in one of the commonest sports of all, swimming, must have had a powerful psychological reason for not learning. . . . He knows the truth about himself. He knows he's no hero, that in reality he's an inferior human being. But once that incident occurred, once he publicly proclaimed himself a hero as a swimmer— and probably his fear of water was what prompted him to do it—then he shaped his whole future development. He had to repress that sickening truth, in himself as well as to the world, and in order to do so he developed an enormously aggressive personality. Eventually his aggressiveness turned into grandiose channels, and with Abel's implementation of his megalomaniac goals he's become the incredible power he is today."

"And Abel," muttered the Inspector, "Abel's been paying back his debt of gratitude."

"Exactly. Abel was unconscious when he was pulled out; he didn't see who rescued him. He was a young child, and of course he believed the story his big brother-hero told. So Abel has come through these past forty years believing he owes his life to King. And so devoting his life to his savior."

"And Judah," said Ellery, "Judah was cuffed and cowed into keeping his mouth shut—Judah, who had reached the age of twelve scarred by the weight of his Judas cross and the cruelty of his schoolmates, not to mention that of his father. Judah couldn't fight his husky big brother. Judah didn't dare tell the truth. Judah could only watch the credit that belonged to him showered on the unscrupulous bully who had stolen it. There could be only one place for Judah to go, and that was still further into his shell. To complicate matters—the evidence is in these notes—Judah's always been something of a masochist. Deep down he enjoyed his martyr's role. . . .

"There could be only one port for a man like that—and that's where Judah has landed. At the business end of a bottle. He drinks for the reason most alcoholics drink. It's a way of enduring his unhappiness."

"I wonder how Abel found out . . ."

"The wonder isn't so much that he found out as that it's taken him so long. It seems incredible that Abel could have lived and worked by King's side for so many years and remained ignorant of such a simple fact as his brother's not knowing how to swim. But it's not as incredible as it seems. Abel's had a blind spot on the subject. From the age of seven he's *known*—impressed into his brain by a traumatic experience of great force—that King could swim. And King threw up a clever smoke screen. What did Karla tell us? That except for a bit of wrestling and boxing with Max, *King never takes any exercise.* They've led unbelievably crowded lives, and Abel himself is hardly the sports-loving type."

"Then Abel found out—"

"Or Judah, more than usually drunk, told him," nodded Ellery. "Then all Abel would have to do was manufacture a test, as I did today . . . and everything would curdle in Abel. Instantly. To worship your brother for forty years, to dedicate your life to him, and suddenly to find that you've been worshiping a fraud—worse, a cheat. . . . It would be a devastating experience. If Abel's worship of King had blinded him to King's faults, this knowledge would clear his eyes in a flash.

"So Abel drew up a new set of plans. The first plans of which his brother King had no knowledge."

Ellery fell silent, and for some time they sat without speaking, continuing to watch what was going on below them. The launches streaked back and forth, the ships loaded, the cars and trucks continued to stream down from the cliffs, vessels plunged out to sea, planes landed empty and took off full. . . .

"What the devil *is* he up to?" Ellery said at last. "Dad, this looks like a wholesale evacuation of the island."

"I wonder where he is. . . ."

"Who?"

"His Majesty. Do you suppose he's alone?"

"Why?"

"If he is," said the Inspector, "he's not exactly safe."

"He's safe," said Ellery gloomily. "You saw Max go after him. He hasn't let King out of his sight since the night of the attempt. They'd have to kill Max first."

"Well?" said the Inspector.

Ellery stared at him. Then he snapped on the ignition and kicked the starter.

17

THE GUARDS were gone from the foyer of the family's apartments.

The corridors were deserted.

"They're probably at the Home Office," said the Inspector.

"No," said Ellery, "no. If anything's happened, it took place here!"

They pushed open the door and went in. There were no flunkies about. Everything was in disorder.

"Max?" roared the Inspector.

Ellery was already racing toward King Bendigo's private suite. When the Inspector caught up with him he was at the doorway to a great bedchamber, looking in.

"Isn't Max—" began the Inspector.

Then he stopped.

King Bendigo was lying neatly on his bed, his head on the bolster and his open eyes staring up at the canopy.

There was no sign of Max.

The master of Bendigo Island was dressed as they had last seen him, with still-damp slacks and soaked sports shoes, his torso naked. Three trails of blood snaked diagonally down the right side of his face. They led from a hole in his right temple. The hole looked burned; around it the flesh was tattooed with powder.

A revolver with a nickel finish was gripped in the right hand, which lay on the bed parallel with the body.

King's forefinger was still on the trigger.

"S & W .22/32 kit gun," said the Inspector, turning it over in his hands. "One shot fired. Suicide, all right—"

"You think so?" muttered Ellery.

"—if you're blind. Look at the angle of the wound, from point of entry to point of exit, Ellery. The course of the bullet was sharply downward. If King had committed suicide, he'd have had to hold the gun *pointing* sharply downward—which means from above his head. To pull the trigger from such a position and make such a wound, he'd have had to hook his right *thumb* around it. With the forefinger it's a physical impossibility."

Ellery nodded, but not as if he had been listening. "So after everything that's happened—all the planning, all the eyewash—something's gone wrong again," he murmured. "In Abel's hurry he forgot to take into account the angle of the shot. I wonder how he got Max."

"Let's go ask him," said the Inspector.

THEY found Abel in King Bendigo's office. Abel, and Judah, and Karla, still together.

Colonel Spring was there, too. The Colonel was in mufti. Stripped of his beautiful uniform, in a wrinkled and badly fitting suit, he fooled them. But only for a moment. His hand came up with a brown cigaret, and he said something with a lazy sting in it. He was directing the feverish activities of a group of men, also in ordinary clothes. These men were hurrying in and out of the safe vault near the great black desk, empty-handed going in, coming out laden with documents, money boxes, and what might have been precious gems in sealed cases.

The safe was almost empty.

Judah was bundled up in a coat; he looked cold. Karla was in a suit and a long wool coat. Her face was swollen and red.

Abel Bendigo was at his dead brother's desk, going through drawers. A man stood silently by, holding a grip open. Abel was dropping papers into it.

The Colonel and his men paid no attention to the interruption, but the wife and the brothers looked up sharply. Then Abel rose from the desk and made a sign to the man beside him, and the man shut and locked the grip and put the key in his pocket and carried the grip out, past the Queens.

"We're about through," said Colonel Spring to the Prime Minister.

"All right, Spring."

The men went out under their last burdens. Colonel Spring followed them, lighting a fresh *cigarillo*. As he approached the Queens he looked up, smiled, spread his hands in a charming gesture, shrugged, and passed on.

"Getaway?" said Ellery.

"Yes," said Abel.

"You seem to be doing it on a wholesale basis, Mr. Bendigo. Who gets left holding the bag?" the Inspector asked.

"You'd better get ready, too," said Abel. "We're leaving in a very few minutes."

"Not before you answer a question or two, Mr. Bendigo! Where is Max?"

"Max'l?" Abel sounded preoccupied. "I really don't know, Inspector. When the evacuation started, he disappeared. Search parties are looking for him now. I'm hoping, of course, that he'll be found before we leave the island."

The Inspector's jaws worked.

Ellery stood by in silence.

"And where," rasped the Inspector, "have you and Mrs. Bendigo and your brother Judah been since you left us at the pool?"

Abel's stare did not falter. "The three of us—I repeat, Inspector, the three of us—went directly to the Home Office, and we've been here, together, ever since. Isn't that so, Karla?"

"Yes," said Karla.

"Isn't that so, Judah?"

"Yes," said Judah.

"You haven't left this room, I suppose," said the Inspector, "not one of you?"

The three shook their heads.

"When did Colonel Spring and his men get here?"

"Only a few minutes ago," said Abel with a faint smile. "But that's of no importance, is it, Inspector Queen? Since the three of us vouch for one another?"

Now the Inspector was silent. But then he said, "No. No,

if you vouch for one another, I don't suppose it is. By the way, my condolences."

"Condolences?" said Abel.

"I'm sorry, Mr. Bendigo. I thought you knew that your brother King is dead."

Karla turned away. She faced the wall, and she remained facing it.

Judah took a flask from his coat and unscrewed the cap.

"We know," said Abel. "I wasn't sure you did. My brother's death was reported to us—a few minutes ago. I'm told he took his own life."

"He was murdered," said Ellery.

They stared at each other for a long time.

At last Abel said, "If there were time to go into it . . . But of course there isn't, Mr. Queen. You understand that?"

Ellery did not reply.

Abel came around King Bendigo's desk and took his sister-in-law's arm gently. "Come, Judah."

"But are you going to leave him lying there—" began the Inspector.

"My brother," said Abel, and before his stare the Inspector felt himself tighten all over, "will be buried in a fitting manner."

A HALF-HOUR later the father and the son were in a launch, with their luggage, roaring up the bay. Ahead of them sped another launch, a larger one, with the two Bendigos and Karla.

The Queens said nothing to each other. The Inspector was sunk in something remote from launches and islands and people who did murder in such a way as to confuse and defeat a man, and Ellery was taking in the fantastic scene on shore and in the bay. He had never seen so many ships, such a variety. This is what Dunkirk must have been like, he thought, minus the bombs. The whole island seemed on the move, converging in its thousands on the little harbor. Far out to sea scores of other ships lying low in the water were hove to, as if awaiting something—a signal, or nightfall. Overhead, the planes screamed and streaked, most of them leaving the island, some of them still coming in. *He must have put in a call for every seagoing vessel and aircraft in the Bendigo empire. . . .*

When they climbed aboard the big cruiser, a seaman saluted and conducted them to the chartroom. There they found the Bendigos and Karla, looking back at the harbor through glasses. Two pairs of glasses were waiting for them. In silence Ellery and his father each picked one up. In silence the five kept their eyes on the island.

The activity had noticeably slackened. The gush of vehicles down the cliff roads had dwindled to a trickle. Most of the bay spread clear; the piers were still crowded, but things were coming to the end.

The end came ninety minutes later.

The last ship edged away from the dock and headed up the bay.

The roads, the piers were deserted. From one cusp of the harbor to the other, nothing moved.

The last flight of planes rose from the heart of the island, circled once, gaining altitude, then straightened out and skimmed off into the remote skies.

A REDFACED man in a brass-buttoned blue uniform and a cap visored with gold came in.

He said to Abel: "All ready, sir. There is no one left on the island."

"There's at least one," said Inspector Queen. "King Bendigo."

The officer looked at Abel Bendigo, startled.

"My brother," said Abel steadily, "is dead. I'm in charge now, Captain. You have your orders."

Ellery put his hand on Abel's arm. "Dr. Akst?" he asked.

"On board. Safe and well."

THE *Bendigo* got under way slowly. Slowly the cruiser headed out to sea.

They were all at the railing in the stern now, watching Bendigo Island shrink and lose color and definition.

Gradually the cruiser picked up speed. The sea was calm; the air was mild.

The armada of small ships and medium-sized ships and large ships was at full steam. Most of them had already vanished over the horizon.

Through the strong glasses Ellery kept watching the island. Nothing on it anywhere moved. Nothing lived.

Five miles from the island the cruiser's speed slackened, the seas churning. Gradually they subsided, and the vessel lifted and fell gently in the swells.

And suddenly, very suddenly, the whole island rose in the air and spread itself against the sky. Or so it seemed.

A great puff of smoke rose swiftly from the place where the island had lain. It mushroomed like a genie.

The cruiser trembled. A blast of sound struck the vessel, staggered them.

And then there was another explosion, and another. And still another.

And another. . . .

They had no consciousness of time.

Eventually the smoke pall drifted clear, and the débris sank and vanished.

And a sheet of flame stood out of the sea from one end of what had been Bendigo Island to the other. The entire island was burning—the ruins of the exploded buildings, the trees, the roads, the very sands. When it should burn itself out, in the course of days, or weeks, there would be nothing left but a flat black cinder on the surface of the sea.

Ellery turned, and Abel Bendigo turned, and their glances met. And Abel's glance seemed to say: *Trust me.*

Ellery's remained opaque. He was deeply troubled.

But the Inspector said with bitterness, aloud: "And what difference will this make? Nothing has changed. It's one king or another!"

"Something has changed," said Abel.

"Yes? What?"

"It's me now, not him."

"And will that make a difference?" cried the Inspector.

"Yes. There's nothing wrong with power. The world needs power. The world needs power more today than ever before in history. Enlightened power—if you won't laugh. Power directed toward the good. Instead of the other way." Abel spoke awkwardly. His eyes were on the flames now.

"Do you think I believe that?" said the Inspector scornfully. "That the leopard can change his spots? You were in it up to your neck for twenty-seven years."

"My brother always spoke to me of a dream he had," murmured Abel. "A dream of a glorious world, a dream that could come true only if power were absolute. I believed his dream. I convinced myself that the end justified the means."

Abel stared at the flames, one hand over Judah's on the rail, the other over Karla's. "But then I discovered that my brother was a liar and a cheat and that there was no good in him at all. And I saw how a man can fool others with 'ends' while he plays with rotten means. Because, when you get right down to it, no end is worth a damn that isn't the sum total of all the means used to reach it. And I knew that if the power ever passed into my hands, I'd use it differently. And Judah and Karla," he pressed their hands, "agreed with me."

Abel turned then and glanced up at the bridge.

He raised his arm.

The seas churned and ran white again.

The *Bendigo* moved.

Judah Bendigo stirred. His hand went up to cup his eyes as he stared back at the burning island.

Karla turned from the rail. Her eyes were full of tears. She walked away, looking down at the deck.

Abel Bendigo put his coat collar up. His lips were compressed, as if he were making some great effort.

"So the King is dead," said Ellery in a bleak voice. "The King is dead, long live the King. Point of information: Now who keeps an eye on the incumbent?"

Judah Bendigo looked over his shoulder. One eye was visible, and it was fixed on his brother Abel. It was a bleary eye, but it held remarkably steady.

"I do," said Judah.